The
BEACONS
of Larkin Street

By Judith Favor

APOCRYPHILE
PRESS

The Apocryphile Press
1700 Shattuck Ave. #81
Berkeley, CA 94709
www.apocryphile.org

The Beacons of Larkin Street
Copyright © 2017 by Judith Favor
ISBN 978-1-944769-48-2

Cover art by Nancy Earle

Printed in the United States of America

Please join our mailing list at
www.apocryphilepress.com / free
and we'll keep you up-to-date on all our new releases
—and we'll also send you a FREE BOOK.
Visit us today!

CONTENTS

ACKNOWLEDGEMENTS

The main thing to acknowledge in writing this book is the power of kindness.

Beloved Pete is the kindest man I know, and my greatest source of inspiration. A year after I began this novel, he was diagnosed with Parkinson's Disease. This is an unpredictable disease with symptoms as unique as each person who suffers from it. Pete is open about his condition, honest about losing strength, balance, memory and vitality. Cognitive impairment is a marauder, but each loss has brought gracious assistance from caregivers and neighbors at Pilgrim Place, our intentional community.

Parkinson's is not all bad. Far from it. PD has helped us learn to live in the moment and to pay attention to what matters most. Parkinson's has prompted us to rest more, to appreciate moments of simplicity and peace, joy and contentment. Pete and I have discovered greater kindness within us and around us than we ever guessed possible. We hug each other a lot, and he now offers world-class hugs to many others.

Nearly every day, when he senses I need a break from the keyboard, Pete invites me to join him for 'foot time.' We go into the living room, sink into two wide leather chairs, place the soles of our bare feet together on the big blue hassock and share a sanctuary of quiet listening. Nearly every night he offers me a foot massage.

This book has come alive through the help and patience of so many kind people. First, kind thanks to my developmental editor, graphic designer, lifetime web-master and great friend Michael Kirk. I honestly could not have done it without you.

Kind thanks to Nancy Earle for her fine cover art, and to John Mabry for publishing the first in a trilogy featuring the Beacons, the Rev and the city of San Francisco. Your faith in me means more than I can say.

Kind thanks to Claremont Writing Club colleagues BonnaSue, Don Coleman, Connie Green, Don MacKay, Eleanor Scott Meyers, April Nakamoto, Lissa Peterson, Peggy Redman, John Rogers, Laura Saint Martin and Teri Tompkins for making *The Beacons of Larkin Street* so much better with your insights, prompts and challenges.

Kind thanks to Lois and Ward McAffee for the sanctuary of your mountain cabin during periods of inception and integration, and to Penelope and Doug Wyllie for giving me shelter in your Castro Street home during periods of research in San Francisco.

Kind thanks to Mary Atwood, Wendy Bayer, John Brantingham, Jacqueline Chase, Gail Duggan, Carol Billings Harris, Jean Lesher, Penelope Mann, Frank Rogers, Jo Scott-Coe, Alicia Sheridan, Julie Steinbach and Janet Vandevender for caring so deeply and for supporting my writing over so many years. *The Beacons of Larkin Street*, my first novel, grew from trusting that I am grounded in your care, knowing I am guided and loved, heard and held in compassion.

The forceful power of kindness now brings *The Beacons of Larkin Street* into the world. I give thanks for emotional and physical help from friends, colleagues, editors and publishers. I give thanks for practical help from booksellers and librarians. And I give thanks in advance for reviews from readers like you. Reading groups and church women who select *The Beacons of Larkin Street* will find guides and study questions posted on my website www.judithfavor.com

For **PETE**

CHAPTER 1

THE GATE

Entry Points

THIS ONE

"I'm fed up with the old boys club!" Dot pounded a fist on the table where five Beacons—the deacons of Saint Lydia's Church—sat trying to decide who they should hire to become their new pastor. "We need a *woman* minister this time!"

"You bet," nodded Hope, "especially after that scummy Reverend Petersen."

"Was I ever glad to see the rear end of that prick!" huffed Dot.

"Dot! Language," Paige objected, but the big black woman hooted.

"I cleaned it up 'cause we're in church, girl. You want language, try my neighborhood. They'd say he screwed himself, getting cock-deep in a prostitute."

"Such abominable words as no Christian ear can endure to hear!" Paige shook her head and wagged a finger at Dot. Paige was pretty sure she was the only one in the room who recognized the quote from Shakespeare's "Henry VI."

Beka ignored them both. "We do need a woman pastor, and soon."

Lord, was she tired! Beka Ash had kept the church going since they forced the exit of Saint Lydia's minister, the one dubbed Pastor Peacock. As Head Beacon, Beka wound up talking to reporters, ordering supplies, collecting data, calling meetings, leading meetings, strategizing, organizing, arranging funding, constructing endless progress reports, even handling the weekly preaching. Plus a host of other functions. Tending heartbreak. Her own heartbreak. The founding elders' heartbreak. The kids' heartbreak. The choir members' heartbreak. The teachers' heartbreak. Also: baking muffins for homebound grannies, locking and unlocking doors, replacing paper towels, comforting tearful little girls, bringing milkshakes to ushers who were getting sober and raising hell with ushers who weren't.

The Head Beacon heaved a huge sigh. "I am more than ready to turn over the keys to a strong, confident female," she declared. "We need a minister who can handle all the pastoral and administrative responsibilities at Saint Lydia's."

"You've done a great job holding the church together since you and Dot sent Pastor Peacock packing." Millienne spoke in a Haitian lilt. She pulled her shawl close, leaned across the table and lifted one of three folders under consideration. "I like this one. She has kind eyes." The Beacon wanted to hire a tender-hearted woman like herself, a sweet soul to care for the congregation's jumpy children and shaky elders, folks like Miz Washington, members of Saint Lydia's since 1948, back when Howard Thurman started the church on Larkin Street. Yes, Millienne wanted the pastor with gentle eyes.

"Not enough gravitas," Dot decided. "I like *her*." She smacked down a different folder, one with REV DR. RUTH RIDLEY SALTER scrawled across the top.

"But she's white," Hope pointed out.

"So?" Dot said. "What are you, racist?"

"No, but..." Hope fumbled for words. Her North Dakota uncles were racist, but when she'd had enough of their Lutheran piety she came west and joined an inter-racial, non-denominational church. She got along fine with black folks and white folks, but she yearned for a *close friend*. She wanted someone to confide in, a pastor who could be her *close* friend. Millienne's choice suited Hope. This kind-eyed woman looked like she would enjoy knitting. Maybe she could help organize the annual rummage sale.

"This Ruth Salter sounds as deeply committed to social justice as I am," declared Dot, "so I want her. We need a woman with her credentials to organize the people of Saint Lydia's. Our congregation has gotta get busy feeding the hungry!"

"There's more to ministry than that," cautioned Paige. She reached for the file and studied the resume. "Alright, I can go with Reverend Salter because she's grounded in the classics of western Christian spirituality." The poetic Paige longed for a scholarly pastor, one who would understand and champion her mystical ways.

Beka picked up the 8x10 photograph and studied Reverend Salter's chiseled, matronly face. The Head Beacon knew her opinion carried weight. It was only because she was so well respected that she'd been able to force the resignation of Pastor Peacock, and even then things had been tricky for a while. Many folks were relieved when he left, though Saint Lydia's lost quite a few members during the ensuing scandal. But everyone knew it had been Beka's steady hand on the tiller that moved the congregation safely through the storm.

"Saint Lydia's Church does need an ordained woman," she repeated, "but there aren't many ordained women to choose from. Our congregation also needs a visionary leader," she announced decisively, "and I respect the way the Reverend Doctor Ruth Ridley Salter stood up for women's rights in pursuing ordination. She prevailed under tough opposition. I like this one. I think she's the right woman for us."

"Beka's right," announced Dot. "I say we hire this one from Cleveland and bring her to San Francisco as soon as she can get here."

TERTULLIAN

Key in one hand, cane in the other, the white-haired Reverend Doctor Ruth Ridley Salter unlocked the study at Saint Lydia's Church on Larkin Street and wrinkled her nose at the musty smell. Steely eyes traveled to the desk, neglected since her predecessor's hasty departure. *Sex has led to trouble for many a man of the cloth*, she mused, *but that is no excuse to neglect the pastor's study.* She would speak sharply to the janitor about this. The patrician pastor did not mind dust bunnies, but she did insist upon a clean work surface.

The desk calendar was open to May 20, 1976. She flipped the pages on its curved spine to September 12. Excitement shivered her own spine. Here she was, finally getting a church of her own at an age when most pastors were retiring to play golf. She also felt a mild shudder of embarrassment on behalf of her fellow priest. *Whatever his sins, it must have been quite a debacle to drive the Reverend Perry Petersen from Saint Lydia's.* She had not heard the details, but clerical gossip would have to wait. One hated to see a colleague tossed out on his rear, but right now she had work to do.

A clutch of anxiety grabbed hold. Only two days to prepare her first sermon. Rev Ruth let out a gust of air and eased her bony haunches into the chair. One caster wobbled beneath her; another creaked. *This will never do; must get the custodian to fix it.* The very thought tired her. Moving from Cleveland to San Francisco had worn her out, which should come as no surprise. As Timothy caustically reminded her, "Mother, you're no spring chicken."

Rev Ruth wanted to make a good impression on her new congregation. What to say to a crowd of strangers? She fretted, massaging arthritic knuckles. There was no time to compose a sermon from scratch so she flipped through notes from student days at General Theological Seminary. Where to start?

Tertullian came to mind, a biblical scholar from antiquity. Seminary classmates had once praised her sermon on

Tertullian. That's it, she decided. These San Franciscans have not heard a woman priest. They may think I'm just some dumb dame, but once I step into the pulpit and present Tertullian's complex theology, they won't think I'm nearly as shallow as they expect me to be.

FOUND

The Reverend Doctor Ruth Ridley Salter was "irregularly ordained" in 1974 before women were legally allowed to become priests in the Episcopal Church; she'd been watching for pastoral openings for two years. When she learned about the interim position at Saint Lydia's Church, she'd persuaded Bishop Tuttle of Ohio to release her. "You have to give me a chance," she'd insisted. "You know how old I am. This may be my last chance to serve a local parish."

In San Francisco, her face showed pleasure in having been found as she turned questioning eyes toward Beka Ash. "How did you know where to find me?"

"I learned about you from Bishop Edward Stiles." Beka looked a bit smug as they chatted in the pastor's study.

"And how did you meet Bishop Stiles?"

This reverend reminded Beka of a terrier with a bone. "With nerve born of desperation," she said, dramatically. "He is known as San Francisco's most liberal churchman, so I phoned his secretary and pleaded for an appointment."

"Bishops are busy men. How did you get in?"

"Threw myself on his mercy. Told him Saint Lydia's needed his high-powered assistance to find a high-powered woman priest."

Reverend Salter had the grace to blush. "Did Bishop Stiles mention that he and his cronies put me through an ecclesiastical trial after the ordination they insisted upon calling irregular?"

"He didn't say, but he did express regret about Saint Lydia's sex scandal. I think that's why he took pity and invited

me to Grace Cathedral. What an elegant office, like a castle."
Beka widened her eyes and spread her fingers. "Thick Persian
carpets on old stone floors. Oil portraits of California bishops
lining the walls, watching over us."

A quick vision of Bishop Tuttle in Ohio—the old goat—
made the priest's lip curl. "What is this one like?" she asked.

"I'd heard that Bishop Stiles was iron-willed so I was
expecting a stern old man, but he has a kind face and a warm
laugh. I also like the way he dressed, a bright purple shirt with
a cross tucked into the pocket."

"That's encouraging. What did you tell him?"

"That Saint Lydia's Church was founded in wartime but
now, thirty years later, there's a different kind of war going
on in San Francisco. People want a church where they can
belong, where they can trust each other. I told him our congregation wants to be more than just good, boring Christians. We
want to build a bigger, more inclusive church. A more feminist
church."

"I'm in favor of that." Rev Ruth nodded vigorously, rub-
bing her hands.

"After he heard my plea to find a visionary woman leader,
he told me that he, too, senses a growing hunger among people
of faith for women priests to feed them. That's when he said he
might know of someone who could do the job."

"Interim ministries do strange things to people," San Francisco's liberal Bishop later warned Reverend Salter during a
telephone consultation. "Saint Lydia's is quite a legendary
church, and very independent. My diocese has no official oversight, so you'll be on your own, without a Bishop to call upon.
Saint Lydia's is bound to challenge you, but it may also be the
making of you."

Was the Bishop serious or joking? She hadn't seen his face,
so she couldn't tell. Despite his word of warning, Rev. Ruth
was delighted to be the one chosen from a cadre of candidates.
She also felt a bit guilty that her chance came at the expense
of Pastor Petersen, but that's how it went. The silly Casanova

brought about his own downfall. One man's disgrace was one woman's gain.

POETIC WELCOME

To Reverend Doctor Ruth Ridley Salter, Interim Pastor
From Paige Palmer, Beacon of Saint Lydia's Church

San Francisco has magnetically beckoned you
    into our gravitational field
To face a multitude of challenges, friendships,
    traumas and healings
In our interracial, interdenominational,
    transformative church community.
Members of multiple races and languages,
    creeds and spiritual practices
Heterosexuals, homosexuals, bisexuals,
    transgenders and fluid identities
Make androgynous imprints on art and culture,
    philanthropy and politics.
Some see San Francisco as a happy place,
    a crucible of possibility
Others view San Francisco as a wild town,
    with hidden dens of danger
Residents include risk-takers and idealists,
    innovators and opportunists.
The Golden Gate is entry point for sailboats,
    cargo ships, military fleets
One tunnel—The Broadway—plus
    a vast underground Muni network
The historic Embarcadero includes
    multiple wharves and piers.
Two grand bridges span narrow Golden Gate
    and wide San Francisco Bay
Seven hills comprise the heights and valleys
    of city grit and glam

Thousands of streets and avenues
    thread through seven square miles.
Dramatic shorelines edge the ocean and the bay
Poetic light filters through thrilling layers of clouds
Refreshing winds criss-cross the mighty Pacific.
It is good to stand in San Francisco
    —anywhere will do—and
Consult your heart: What do you want from this city?
Consult your mind: What do you bring to this city?
Whether you stand shy in the shadows
    or bold on a promontory
No one—old-timer or newcomer—
    can take the city's full measure
For San Francisco remains elusive,
    immeasurable and unpredictable.

FRESH BEGINNINGS

The female priest from Ohio was said to possess qualities
that made Saint Lydia's church leaders tremble with excitement. After they booted out Reverend Petersen, the legendary non-denominational church appointed five women—
Beka Ash, Hope Hudson, Millienne Guillernos, Dot Davis
and Paige Palmer—to provide ministerial oversight. When
citywide publicity rocked the historic church, some folks fled
to calmer pastures. The five lay leaders did their best to shepherd what was left of the flock. They worked hard to find and
hire the Reverend Doctor Salter, and now she was here. The
pulse of new beginnings pressed its mystery into their hearts.
All were ready to celebrate the highly anticipated arrival of
Saint Lydia's first woman pastor.

ITCHY

We've waited long enough, mused Beacon Millienne Guillernos, rearranging her wide hips on the hard pew, and now she's

about to speak. She gazed around Saint Lydia's sanctuary; everyone was dressed in Sunday best. Some squirmed with excitement; others sat tense with nervousness. Many eyes were closed in prayer, so she closed hers, too.

The congregation held a vibrant hush as the esteemed Reverend Doctor Salter took her place on the dais. Her gold and purple vestments were dazzling. An angled sunbeam lit the sharp corners of her face. The sanctuary was filled with sacred choral harmonies; the air was rich in oxygen.

She's dressed more elegantly than the rest of us, thought Millienne. Looks like an aging model on a Vatican TV show. But why does she speak so rapidly? The peasant woman from Haiti lost the thread when the preacher quoted Tertullian: "*Enoch predicted that the demons and the spirits of the angelic apostates would turn into idolatry all the elements, all the adornment of the universe, and all things contained in the heaven, the sea, and the earth, that they might be consecrated as God in opposition to God. All things, therefore, does human error worship, except the Founder of all himself. The images of those things are idols; the consecration of the images is idolatry.*"

The reverend thrust out her chest and straightened her back as if to look taller. Her satisfied smile and steepled fingers looked to Millienne like she was bragging. From time to time, Reverend Salter stretched out her arms in an expansive gesture, but it didn't help. To Millienne, with just enough education to certify as a licensed vocational nurse, it was like listening to someone preaching in Latvian.

The sermon went on too long. Millienne pushed off her Earth Shoes and pressed her toes into the hardwood floor. She wanted to be outdoors. She wanted to smell the wild grass and inhale the scent of soil. She wanted to touch pine bark. She raised her chin and looked to the ceiling, where she imagined the preacher's words hanging like moths, a flock of big, complicated words that made her ears itch.

JITTERY

Beacon Paige Palmer placed both freckled hands on her flat abdomen. She had a sour stomach, which made it hard to sit still during the sermon. She adored the writings of Saint Thomas Aquinas, but Tertullian's ideas made her nervous. *"We ourselves, though we're guilty of every sin, are not just a work of God; we're image. Yet we have cut ourselves off from our Creator in both soul and body. Did we get eyes to serve lust, the tongue to speak evil, ears to hear evil, a throat for gluttony, a stomach to be gluttony's ally, hands to do violence, genitals for unchaste excesses, feet for an erring life? Was the soul put in the body to think of traps, fraud and injustice?"*

The new pastor had a knowing smile and a scholarly brain, but where was her soul? For Paige, who lived alone and worked at home transcribing medical records, spiritual thirst was best quenched by contemplative pauses, but this new reverend was all about energy and drive, guilt and unchaste excesses.

Paige lifted her eyes and scanned the water-stained acoustical tiles, searching for angelic patterns in the sanctuary ceiling. Spotting an angel might soothe her turbulent gut. The ploy didn't work. "Excuse me, excuse me," she whispered, knocking knees with parishioners as she hastily exited the pew.

She locked the door of the ladies room and hoped no one would need it. Head in hands, pale and shaky, she sat on the toilet, a position familiar from years of irritable bowel syndrome. No one knew the appalling weight of her secret; the superhuman effort it took to appear normal. No one guessed how lonely she felt, or the strain of trying to be part of things that came easy for others.

In the privacy of the stall, Paige pondered the sermon. Why preach to San Franciscans about an obscure Christian scholar? From what she'd heard about Reverend Salter, she'd expected a sermon worthy of Saint Hildegard of Bingen. And with a famous priest in the pulpit—a woman at last—Paige had not expected to be bored. She loved worship but hated boredom.

More to the point, she hated hearing people muttering during the newcomer's sermon. Didn't the new reverend know Saint Lydia's was a sanctuary for the oppressed, not a chalky lecture hall? Scholarly sermons might be acceptable where she came from, but not here in San Francisco's most progressive church.

Paige felt burdened by responsibility. She had agreed to hire the Reverend Doctor Salter and —until today—thought that she and the Beacons made the best choice.

What have we done?

Whatever have we done?

It was enough to make her moan, *Shit!*

BRUSHED OFF

Sermons are meant to be nutritious, thought Beacon Hope Hudson, but this one made her gag. *"The flesh feeds on the Body and Blood of Christ that the soul may be fattened on God."* She had no idea what Tertullian was talking about. The word of God is supposed to feed the hungry soul, but these words were dry as bone. Hope was impressed by the preacher's self-introduction, though; twenty-two lines in the newest edition of *Who's Who in America*.

The day had started juicy with a sense of harvest, but the sermon—which seemed two hours long—made her both pensive and hungry. Hope pictured the empty sugar bowl on her kitchen table and imagined tilting the C&H bag to fill it. She pictured the shiny new answering machine on her desk, a gift from son Cody, and wondered if anyone had left a message on it.

Hope's insides were all a-flutter. The oldest Beacon wanted to make a good impression on the new church boss so she got a perm and wore her best dress, the blue one purchased for little Rex's christening. She'd come to church early so she could impress Reverend Salter by artfully arranging fragrant glazed donuts on the gold-trimmed china platter. Remembering the donuts made her mouth water.

At the welcoming reception in Fellowship Hall she watched usher Billy Cobb bring a chair, but the aristocratic reverend barely acknowledged his kindness.

When it was Hope's turn to shake the hand of the famous pastor, she felt curiously tongue-tied. She held out her hand; the priest took it, then quickly pulled away and smoothed her skirt as if the Hope were a wrinkle she needed to brush off. The reverend did not even wait to hear her name, already smiling up at silver-haired Judge Webb in his three-piece suit.

It occurred to Hope that the new boss was one of those people who preferred to converse with higher-class folks. Stung, she stepped away with neck straight and chin high. She checked the coffee level in the percolator, refilled the cream pitcher and rammed half a glazed donut into her mouth. Just as Billy Cobb asked what she thought of the sermon, the donut lodged in her throat. Hope could feel the usher's eyes on her but could not possibly look up. She gave a gulp that sent the sugary lump squeezing past her tonsils. It hurt all the way down.

SPINNING

Head Beacon Beka Ash hurried into Fellowship Hall, trying to appear competent and spiritual. She greeted Miz Washington, the ancient church founder with her fierce walnut face and flowered hat. That courtesy completed, Beka straightened her navy blazer, turned on her mid-high heels and moved on. She looked efficient from the outside, but inside she was vigilant, flooded by complex and contradictory feelings, watching for trouble. She wanted Saint Lydia's folks to like the ordained woman she had gone to great lengths to find, but after that sermon she realized there was nothing she could do to make them accept, let alone approve of, the Reverend Ruth Ridley Salter.

Beka saw an usher conduct the new interim pastor into Fellowship Hall; she watched the priest slide her cane out of sight beneath the chair and hold out a hand as though offering it to be kissed. Most folks watched from a distance as the *Who's Who In America* personage greeted a few bold members of the congregation. The white-collared priest smiled enchantingly but the only thing the Head Beacon could do was turn like the ballerina on top of her mother's jewelry box, keeping an eye on everyone.

Beka flashed on a memory of Grandmother Ash in Los Alamos, spinning in her kitchen; looking for her husband, looking for her spatula, looking for her future.

What was the Head Beacon supposed to do now? Her stomach clenched. She had expected that bringing this famous woman to her beloved congregation would change everything, or at least change something, but now she just didn't know.

Beka's vision blurred with fatigue. Her exhaustion stemmed from confusion. She shook her head to clear it, but thoughts flapped around incoherently. When she spotted Millienne in the crowd, approaching from the far side of Fellowship Hall, the knots in her stomach eased a bit.

"Are you okay?" asked the big woman.

Beka squinted her eyes, as if trying to read print that was too small. She looked away. "I don't know," she said, speaking toward the window.

"I don't know, either." Millienne spoke over Beka's shoulder, to the wall.

They were both afraid to take a deep breath.

ROCKY ROAD

Beacon Dot Davis had wanted to jump up and interrupt the dominating white woman preaching with uppity diction. *"Every soul, then, by reason of its birth, has its nature in Adam until it is born again in Christ; moreover, it is unclean all the while that it remains without this regeneration; and because unclean, it is actively sinful, and suffuses even the flesh (by reason of their conjunction) with its own shame."*

Dot had wanted to shout out, "Tell us about the love of Jesus, not the theology of Tertullian!" Her fists clenched in fury, apricot fingernails digging into palms. Frustration formed a tight band across her broad black forehead, giving her a headache. During the sermon she'd raised her eyes, hoping to see Jesus up there, waving. A short laugh got past her lips before she clamped them tight.

She was too antagonistic to stand in line for coffee, and seething too hard to introduce herself to the new pastor. *Interim pastor.* Dot had agreed to serve on the Board of Beacons—against her better judgment—because the last bunch of men hired such a scumbag. It had taken great cunning and courage for the women of the church to get rid of Pastor Peacock, the slimy predator. Dot had declared she would do anything to get a good woman pastor at Saint Lydia's, and since that meant serving a two-year term on the Board of Beacons, then by God, she would do it. Reverend Salter's paperwork showed a woman with high credentials, but today's sermon stunk.

Just then, Dot heard the ice cream truck jingling on Larkin Street. That does it, she decided, I'm outta here.

She waved across the room to Beka and headed for the door. It's never too early for Rocky Road.

GLORY

After her first sermon in San Francisco, the seventy-year-old pastor felt as if she'd landed in heaven. The city was lovely. The wind was gentle. The sky was cloudless. The lay leaders of Saint Lydia's—all women—really wanted a female priest. They'd hired her despite the fact that she lacked parish experience, so here she was.

If only Bishop Tuttle could see her now. He'd done his best to prohibit her from taking the job in San Francisco, as if he had the power to keep her in his Ohio cage. Two years ago, during the brouhaha that followed her irregular ordination, the old goat had actually filed charges against her in the House of Bishops. His cronies grilled her on points of theology and ecclesiology but never listened to a word she said. Nine bald white men raised questions in one breath and answered them in the next, drawing theological conclusions about her and imposing ecclesiastical sanctions on her, but she had come west anyway. Since Nolan's death nearly a decade ago, she made her own decisions.

With the clerical trial in Ohio behind her and no California bishop standing in her way, Ruth felt supremely lucky to finally be in charge of her own church. Ordination had taken a lifetime, but becoming the first woman priest in San Francisco would make her even more famous. All she had to do was keep giving great sermons.

As the sun sank toward the Pacific, she savored the vision of a bright future. Ohio and its conflicts lay behind her. Ahead stretched the possibilities of Saint Lydia's Church in the grand city of San Francisco. As vivid orange and violet clouds smeared the western sky, the Reverend Doctor Ruth Ridley Salter could foresee the glory of her great success in ministry.

For the second night in a row, she slept until dawn without being troubled by a single bad dream.

CHAPTER 2

THE SHORES

Land's End

HEART TROUBLE

Ruth didn't know which was worse, the numbing shock of learning that people hated her sermon or the galvanizing fury that came next. How dare they criticize her scholarship! Had these westerners no manners? Had they any idea how much she'd suffered to achieve ordination in a church opposed to women priests?

What if the Saint Lydia's told her to leave? What would she say to her family? Her sons—well, one son—sent her off to San Francisco with good wishes and an armload of orange chrysanthemums. Never mind that she'd abandoned the bouquet in an airport restroom. How else to manage her bag and cane?

Ruth considered telling granddaughter Caro that she'd made a mistake, but that would cause too much family furor. She couldn't bear the thought of admitting defeat. Besides, her sons would think she'd taken leave of her senses. They'd either stick her in the loony bin or some damn nursing home. No, she could not risk admitting failure.

The interim pastor drew in a breath so sharp she bit her tongue. She paced the worn carpet; strode into the bathroom; bent beneath the sink; grabbed a bottle of Lysol and shot the spray over fixtures and faucets. After a blaze of disinfecting righteousness, she collapsed on her single bed.

Alarm came over her in a rush; panic left her skin prickling. She wanted to scream, but knew she mustn't. Her heart fled in fright, the agony of failure. How could she get her heart back into her chest? She must remain very still. No one must know she was missing her heart.

ILLUSTRIOUS HISTORY

When she'd first learned about Saint Lydia's, Reverend Ruth was impressed by its illustrious history. The church boasted a famous Negro founder, Reverend Doctor Howard Thurman, who'd collaborated with the Fellowship of Reconciliation to start the church in post-war San Francisco. She liked that it was non-denominational, multi-racial and multi-faith, founded to serve African-American families who came from the Deep South to build warships. The church now drew members from all across the Bay Area.

During her single year of seminary training, Rev Ruth interned in a mixed-race congregation; she liked hearing black and white voices harmonizing on the hymns. Here the choir stood near a mighty organ brought 'round the Horn by the Reverend Gustav Niebuhr, a theologian Rev Ruth once studied. She was uneasy about the Altar Guild, though. In Cleveland, Altar Guild was a traditionally feminine bastion but here at Saint Lydia's it was manned by homosexuals. She could not imagine anyone except ladies creating floral arrangements for the altar.

Sitting at her ugly desk in her ugly study, Rev Ruth did wish someone—even a swishy guy—would bring her a lovely bouquet. In Cleveland, she took beauty for granted; here she missed it. She was depressed: cluttered corridors, low ceilings lined with sputtering fluorescent tubes, a long, skinny sanctuary. The whole church was skinny, hemmed in by apartment buildings that cast dark shadows over her workspace.

Where was the lovely rose window casting beams of sunlight onto the altar?

Where was the meditation garden, graced by neatly trimmed shrubbery, sturdy stone benches and a bubbling fountain?

Saint Lydia's had no sunlight. No lawn. It was the gloomiest church she had ever seen. The only way in was through heavy doors that reminded her of a wartime bunker. Five steps up to Sanctuary and Christian Ed rooms. Five steps down to Fellowship Hall, kitchen and pastor's study. She missed the grandeur of Saint Mark's in Cleveland.

At least her disgraced predecessor had a sense of humor. The two-level wooden in-box Reverend Perry Petersen left on the desk was labeled *Sacred* and *Top Sacred*.

Ruth recalled nothing about an odd group calling themselves the Board of Beacons in the church profile. Would she have come to San Francisco if she'd known a gang of five untrained laywomen held power that was rightfully hers?

What would she say to Caro? The girl had been so encouraging.

CARO

"Here, Carrie, you drive today." Ruth tossed the car keys to her granddaughter.

The girl's slender fingers easily caught the keys. "Caro. My name is CARO now." She flashed snappy brown eyes at her Gram as she opened the passenger door. "And when did you get so generous, letting me drive your beloved Buick?"

"Since last week's fender bender," Ruth said sheepishly, glaring toward the crumpled front end. "Crunching into a fire hydrant convinced me that this is the time to get out of one fast lane and into another."

"Stop talking in riddles. I'm not a kid anymore."

Caroline Evelyn Salter, confident in slim white jeans, red rubber boots and a long-sleeved blue and white Wellesley

pullover, strode around the front of the Buick. Dangly earrings danced as she wiggled the twisted bumper, decided it
was secure enough to drive, and shook her head at the fender
damage.

Thunderclouds heaped along Cleveland's horizon made a
low rumble. "Storm on the way," said Caro, "but not before
we reach our lunch place. Where to?" she asked, turning the
ignition key and revving the engine.

"This is your back-to-college farewell lunch, so you
choose." The Reverend Salter arranged her narrow face in a
wide smile and wiggled her raggedy eyebrows at the driver.
"Take me wherever you want. I am in your hands."

"All right, then, we'll go to the Great Lakes Brewing Company."

Trying not to act shocked by the destination, Ruth bit back
the impulse to scold Caro about drinking. Instead, Ruth asked
about college; they both recognized this as a ruse meant to
deflect the girl from criticizing Gram's driving. The twenty-
year-old had plenty to say about why she'd changed her major
to political science, and even more to say about her romance
with Rosa, the hot Latina who'd tossed her childhood nick-
name and re-named her Caro.

They were on West Boulevard, approaching the World
Publishing Company, when Ruth gestured up at the globe
bulging out of the landmark building. "That's where I want to
go!" she exclaimed.

Caro tilted her rather plain face up toward the bronze
globe. "You want to go around the world?"

"Not quite. Just to the west coast. I'll tell you more while
we eat."

They both ordered cheeseburgers with a slice of raw onion.
Although fifty years apart in age, the Salter women shared
similar tastes for rare steak, Junior Mints and old-fashioned
Alpine house shoes made of mouse-colored felt. They also had
identical skeptical streaks, strong opinions and oversized egos.

"So, tell me about going west," said Caro, sipping suds from a chilled mug.

"I am so excited! I have actually been called to pastor a church," Ruth exclaimed. "The leaders—all women—at Saint Lydia's Church want me to move to San Francisco and become their priest. Imagine that!" The old woman's deep-set eyes and wide smile lit up the wide, noisy afternoon.

Caro's face turned a hectic red. "What a nutty idea," she managed, choking on her beer. "To start from scratch in California, at your age!"

"But you know how long I've wanted to be a parish priest!" Ruth's insistent tone was underscored by percussive rhythms from the brewery's gigantic stereo speakers. "And you've heard me tell how cranky old Bishop Tuttle managed to block me from pastoring a church in Cleveland!"

"So you would go to San Francisco to do the ministry you've waited all your life to do." Caro narrowed her bright brown eyes. "I understand that." Her face took on a pensive expression and her long silver earrings jangled as she nodded her head, which she kept doing. "This whole thing strikes me as pretty silly, Gram, but it's also kind of brave to go west in old age."

"I'm not so old," she protested. "Only seventy."

"Most seventy-year-olds are enjoying their golden years."

"The chance to do ministry in San Francisco gives me the biggest gold rush I've had since I met your granddad," retorted Ruth.

Caro grinned but was not about to be sidetracked. "I think it is totally wild for someone your age to leave Cleveland and go west, all by yourself." She scratched the side of her head, rearranging her short brown hair. "The idea is definitely nutty, Gram, but it could also be a sign of your brilliant eccentricity."

The Reverend Doctor Ruth Ridley Salter, a trailblazer in the fight for women's ordination in the Episcopal Church, always wore trousers. And she made sure her trousers had pockets because she always carried a Chap Stick. She took it out now and rubbed it across thin, dry lips.

Caro gave her an assessing look. "Your white clerical collar contrasts nicely with your tailored navy pantsuit," she said appraisingly, "but don't you think your black lace-up oxfords are too mannish?"

"My shoes are my own business." Ruth raised her chin and glared. "Who are you to give me fashion advice." It was not a question.

"C'mon, Gram, I may be a lesbian but I'm not a bull-dyke. And you're not a lesbian but the way you dress makes you look like one. You don't want to give those San Francisco women the wrong impression, do you?"

Ruth squeezed her eyes shut. *Too mannish.* She took a deep breath and buried her anger. *Bull-dyke.*

This was her firstborn—and favorite—grandchild. Ruth, not known for her patience among family, church folks or political enemies, found enough patience to calm down. Gazing at this gleaming girl in her royal blue and white striped Wellesley shirt, Ruth raised her hands, gave a big, noisy exhalation and said "Okay, okay."

While they were eating, the temperature dropped outdoors and the wind picked up. Just then, a summer rainstorm let go, pounding so hard on the metal roof of the brewery that all conversation was drowned out.

Ruth rose stiffly, wielding her cane like an Old Testament staff, and marched to the restroom. By the time she returned, the rain had let up enough that they could hear.

Caro cocked her head and gave a quick shrug. "So, let's talk about names. I got my new name in college, from Rosa, and I love it. Now you need a new name. Before you go to San Francisco."

"My name is perfectly suitable," sniffed Ruth. "I carry your grandmother's maiden name and your grandfather's last name."

"But what do you want people to call you?"

"By my own name, of course." She brushed away a stray eyebrow hair.

"What title, I mean. Father Salter? Mother Salter? Reverend Salter?"

It took a while for Ruth to respond. After an appropriate pause to establish who was in charge, she blurted "Lady minister. I hate that term."

"Why?"

"I hate being called a lady minister because it confuses the aristocratic with the biological, and layers both on top of the vocational."

Caro's eyes widened. "Wow, I never thought of it that way."

"I've never said it that way before." Ruth looked proud of herself.

"Is that why you never wear a dress?" asked Caro.

"Exactly!" Ruth said. "I will not wear a dress because I will not give anyone an excuse to call me a lady minister."

"Okay, I applaud you for sticking to your guns about skirts, but I still need to hear how you want the people in your new church to address you."

"Does Reverend Salter sound too formal?"

"It sounds too mannish. Salter was Grandad's name."

"I've always rather liked the sound of it," mused Ruth, "because it reminds me of the Psalter, which I adore."

"I don't read the Psalms every day like you do, but our name does make us sound salty," laughed Caro.

"Salt of the earth," agreed Ruth, "but that's not hefty enough for a title..."

"I know!" proclaimed Caro. "Rev Ruth!"

"Rev Ruth." She paused, looked toward the ceiling where rock music blared from oversized speakers, then repeated it. "Rev Ruth. Yes, I do like the taste of that. The brevity. And the clarity."

"Congrats, Rev Ruth. You are the first priest in Cleveland to survive a title transplant."

Ruth gave the girl a fond smile. "You may be as bossy as your father, but you are also the most clear-eyed, tough-minded lesbian I know."

"C'mon, Gram, you don't know that many lesbians."

"Only you, Caro, and one is quite enough."

Puddles filled the parking lot. Ruth plowed through several on the thick treads of her black oxfords, then stopped and took her granddaughter by the arm. "See the rainbow in this puddle? The gasoline rainbow?"

"What are you talking about?"

"Don't you remember Holden in *The Catcher in the Rye*, exclaiming about seeing a gasoline rainbow?"

"Gram, I haven't read Salinger since I was a sophomore in high school. How do you expect me to remember stuff like that?"

"And people think oldsters are forgetful," smirked Ruth. "But you do see the rainbow, don't you?

Caro snickered, then nodded.

"This rainbow is a sign of God's promise! Even if it comes from an oil slick in the parking lot, the iridescent play of color in this rainbow—right here—is a sign that I am on the right track. San Francisco, here I come."

THE CHALICE

Timothy, her firstborn, was just as bull-headed as Ruth herself. She was determined—desperate—to get her own way, but Timothy criticized her for threatening to fritter away her old age in San Francisco. "You were born in Cleveland. You can't just leave all this behind." He was yelling now. "You need to stay here! And die here. Remember, you only have one life to live!"

"Only one life," she scoffed. "My father repeated that tired old phrase more times than I can count, and your father, too, but I don't believe it any more. Only one life implies that what I did yesterday determines what I must do tomorrow."

She was yelling, now, too. "San Francisco is my chance to do something new, so don't you try to set my future in cement!"

He blew up then, turning into a tornado that wouldn't hold still long enough for a civilized discussion. As Timothy stalked out, she shouted after him "I want to be more than a dull old chemist! More than a stuffy old church trustee! I want to be a priest!"

Timothy, she decided, was a demanding son; demeaning, too. He was acting unspeakably rude. Her natural inclination was to loathe him. She wanted, in fact, to strangle him, but no good mother could do that. She held extra-high standards for herself as a mother, just as her own mother had. She also held extra-high standards for herself as a priest. The idea of giving up this opportunity at Saint Lydia's—her only chance—to have a church of her own made her insides clench with determination.

Ruth had been a clumsy adolescent, tall and pimply. "Frankly," she once heard her mother confide to a friend, "I don't know how I wound up with such a homely daughter." In the emotionally chilly and undemonstrative Salter family, the girl often hid behind a wall of despair, though sometimes she lashed out. Those were agonizing years, living with parents who scowled judgmentally whenever she tripped over her own feet, which happened often.

And now she was tripping over her own words, unable to convince her sons how vital —essential— it was for her to move to San Francisco. Timothy enlisted both brothers and all three battered her with reason, medical facts and, finally, shattering guilt. Their male opinions were compellingly rational, which made them worth fighting against. And fight she did, for all she was worth.

For Ruth, one thing was certain: she must satisfy her expectations of herself as a priest, no matter what it cost, even if it meant sacrificing her expectations of herself as a mother. The conflict tore her up. She brooded and brooded on it until her mind was limp and her heart was sore.

Although her parents had been vociferously opposed to Christianity, young Ruth found great comfort in attending services at Saint Matthews, the nearby Anglican Church. During Lent, midway through her junior year in high school, she decided to go to confession. "I am such a bad person," she began.

"Tell me why," said Father Powell. He had a kind voice.

"I don't know if I can," wailed Ruth.

"Tell me the worst," he coaxed, in a way that reminded her of Friar Tuck.

"But I can't," she protested, through tears.

"You must speak and I will listen. That is why we are both here."

So she'd poured it out, not all of it, but enough to ease her sore heart.

Not long after that, she brought a dream to confession. In the dream, Ruth had been looking in a mirror. There she saw herself reflected to the waist, able to see through her clothes, even through her skin. Inside herself she saw only darkness, a black shadow that filled her with shame, yet she could not look away. Then it seemed as if she was moving, as if she had passed through the mirror and gone deep into the shadow. She went on blindly for a time. She feared there was no end to this darkness, then sensed something ahead, glimmering. As she moved closer to the silvery shimmer, she recognized what it was: a chalice—beautifully engraved. A silver communion chalice.

She wept softly. Father Powell held the stillness for a while then asked what the dream meant to her.

"It's mine," she gulped. "I knew it was mine but, in the dream when I reached for the chalice, it disappeared."

In Cleveland, late in the summer of 1976, it was Caro who turned the family tide. She managed to convince her oppositional father and uncles they must give Gram the chance to test out the parts of her self she'd had to keep hidden during all her years of responsibility and respectability.

"Moving to San Francisco requires the curiosity of a five-year-old and the confidence of a teen-ager," Caro said, "and I see plenty of both in Gram. There's nothing she can't do if she wants it badly enough."

Ruth nodded vigorously. "I've always wanted to be a pastor, you all know that. You also know I have never have had the chance to try." Her voice sounded close to tears, through her face was set in granite. "Heaven knows, I don't want to turn into a fossil, but I will if I stay in Cleveland. God only knows how much time I have left on this earth. And I want to spend it doing something glorious!"

"Go, then!" instructed Caro. "Follow your heart, for God's sake."

Timothy refused, but Simon and James helped their mother put furniture into storage and place family treasures into the hands of their wives.

Following a farewell lunch at Saint Matthew's, hosted by The Daughters of the King, Rev Ruth packed her clothes, her Bible and her Book of Common Prayer. She turned over the apartment key to the manager and the Buick key to her granddaughter.

"Grow old along with me!" Ruth jazzily quoted Robert Browning as a flinty-eyed James drove her to the airport. "The best is yet to be," she sang, "the last of my life for which the first was made."

The BOARD OF BEACONS

"I called tonight's meeting because our interim priest," said Beka, tilting her head toward the Reverend Ruth Ridley Salter, "has raised objections to the way we do things."

"You bet I have." Rev Ruth glowered from the foot of the table. "Any church worth its salt has DEAcons, and I know what Deacons do, but…"

Beka cut her off. "At Saint Lydia's, Beacons are selected by the congregation to plan for the needs of the whole church, not simply our own interests. We're here tonight to explain who BEAcons are, what BEAcons do and why Saint Lydia's chooses to have BEAcons. So, hang on while we explain."

Rev Ruth's face tightened, one fist wrapped around the head of her cane.

Beka gestured around the table. "Raise your hand when I say your name, and say a bit about how you became a Beacon so our new priest can connect your face with your story. Newest member first. Millienne Guillernos."

"It took mighty strong convincing to get me on the Board." Millienne's voice had a Caribbean lilt. "I stuttered like Moses. Who am I, to think God would use me? So I said no. Until Beka read Jeremiah to us, *O Lord, thou hast duped me.*"

The Beacons took it up, chanting the rest of the verse in unison, *Thou hast outwitted me and Thou hast prevailed.*

Dot exaggerated the next part, leaning back with a hand to her brow like a comic-opera singer. *I have been made a laughing-stock all the day long; everyone mocks me.*

Paige picked it up, speaking above the laughter. *But his word was imprisoned in my body,* clutching her flat chest, *like a fire blazing in my heart.*

"Quite a performance," said Rev Ruth, applauding despite herself.

"Sooo-ooo-oo, ladies." Beka raised an arm to get their attention. "Let's settle down. Hope Hudson."

"I want everyone to like me and approve of me," said Hope in her merry, self-deprecating way. "That's why I said sure, I'll be a Beacon."

"Thumbs up," said Dot, and everyone except Rev Ruth raised two thumbs amidst a flurry of whistles and cheers.

"As you can tell," Beka glanced at the pastor, "we regularly tell Hope how wonderful she is." Big grins; sparkly eyes all around. Even Rev Ruth cracked a smile.

"Okay, Paige Palmer."

"I said no to most church committees, but the Board of Beacons appealed to me," said Paige.

Rev Ruth's chin came up fast. She peered hard at the woman whose voice registered somewhere between alto and tenor.

"I'm more of a pray-er than a do-er," Paige went on. "I need a lot of time alone, which means I only say yes to things that mean a lot to me." She clasped her hands in prayer position in front of her heart. "Christ comes to guide me, to guide us. As Beacons, it is our job to listen."

"That makes sense," blurted Rev Ruth. "So go on, I'm listening."

"I joined Beacons because each one of us"—she glanced around the circle— "shares the same commitment to listen for the Holy Spirit. *Where is your heart?* we ask each other. *What do you care most deeply about? Which visions touch you? What grieves you so much that you're willing to work hard to change it?* Beacons make decisions based on questions like these rather than rules."

"Are you trying to tell me everyone at this table is a saint?" Rev Ruth stopped fiddling with her wedding ring and began picking at her cuticles.

"Heavens no," said Paige. "We have our share of problems, just like everyone at Saint Lydia's. We're a mixture of loving community and doctrinal frustrations. Some members are idealists and some are skeptics. Some love the sacraments and others avoid them. We pray for help with our troubles, but Beacons aren't slackers when it comes to doing the work of the church. Following God's call is difficult enough without acting holier-than-thou."

"Thank you, Paige," breathed Beka. "You explained us better than I could. Now, Dot Davis, your turn."

Dot lifted both hands and held them out, pink palms up, toward Rev Ruth. Her straightforward gaze caught the priest's eye and conveyed, 'don't mess with me.' Ruth glared back.

"Willing to be led by the Spirit, that's what it means to be a church leader," Dot asserted. "We keep each other honest, and we help each other listen for 'the still, small voice.' Spiritual guidance isn't something that is just granted to special people. To ordained people." She firmed her jaw and flashed her eyes.

Rev Ruth crossed arms over her chest and pressed her lips tight. Her breath came faster and coarser, but before she could say something rude, Millienne spoke up. "I was tempted to back down and step away from the Beacons when things got in such a mess with Pastor Peacock."

Beka almost raised a hand to quiet her, but stopped because she knew the big woman well; Millienne would not interrupt unless it was important.

"I am a peacemaker by nature," she said. "I *hate* conflict but once it became clear that we had to get rid of him, I had to stay involved."

"It's about integrity," added Dot, her voice firm. "That's the fire blazing in my heart. Integrity."

"And mine.

And mine." Each Beacon chimed in.

Their declarations clearly left Rev Ruth in turmoil. "Didn't anyone criticize you or discredit you for humiliating Pastor Peterson in public?" Her tone was smudged with rivalry.

Hope spoke first, with a smirk. "Two guys called us hysterical women."

Dot came out swinging. "Yes, we had detractors, but they had to face the dirty facts when our cameras caught him with the prostitute." She beamed with satisfaction. If the interim pastor wanted to pick a fight, the middle-aged Beacon was ready to spar.

Paige put in a softer word: "Some of our dear old men could not see the priest's behavior as acts of lechery."

Everyone could sense the competitiveness rising. To head off an outburst, Hope changed the subject. "Just like some women will not admit their own racism." Her face reddened.

"Thanks for reminding us of that, Hope." Beka glanced from Rev Ruth to Dot. They both looked ready to spit.

Beka hurried on. "Paige, Hope and I enjoy more privileges because we're white. And so do you, of course." She nodded toward Rev Ruth. "So whenever Millienne and Dot question our reasoning or make us explain ourselves, we all learn and grow."

"And then we pray for each other," added Paige, glancing around the circle. She was highly sensitive to flushed cheeks, pinched expressions and tight jaw muscles.

"Don't you get frustrated?" Rev Ruth baited them.

Dot scowled, aware that she wanted the Beacons to falter or show weakness.

"All the time," said Beka smoothly. "But once we accepted the mission of bringing a woman priest to Saint Lydia's, integrity wouldn't let us act bitchy."

Rev Ruth raised a foot as if to kick the leg of the table, then planted her oxford back on the floor.

Dot raised open palms to the sky and looked up. "We, the Beacons, believe in a church without barriers," she declared. "That's why we put our mouths and our money into making sure that Saint Lydia's is the most honest church in San Francisco."

"The kin-dom of God is what we're after here," said Paige quickly.

"Not just our own comforts and conveniences," added Millienne, patting her ample belly, "though we seldom go hungry."

Rev Ruth cleared her throat and adopted a sullen look.

Paige tried to regain the pastor's attention. "We started Lydia Circle to focus inward, to nurture our spiritual growth," she explained. "When we're intentional about praying together, sharing worries and joys, we are given the strength to focus on our work as Beacons."

Hope grinned, twisting her wrists like a prizefighter. "And these good women tell me I'm wonderful often enough that I'm beginning to believe it myself."

"Soooo-ooo-oo, to sum it up," Beka paused, glancing at her watch, "not every member agrees with our decisions and many don't see how we seek divine guidance, but things have settled down in recent months and the congregation appreciates a more peaceful church. Our leadership seems to affect everyone."

WAM

The Board of Beacons went over paperwork with Reverend Salter, confirming a one-year interim ministry contract. Beka deftly led the process, confirming that the Beacons would serve as her supervisory team. They would conduct a performance review at the end of each quarter. If, by September 1977, Rev Ruth and the congregation were getting along well, and if she was meeting their expectations for shepherding the flock and increasing the membership rolls, the contract would expand into a permanent position.

"Wait," cried Hope, pointing to the clock. I know it's late, but before we go, tell her about WAM."

"*WAM?*" Rev Ruth wrinkled her brow. "Sounds violent."

"Worship, Arts and Music," explained Beka. "After Pastor Peacock left, we called our members together and asked for their help. How could we work together to make our worship services more beautiful? More lively? More sacred?"

"But...but...worship is the pastor's job," sputtered Rev Ruth. "Ordained ministers are the ones who lead services of worship. What do you think we do in seminary! We're trained in liturgics." She briskly rubbed her forearms and massaged her upper chest as if pained.

"Well, "murmured Paige, "we have some very creative people at Saint Lydia's and they like to help lead worship."

Rev Ruth bit off each word and spit it out. "But. That. Is. What. You hired ME to do."

Congregational criticism had tilted Ruth's inner world so far out of control it was making her crazy. Once a successful chemist at Dow, she was terrified of being exposed for the incompetent imposter she believed herself to be. She tried to convince herself that graduating *summa cum laude* from Vassar, and earning a PhD from the University of Chicago qualified her to lead Saint Lydia's, but those achievements did not matter to these San Franciscans. They wanted more from her than she could deliver.

Critiques from the Beacons—or from anyone at Saint Lydia's—devastated her for days. Her own inner voice of self-contempt savagely picked her apart. Anxiety all but paralyzed her even when she tried to prepare a sermon.

Rev Ruth suspected she was acting irrationally but couldn't stop herself. She had always been driven to succeed, which now meant being the perfect pastor, while being painfully aware that she fell far short. Truth be told, ministry was more difficult than she had imagined, and a single year of didactic seminary classes had left her ill-prepared.

SLEEPLESS IN SAN FRANCISCO

At first, Beka was convinced Rev Ruth would be a hit with everyone. The Beacons had developed such a good plan and had, with the help of a friendly bishop, located the best and brightest woman priest in America. When they'd learned from her resume how Rev Ruth publicly supported the Cleveland electoral campaign of Carl Stokes, the first freely elected Negro mayor in the United States, they figured she would fit right into Saint Lydia's mixed-race congregation.

Dot pulled political strings and managed to rent a furnished studio apartment on Larkin Street for the interim pastor, just three blocks from the church. Everything seemed to be coming together perfectly, until Rev Ruth actually started work. Now everything seemed to be falling apart.

After the Beacons meeting, Beka could not get to sleep. In her head, she kept going over all the troubles since Rev Ruth's arrival. Bad sermons and negative reactions. Judgmental attitudes between pastor and people. Beka's own awkwardness in trying to make Rev Ruth understand what Saint Lydia's was all about. The Beacons' careful explanation of what they did at Lydia Circle, and how much their spiritual practices meant to each woman. Even when Beka wanted to think about something else, she couldn't stop hearing the arguments and feeling the turmoil. She couldn't stop worrying about Hope's flaming face and Dot's clenched fist. The smallest details lurked in her mind. The bad feelings upset her stomach; nausea kept her awake.

She knew she should speak to Rev Ruth, but didn't know what to say. Things were still too confusing. No matter what she did, she was afraid she'd look bad and sound stupid. And Beka could not bear the thought of feeling stupid. The very idea made her pulse beat against her throat so fast she feared she was having a heart attack.

The next night was worse. She couldn't understand how anyone slept. Beka lay very still and held her breath, waiting for unconsciousness. Sometimes a moment of blankness would steal over her, then she'd be awake again, remembering again. How could she have been so wrong about Rev Ruth?

NUTTY FAMILY

"When I was a kid and things went wrong at home, my dad would always shake his head and mutter 'Luck of the Jews.'"

"Why?" Hope aimed a puzzled look at Beka. The Head Beacon said she needed advice and asked Hope to meet for afternoon coffee at Minerva's Greek Café.

"According to Dad, the bad luck started with our ancestors. Did you know I'm descended from one of the twelve tribes of Israel?"

Hope shook her head no.

"The tribe of Ashkerath. Grandpa Ash simplified his name when he came to America." Beka squished her eyebrows together and took a tiny bite of honey-layered *baklava*. "I wasn't raised Jewish, but did grow up convinced I was born to be unlucky."

"Why are you telling me this now?" Hope's expression turned thoughtful. "What's bothering you?"

"Rev Ruth. She's so stubborn, and she acts so self-righteous. I wish I could undo my decision to hire her." Beka's eyes went dark and serious.

"Blaming yourself, are you?"

"Dad could turn anything into an occasion for blame." Beka bit her lip and spoke in a monotone. "Unluckiness hangs over me like a storm cloud."

Her gaze landed somewhere in the air beyond Minerva's bakery counter, so she missed seeing her friend's half-smile.

Hope raised an arm and leaned back with exaggerated casualness. "So, you're showing me a glimpse of your Jewish dark side, then?"

They exchanged tight smiles. Beka's body posture collapsed. "I'm not sure why I'm telling you this. I don't usually talk about my nutty family. They didn't raise me with any sort of religion, they just raised me to feel unlucky."

Hope gave another knowing smile over the rim of her cup.

"Growing up in that crazy house left its mark. Dad still makes me doubt my capacity to make good decisions, as you can tell."

"You are not to blame, Beka." Hope spoke calmly. "You may have a nutty family, but everybody is subject to bouts of self-doubt. Remember, it was a group decision. We all agreed to hire her. And remember, too, this is not forever. If she doesn't shape up, we'll send her back where she came from."

LONELY

Hope Faith Hudson was lonely, but found it impossible to admit out loud. The idea of talking about her loneliness was too difficult, too embarrassing. If someone asked why she hid it, Hope would have been stumped. If someone were to ask

'Have you been lonelier since Hank died?' she had no idea how she'd answer. Hank had been a Boy Scout of a husband. Loyal. Thrifty. Trustworthy. No, this wasn't about him.

Dank thoughts seemed to grow around Hope like mold. Her loneliness felt perpetual, no matter how hard she tried to scrub away the mold spores of loneliness. They must have taken root midway through her teens. Now they were impossible to dislodge.

Lonely people are restless sleepers. During her broken nights, San Francisco seemed a place of sewage and seepage. Thrashing beneath her daffodil-yellow chenille spread, she'd think back to how the Fillmore used to be when she lived there in a studio apartment, before she married Hank. She had to be so vigilant, had to steer clear of guys selling heroin in stairwells, derelicts squatting in burned-out buildings and gay men cruising in the shadows.

Hope was engulfed in sweet kisses with a smooth-faced boy when an SFPD siren split the night, plummeting her into a moldy pit of adolescent shame. In her fuzzy siren-addled half-awake state, she tried to define loneliness. It was like being hungry, she decided. In fact, it was like being hungry while everyone around you is not only well fed but also thinks it's shameful to be hungry.

By morning she decided widows are expected to be lonely but nobody wants to hear about it. Loneliness, she heard on a morning talk show, can even be fatal. A doctor on TV said it drives up blood pressure, but Hope would swallow the pills and bear the stigma of high blood pressure rather than admit to being lonely. A medical researcher was interviewed, too; he said loneliness accelerates aging. Well, the date on her birth certificate—1915—matched her thinning hair, wrinkled eyelids and ridged fingernails, so she figured there was no cure for growing old.

Most worrisome of all, another doctor on TV said lonely people are at high risk of losing their marbles. This made the pulse pound in her temples. Hope did not want to go cuckoo.

Okay, I am alone a lot, but that's because I like my own company, she protested to the man on the TV. *And I am not totally isolated. I talk to little Rex on the phone whenever his mother lets him call.*

Her voice sounded wild in the quiet house, even a little wacky. *I cook dinner for my divorced son when he drives in from Fresno. And I visit Laguna Honda Hospital once in a while to drop off batches of knitted lap robes. Is that enough to hang onto the rest of my marbles?*

What am I doing, talking to a guy on TV? Maybe I am going wacky.

Then the truth hit her. Beyond her small and far-away family, if it weren't for the women of Saint Lydia's Church, Hope would see no one at all.

CHAPTER 3

THE TUNNELS
Underneath

PUB TALK

The Beacons came up with a plan. Beka would invite Rev Ruth to mark a day of sunshine with an Irish coffee at a sidewalk table in front of Clancy's Pub on Lincoln.

"No fog," observed Rev Ruth, "but a stiff breeze.'

"Fall is our sunniest season," said Beka, unbuttoning her jacket and hanging it over the back of the metal chair.

"That's encouraging," said Rev Ruth. "I was beginning to wonder if the fog would ever lift."

"Is the wind too cold for you? We could move inside."

"Too noisy in there." Rev Ruth touched both ears with gnarled fingertips. "Thank God I don't need hearing aids—yet—but I don't want to push my luck."

Pedestrians glancing at the good-looking pair may have wondered if they were mother and daughter. There was little physical resemblance but both appeared confident, even elegant, in tailored pantsuits. The white-haired one wore a clerical collar and a gold cross on a slender gold chain. The dark-haired one accessorized her pantsuit with a silk scarf in bold shades of pink, orange and red. The older one wore sensible black oxfords while the younger one bounced a red leather sling-back pump from a big toe bright with lipstick-red polish.

There was a lot to say about what was going on at Saint Lydia's and they said some of it. Then Beka brought up the central conflict. "I'm feeling a bit guilty about acting as if I'm taking over your job," she said. "I don't know why you didn't take me to task on that." This was a conversational gambit. She said it for the sake of form, though her facial expression hinted that she didn't actually feel the emotions behind her words. Growing up with an unpredictable mother had taught Beka how to create a favorable impression on older women, and of course she liked to be admired by people of all ages.

"Mistakes happen," said Rev Ruth sweetly. "I was as much at fault as you."

It was a genial afternoon; they exchanged a few more pleasantries before it was time to head home. Kindness goes a long way, thought Beka after she dropped Rev Ruth at her studio apartment. *Don't do it,* Patty would have cautioned her. *The woman has a jacked-up nervous system and hidden hurts. Training Rev Ruth to be the kind of leader needed at Saint Lydia's is likely to drive you mad.* But Patty wasn't here to counsel her any more. The new interim pastor was tightly wound, and getting along with her was tricky, but the Beacons figured she just needed to be gently handled. Well, kindness it would be then. Kindness is what we shall hope to achieve.

ORIGINAL JOE'S

Rev Ruth, bundled up against the chilly wind off the Bay, was pleased with herself for convincing Beka and Dot to tell her what had happened with Pastor Petersen. They insisted the story must be told over supper at Original Joe's in North Beach. Why here? Because Joe DiMaggio owned the restaurant and Beka adored the baseball star.

Rev Ruth thought Original Joe's was a classy place; it brought her opinion of the youthful Head Beacon up a notch. The walls were covered with baseball memorabilia, oversized pictures of Marilyn Monroe and a huge wedding photo of the famous couple.

Beka flirted with the maître 'd to score a table near the window, then ordered a bottle of old-vine Zinfandel. They sipped as they waited for Dot Davis. "My accomplice has a habit of running late," said Beka.

Rev Ruth nodded without comment, and gestured toward the cathedral across Washington Square. "Grand place to be married."

"That's the Church of Saints Peter and Paul," said Beka, "but Joe and Marilyn only had their wedding photo taken there. They were actually married at City Hall."

"City of Dreams," said Rev Ruth. "Did they serve Rice-a-Roni at the wedding supper?"

"Why?" Beka looked puzzled.

"You know," said Rev Ruth, batting her eyes and humming the tune of a radio advertisement. "Rice-a-Roni, the San Fran-cis-co treat," she sang.

"Even Rice-a-Roni couldn't save that marriage," said Beka. "But we are on holy ground for pasta."

"Which means?

"Original Joe's is the city's oldest Italian restaurant, the birthplace of chicken tetrazzini. Our Hope Hudson makes a homemade version of chicken tetrazzini and brings it to church potlucks. Spaghetti mixed with Velveeta cheese and Campbell's cream of chicken soup."

"I'll skip that dish." Rev Ruth wrinkled her nose and picked up a menu.

They heard Dot before they saw her, classic wooden Dr Scholl's Exercise sandals resonating authoritatively on the plank floor. "Bought them at the drugstore," said Dot, gesturing. "They keep my calves toned." She was the tallest of the three, but tonight there was no question of who was in charge.

"Rev Ruth," declared Beka, "if you're going to be part of Saint Lydia's, you need to know the whole story of how we brought Pastor Peacock to his knees. But first we shall dine on handmade tortellini with spicy Sicilian sausage. I'll order for us."

The pastor gave a phony smile. "I don't see that we have any alternative." She closed her menu. "Tortellini and sausage it is."

"There are always alternatives," said Dot, "but in the spirit of clandestine female bonding, I recommend following our Head Beacon's suggestion." Raising her wineglass, Dot toasted "To the little things."

Beka clinked glasses. "To catching the suspect in his lies."

"Am I missing something?" asked Rev Ruth, peering at their faces.

"All will be revealed." Beka put an actress-y edge into her voice. "First, a good meal then a great story. After cream puffs and lattes, a tour of the alley itself, unnamed but notorious."

PHOTO SHOOT

"We didn't have a Bishop to lean on, no church authorities to step in when Pastor Peacock stepped out of line," said Beka. "We had to do something and Millienne came up with a good plan to trap him. Just two blocks from here." She pulled the bill of an imaginary cap down to shield her eyes. "Ready for a great detective story?"

"I'm all ears," said Rev Ruth, hunching forward to hear over the crowd.

"To set the scene," Beka went on, "the alley without a name has none of the trappings that make North Beach so picturesque. Washington Square draws lots of tourists. You've probably seen photos; old men sunning themselves on park benches; Catholic schoolgirls playing hopscotch; men in tank tops flexing biceps at pretty girls."

"But if you grew up in San Francisco," Dot interrupted, "you'd know North Beach is not so idyllic. Too many old people living in poverty. Too many guys with no place to call home, asleep on the grass. Too many drug dealers and young prostitutes."

"Dot is a loud advocate for social justice," said Beka, flashing a grin across the table. "She can teach you a lot about San Francisco."

"Later," said Rev Ruth. "For now, the alley without a name."

"When we followed him one night, we found his paramour's place in that grimy alley, very narrow and only half a block long," said Beka. "To get to where we could confront him, we had to squeeze past cars pulled up on a narrow strip of sidewalk, then wiggle our hips to move past a huddle of trashcans."

"And avoid stepping in dog litter," added Dot, wrinkling her nose.

"And climb a stairway that stunk of cats and garbage," said Beka.

"And wait nearly two hours at a dark turn of the stairs," said Dot, "holding our noses with one hand and our flash cameras with the other."

Rev Ruth shivered. "Oh, a goose just walked across my grave."

"We were ready." Beka plunged on as if Rev Ruth had not spoken. "Finally, the predatory pastor came strolling down the alley with one arm draped around a curvy blonde woman."

"We let the illicit pair get halfway up the stairs before we flared flashbulbs in their faces." Dot grinned proudly. "'He shouted, 'What the hell!'"

"We got a dozen shots of two wide-eyed and highly alarmed lovebirds before he raised an arm to shield his face." Beka's smile matched Dot's.

"You should have heard my accomplice here," said Dot. "Beka had steel in her voice when she said 'We see you, pastor of Saint Lydia's Church!'"

Their eyes held; both nodded. "Our Head Beacon can be as cold and unbending as a railroad track," said Dot, nodding toward Beka.

"He recognized us. I saw his eyes glitter and heard the tremble in his voice when he asked what do you want."

"Your resignation!" They yelled it in unison, just as they had on that fateful night. Their volume startled nearby diners in Original Joe's.

"Sounds as though you'd rehearsed that," grinned Rev Ruth.

"Nope," said Beka. "Neither of us foresaw the imperfect minister asking the perfect question. Especially so early in the game."

"The creep grabbed for my camera but he didn't get it," said Dot, pitching her voice lower. "He growled, "What makes you think I would resign?""

"My pictures, that's what!" announced Beka.

"And mine," said Dot. "I hollered that last part over my shoulder because by then we were halfway down the stairs. "Tomorrow," I yelled, "both sets of photos go to Herb Caen at the *San Francisco Chronicle* unless your resignation is on the desk by noon.""

"Noon is also the deadline to have your stuff out of the pastor's study," added Beka. "Got that?"

"Got it', we heard him moan," said Dot, "just as we bolted out of the alley." Her smoky alto deepened dramatically. "And that's the last we saw of him."

PREDATORY PRIEST

"What led you to take part in the photo shoot?" asked Rev Ruth, gesturing for a refill on coffee.

"Pastor Peacock had it coming," declared Dot, "and I think he knew it. After I caught him staring down my blouse while I knelt at the communion rail, I confronted the guy. You know," she said, peering hard at Rev Ruth, "I was raised in public housing. It was tough growing up on welfare and I know the cost of poverty. I also know the uselessness of fear, so I was not afraid to confront him. It didn't take me long to tell him I was not about to put up with his lustful stares."

"What did he do?" Rev Ruth stared into her cup.

"When I barged into his office and said my piece, that man did not even look at me. He tried to hide a scornful smile behind his mustache, which was not a good hiding place. And you know what the fool said to me! 'Every clergy man worth his salt has a healthy sex drive and you would, too, if you were a man.'"

Rev Ruth gulped, grabbed her napkin and coughed a little coffee into it.

"He mocked me, like this," said Dot, rolling her eyes toward the ceiling and setting her jaw. "He lifted his eyes toward a holy-looking Jesus on the wall, stood up and stepped right past me, as if I was a dead fly."

"What did you do then?" prompted Beka, wanting Rev Ruth to hear the whole story.

"I watched him strut out, then I busted out laughing."

"Laughing? Why?" Rev Ruth furrowed her brow.

"Because he looked exactly like the perfect man on top of the wedding cake. Parted hair, clipped mustache, creased trousers. No wife in sight, though. Poor, pale Missus Petersen seldom showed up at church. And everyone knew there was no place on top of Pastor Peacock's cake for a woman like me." Dot gazed down at her ample bosom. "No place for a buxom black social worker sporting tangerine polish," she declared, flaring her hands to show ten brightly painted fingernails.

"That's quite a story," said Rev Ruth. "How about you, Beka? What made you take part in the photo shoot?"

Beka hauled in a big breath, then another before she could answer. "I felt like one big bruise after his assault. Six months before you got here, after choir practice, just as I was reaching for my coat, the lecherous priest laid hold of me. Here." She placed a hand on her left breast and worked to calm her hitching breaths. "He twisted my nipple hard enough to leave bruises."

Dot and Rev Ruth held a respectful flash of silence until Beka recovered her voice and went on. "I fled, but when I got home I could not sleep. I listened so hard for his footsteps that the night seemed solid." Her breath came fast and shallow. "I wrapped my comforter around me like goose wings but couldn't stop shivering. I imagined slapping his smirky face. It felt like hitting solid cheekbone, even in my imagination, but I kept at it to get rid of the dirty feeling of being a sex object to my pastor."

Dot nodded sympathetically and covered Beka's hand with her own.

"Most of that ugliness stayed coiled up tight inside. He squeezed every bit of beauty out of me and left nothing but disgust. I had no way to uncoil it until Dot came to see me." Beka lifted her hand from the tablecloth and placed it atop Dot's.

HORTON

Rev Ruth ordered another round of lattes. "And how did Reverend Petersen get along with other people at the church?"

Dot launched into it. "Soon after be groped Beka, Matilda Harris came before the Board of Beacons. She represented the Board of Christian Education and came to report what three Sunday School girls were saying about the pastor."

"Which was?" said Rev Ruth.

"So disturbing that Matilda said she didn't feel good repeating it. She looked down at her tennis shoes for a while, then whispered, 'That's why I asked for a place on the Beacons agenda tonight.'"

"Beka told her we were aware of some problems and encouraged her to go on. Well, the girls told their Sunday School teacher that Pastor Petersen had accused the Head Beacon of being a Jezebel." Dot looked briefly at Beka; they both shook their heads. Dot went on. "Matilda asked if we could do anything about that. Paige said we sure could because the Board of Beacons is empowered to do more than bandage wounds of injuries caused by a wicked man."

Beka broke into the story. "There's one more thing. Matilda was gaining spunk. Reverend Petersen also told three sixth-grade girls that God commands them to remain virgins so they won't get mud on their wedding dresses. She asked us if we believed that and Hope assured her we did believer her. Millienne said we would do something about it, though it may take us a while to figure out what."

"A suggestion," said Matilda with a crooked grin. "An idea from Doctor Seuss."

Dot paused dramatically. "Matilda had our full attention as she recited these lines from _Horton Hears A Who_:
  Call a big meeting!
  Get everyone out!
  Make every Who holler!
  Make every Who shout!

IN CHARGE

Rebekah Miriam Ash had often been told that people saw her as restless, though she preferred to think of herself as direct and competent. Beka had always been ambitious about improving herself; she also got edgy unless she was in charge. By sixth grade, she had gained a reputation for becoming irritable unless people did what she wanted. She thought of herself as a born leader; others complained she was a lousy follower.

Born June 6, 1950 in Los Alamos, New Mexico, she'd grown up surrounded by chain-link fences, identity badges, security gates and uniformed guards. Her childhood was also marked by falsehood, as she saw it, official lies sanctioned by the Department of Energy. Beka was frustrated that her parents hid vitally important things–truthful things—and so did her teachers and her government.

Grandpa Ash had been a nuclear engineer, and she'd trusted him. Her parents were not scientists, although they pretended to have insider knowledge. Rebellious Beka made sure people knew her dad was only a supply clerk at the Lab and her mother was just a housewife. Joshua and Miriam Ash were atheists who adored atomic research; they claimed nuclear fission would solve all the world's problems. Beka suspected this was not true, because Grandfather Ash taught her to use her mind to analyze things in the world around her. He died when she was thirteen, but by then she trusted scholarly data more than she trusted most of the people she knew.

At nineteen, Beka found out she was bisexual. Here in San Francisco, however, she kept quiet about her flirty adolescence, Miss Heterosexual all tarted up in high heels and Maybelline. After Clint Rogers asked her to go steady, oh, how preoccupied she'd been with making herself pretty. It hadn't taken long to lose her virginity to Clint, a clean-cut member of the debate team. "Sex is divine!!!" she confided to her journal the next morning. "Sex got me out of my mind and into outer space."

Along with exciting sex, Clint introduced her to a spiritual "gold standard." A youth member of the Rosicrucians, he convinced Beka that the real work of alchemy was spiritual in nature. Clint shared her passion for research. He whispered Rosicrucian secrets into her pretty ear; methods of distillation, coagulation, and dispersion that ancient alchemists used to turn base metals into gold. Beka was intrigued, eager to learn more about this mysterious process. She also liked the idea of "gold" as a metaphor for the spiritually evolved person. She wanted to become a spiritually evolved scientist, she just didn't know how. Clint wasn't much help with that.

During freshman year at the University of Colorado in Boulder, she fell for roommate Rosa. Their sexual explorations opened Beka to an even richer aspect of "gold." To her surprise, the mystical pleasures of making love with a hot young Latina brought forth Beka's masculine nature, which balanced her female side in a new, and quite powerful, way. "Receptive femininity and assertive masculinity in one unified whole! Now, this is true gold," she exclaimed to Rosa as they raised beer mugs in a post-coital toast.

In San Francisco a few years later, Beka found her soulmate in Patty Rosen. Patty was so smart. So gorgeous. So sexy. Beka couldn't imagine anyone—male or female—being a better match. They'd been so happy until the day after their first anniversary.

Until the trip to Disneyland. Until the accident.

IN LOVE

True, Beka Ash had done some bad things. *Well, that's just who I am,* she would say to herself; *I'm a risk-taker.* She had lied about some things, too, and wasn't about to stop now. She'd lied so often, in fact, and so well that she sometimes got confused about the facts of her own life. In truth, they were simple. She was born in Los Alamos to parents who meant well and did little. She'd taken up shoplifting as a teen, after watching Errol Flynn in *Robin Hood,* though she never stole from the poor. By fifteen she'd decided to work her way out of New Mexico, and soon did that. She liked the thrill of living on the edge, in the moment. On the run, she felt she had something exciting to go to during a year abroad in Madrid, where she not only learned the language but also how to get what she wanted. In conflict, she felt alive. Beka liked the smell of danger, the feel of her blood running hot.

When she came to graduate school at UCSF, nobody knew her. Nobody gave a damn if she was a hero or a thief. But when she first spotted Patty jogging off the softball field after a game in Golden Gate Park, Beka felt her legs give out, like they were made of string. She couldn't even breathe. A strange wheezing took hold of her lungs; she couldn't get enough air.

She'd matched her pace to fall into step with Patty. They walked side by side through the gates of the Arboretum and somehow got on the subject of love. It hadn't taken long. "If you were my sister, you wouldn't even believe in love," Beka declared. "I'll show you what love is." She'd grabbed Patty's hand and pressed it flat against her chest. Beka's skin was hot; her heart was pounding. She knew Patty felt it, too, though she wouldn't meet Beka's eyes. She knew this was a bold thing to do with a woman she met only ten minutes ago, but she loved the feeling of blood rushing to her head. It made everything heightened and fast and wild. "Now you know," she'd said, casting Patty's hand away. "Don't forget it."

The next day Beka lurked at the edge of the softball diamond and watched the game. Patty was playing shortstop. Does she know I'm here? Beka couldn't tell, but her heart was thudding, face on fire. When the game was over, Patty came straight for her and grabbed her hand. This made Beka feel like crying, but she stopped herself because once she started doing that, there'd be no hope for her whatsoever.

Now that Patty was gone, Beka could (usually) keep the tears at bay by staying busy, but the ache in her heart never went away. She figured Rev Ruth wouldn't have a clue what that felt like.

CENTRAL LIBRARY

In the beginning was the word, and Paige's word was *library*. In the beginning, before the Beacons got stuck on points of sacramental theology, Paige took Rev Ruth to San Francisco's Civic Center and introduced her to Central Library. This had been her salvation when she was young. Central Library was almost a hundred years old by the time the two women walked into its domed rotunda, dwarfed by the grand Italian Renaissance pillars and arches.

"Like a cathedral," said Rev Ruth, gazing up into the light.

"The library was my first church. Walk this way and I'll show you my little worship cranny." Paige's whisper turned irreverent. "I got my first library card here when I was in second grade, which took some doing. In 1950, it was easier to buy a gun in San Francisco than it was to check out a book."

"You must be joking." Rev Ruth wasn't yet acquainted with Paige's lopsided sense of humor.

"No ma'am, ah'm telling you the gospel truth." Paige spoke in an exaggerated slang. "Us darkies and Polacks had to fill out seven lines of info-mashun on a long form every time we took out a book." She gestured at the ornate checkout desk in the lobby.

"And to buy a gun?" Rev Ruth grinned to show she could play along.

"Just three lines on one short form. But only males could buy guns." Paige raised one palm and placed the other flat, as if on a Bible. "God's own truth."

Rev Ruth's face registered a mix of disbelief and sympathy. "San Francisco must have been a dangerous city when you were growing up."

"It was, even before the deadly Zebra killer gained fame. Not to mention all the women murdered by our Zodiac serial killer."

Rev Ruth looked alarmed. "How in the world could your mother let you come to downtown all alone?"

"My momma was usually spaced out on painkillers." Paige firmed her jaw. "She paid very little attention to me, so I was free to roam all over the city. I felt protected here in the library, despite the winos and crazies then"—she gestured around the marble lobby—"and now."

Rev Ruth nicked her head toward some men in baggy clothes. One was slumped forward, his disheveled head resting on a desk.

"But the librarians kept me safe," Paige nodded, "and reading kept me sane."

"What did you like to read when you were in grade school?"

"Everyone but Mark Twain." Paige grimaced.

"Why did you boycott America's favorite writer?"

"Because he was a dirty old man."

"How'd you know that?" Rev Ruth lifted tousled eyebrows.

"I saw a photograph of Twain wearing his white suit, posing with his arm around a little girl in a white slip. He had her head pulled tight against his chest and looked down at her in a repulsive way. It creeped me out. I decided I would never read anything written by an old man who fancied little girls."

Before Rev Ruth could think what to say, Paige turned away. "We'll go down this hall. I want to show you the walnut-paneled niche in the Reading Room where I first met Saint Thomas Aquinas."

COLORED

Dot Davis grew up in the Fillmore so she figured it was her duty to educate the new minister by showing her around the old neighborhood. During the war, The Lower Fillmore had been a maze of narrow streets and noisy, crowded clubs; in the light of peace, it was a less veiled district. It was safer to take Rev Ruth into the Fillmore during daylight; after dark it was a place of secrets that excluded white folks. Layer upon layer of secrets.

Dot's life sometimes felt puny against the backdrop of so much history. A native San Franciscan, she found a strange comfort in recalling how many good people had gone before and a strange uneasiness in remembering how many had already been forgotten. This was, she supposed, the natural order of things but she didn't like it.

"Careful," she said, guiding Rev Ruth into a covered walkway. "This area is in transition." They carefully made their way around the perimeter of a construction site where a bulky brick building was going up. "Looks bad enough now, but they had pig farms here in the late 1800s." Her Dr. Scholl's sandals clattered on the plywood walkway.

"At least the pigs are gone now," said Rev Ruth, stepping over a gap.

"Trouble is, they've been replaced by racist cops," muttered Dot, shooting a glare at a white policeman with belly spilling over his belt buckle. The jelly donut in the cop's hand quivered as he stared at Dot's curvaceous figure.

Dot changed the subject with a wide gesture. "Over there was Winterland, the ice-skating rink," she said. "We loved to skate there when we were kids, but it was bulldozed during the redevelopment project in Fifty-Six. The city knocked down homes and forced out countless families to widen Geary Boulevard. My people called it the Negro Removal Project."

"All in the name of progress I suppose," said Rev Ruth. "I am so sorry."

Dot changed the subject, not ready to reveal her angry sorrow. "After Winterland, we lost the boxing rink, then the whole Jazz District. See the Marcus Bookstore over there?" She flung out an arm. "Jimbo's Bop City used to be there. That's where Dick and I went on our first date."

Rev Ruth's gaze followed Dot's hand, taking in the Fillmore's uneasy mix of shabby three-story Victorians, cement-block apartment buildings, cut-rate liquor stores and greasy-spoon cafes. She had run out of responses.

Dot went on. "You can't see the civic scars, but we feel the losses every day. Negroes had a thriving community but urban removal uprooted thousands of us to make space for luxury condos and trendy restaurants. The Jazz District here dated from World War Two, when thousands of Negroes from Alabama and Mississippi were recruited to work in the shipyards. Freddy's Bistro, in the next block, was where Dick liked to take me on dates. Now we have to cross the bridge into West Oakland to hear good jazz."

By the time she ushered Rev Ruth into Ernie's Café, she had run out of things to say about the Fillmore. "Welcome to the home of Giants paraphernalia and mismatched mugs," she joked. "Ernie's is famous for buttered grits so that's what I'm having." Rev Ruth ordered coffee and a chocolate glazed donut.

Two gray-haired black men sat in an adjacent booth, eating grits and engaging in lively conversation. "You know, seems only a little while ago I was a Negro, then pretty soon I was black," one man said with a chuckle.

"Not real descriptive, since we're mainly brown," snarled the other, "but what the hell."

Dot and Rev Ruth bottled up their breath to try and keep quiet.

"Next thing I know," declared the first man, "black's out and African-American is in. What a mouthful."

"Well," asserted the second, "t'other day my neighbor kid—goes to City College—he tells me that's out, too. Now we are people of color." Both old guys let out a hoot at the same time, and it was all Dot and Rev Ruth could do to stifle their own.

"So I says to the kid what color is that? Back when I was your age we was colored people. The way things a 'goin', pretty soon we gonna be niggers again. The young man, he did not find it funny."

Rev Ruth did, though, and couldn't hold back. High color flushed her face as she flung out both arms and burst into raucous laughter. A split second later, Dot joined in. Their hilarity could not be contained. The white woman and the black one whooped and hollered with two old men of color, slapping tables and hooting until tears splashed into their saucers. A wave of happiness washed over them, erasing a bit of the tension prickling between the Beacon and the Rev.

CHAPTER 4

THE HILLS
Steep Climbs

FEARLESS

The Reverend Ruth Salter liked to think of herself as a brave player in the arena of church politics. She grinned, remembering the clever deal she'd struck with Bishop Tuttle in Cleveland. "I'll get out of your hair – what's left of it – if you'll send me to a church that won't stone a woman priest," she'd declared. The gambit had worked. She aimed a little prayer of thanks in his direction.

During the long controversy about ordaining women, and especially since her "irregular" ordination in 1974, Rev Ruth had been a thorn in the ample flesh of Bishop Tuttle, as he had been in hers. If he was relieved to get her out of the Diocese of Ohio, she was even more relieved to finally get a church of her own far beyond his jurisdiction, especially at an age when most priests were retiring from parish work,

People always told her they saw her as fearless. After nearly flunking out of Mrs. Oliver's School for Girls, Ruth set her heart on qualifying for admittance to Vassar and by God she did it—with the help of an expensive tutor. When the Dean of Students asked what she wanted to do after graduation, Ruth confessed she wanted to be a priest. "By the time you graduate, the Church will be ready for women priests," the

Dean insisted. Ruth could always get a laugh by quipping that she'd only been off by half a century.

And, of course, fearlessness was crucial in getting admitted to a graduate program in Chemistry. Ruth had to challenge some powerful men in order to earn her PhD, and many more to earn her place in scientific history. All along, though, she kept her sights on the Episcopal priesthood, refusing to be deterred by the fact that her church had never ordained a woman. The sin of exclusion fed Ruth's fiery fearlessness until she and ten determined women stormed the barricades and—with the help of two retired bishops—finally secured women's right to ordination.

In her mind's eye, Rev Ruth proudly reviewed her entry in the newest edition of *Who's Who In America*. Twenty-two lines! I bet nobody at Saint Lydia's can beat that. In fact, I doubt anyone in San Francisco is more famous, or more fearless, than I am.

By the time she was appointed interim priest at Saint Lydia's Church, the feisty Rev Ruth had been challenging authority for so long that she didn't know how to stop. But what nobody else knew, what she barely knew herself, was how the wily demon of self-doubt could still sneak up and grab her by the throat.

CIRCLE OF SAINTS

"Circle? What kind of a group is that?" sputtered Rev Ruth. "In Cleveland, we say what we mean. Ladies Aid Society means helping the downtrodden. Altar Guild means ironing napkins and polishing candelabra. So what do you San Francisco ladies do at CIRCLE? " Her tone had a sarcastic edge.

Beka Ash had stepped into the pastor's study to invite Rev Ruth to be their guest at Lydia Circle. She took a deep breath and studied the white-haired priest. Ropy arms crossed over a narrow chest. Wrinkled cheeks, sucked in. Stiff neck cords standing out above her white collar. Raggedy eyebrows lifted in challenge.

"In Circle," she said slowly, "we talk and listen. Pray for one another."

"Oh, it's a prayer circle then."

"Prayer and more. Circle is where we get real. Tell our own truths and hear each other's truths." Beka felt the sweat breaking out on her forehead.

"So it's a women's lib group." Rev Ruth nodded as if she had the gist of it.

"Yes. No. More." Rising color stained her cheeks. Beka Ash, scientist and scholar, was embarrassed to be stammering. Usually the most articulate woman in the room, she was not accustomed to being verbally cornered, especially by the priest she had expected to admire. Beka cringed at the possibility that the sweetness of Circle, even its sanctity, could be challenged by the very woman who was supposed to be their spiritual leader. Would her dear Beacons feel safe with the tart-tongued priest? Would she?

Turning her body at an angle to shield against Rev Ruth's judging gaze, Beka tried again. "Lydia Circle is where we help each other heal from our hurts. Where we explore spiritual practices and test new ideas." Her voice grew in volume and confidence. "We take turns leading the group. Each leader brings a topic that matters. We follow guidelines of courtesy and respect. In Circle, we grow closer to God and each other. It's our sacred place."

Rev Ruth's *hummpppph* was accompanied by audible blasts of air through both nostrils. "That's what church is for. But I'll come to your circle."

After they parted, Beka worried. Had she endangered her friends by inviting Reverend Salter? She called Hope Hudson, who let her fret and helped her settle down. She called Dot Davis, who told her to snap out of it. She called Millienne Guillernos, who assured her everything would be all right. She called Paige Palmer, who prayed with her. Together they came up with a strategy.

The leader usually hosted Circle in her home, but Beka's apartment in Upper Castro was in such a steep neighborhood that it had concrete steps built right into the sidewalks. Because the elderly priest had a bad knee, they decided to meet at Saint Lydia's. Beka arrived early to set the Circle, light the candles and cue the cassette tape.

Paige came next, carrying her usual aura of stillness. Hope, Millienne and Dot were uncharacteristically quiet as they settled into folding chairs in Fellowship Hall. Everyone shifted nervously when the priest limped in. We're all anxious, thought Beka with someone as famous, as outspoken and as unpredictable as the Reverend Doctor Ruth Salter. Time to show her who is boss.

"Tonight our topic is SAINTS." Beka spoke confidently. "Soon we will take a few minutes of quiet to ponder the question *Who is your saint?* I chose this theme as a way to include our new interim pastor and get to know her." Beka and Ruth nodded curtly to one another. Neither smiled.

"A little background," Beka went on. "The Greek word for saint is *aghios*. It comes from the same word as *sanctify* and it means 'to make holy.' Saint Paul used the word *aghios* to describe Christians because he said each of us is made holy by baptism. So, who makes life more holy for you? You can name someone living or dead, someone you know personally or someone you have heard or read about. We'll listen to the Monks of the Western Priory chanting the Psalms while we reflect on our favorite saint." She concluded by clicking on the cassette player.

A few minutes later she clicked off the music. "I'll begin, then we'll go around the circle to my left. You're invited to name someone you consider a saint, and tell a bit about why. I name Saint Anna, wife of Joachim, because she said yes to God. She'd been childless for twenty years when she got pregnant with Mary, the Mother of our Lord. She was thrilled, even though it was dangerous to bear a child in old age, and—"

"Wait a minute," blurted Rev Ruth. "Saint Anna is the prophetess in Luke. Where did you get this other Anna?"

"In the Apocrypha." It was all Beka could do to keep her voice level. "And we do not interrupt here in Circle. As I was saying, Anna is my saint because she raised her daughter to listen for the word of God and follow it. Saint Anna protected young Mary when she got pregnant out of wedlock and—"

"The Apocrypha? You read heretics?" Rev Ruth sounded scandalized.

"Yes." Beka sounded curt. "We sometimes read scriptures hidden by the early Greek church, but right now I must insist on keeping our guidelines."

Beka rolled her shoulders, releasing tension. Millienne and Dot did the same. No one looked at the priest. Rev Ruth blew out a noisy breath and stopped interrupting.

"So, Anna, the grandmother of Jesus, is my saint because she protects women who are vulnerable. That's all I wanted to say. Now," Beka turned to her left and nodded at Paige. "Who is your saint?"

"Saint Paul, because I was named for him and also because the word *aghios* can mean someone who is set apart. You know I choose to live apart from commerce and conflict. My *poustinia* keeps me separated from all that is not of God." She heaved a deep sigh and closed her eyes. A hush fell over the group. The Beacons had seen how Paige's dual gender set her apart, and how her sister's disappearance had separated her even further from the family relationships that most of them enjoyed. They respected Paige because she carefully avoided distractions that kept most people from wholehearted commitment to the living Christ.

Paige's eyes were closed, face serene beneath her five o'clock shadow.

With a nod, Beka signaled to Millienne. "I name Paige as my saint," she whispered in her lilting voice.

Paige's eyes flew open. A surprised intake of breath moved around the circle.

"Because," Millienne emphasized, drawing out the word and repeating it, "beeecaaaause Paige lives like the saints of old. She is not cruel or selfish. When temptations come her way, she takes 'em to the Lord in prayer." Heads nodded; eyes met. "And beeecause she reminds me of Erzulie, the Haitian saint my aunts worshipped when I was a girl. Erzulie loves mirrors and sweets, like I do, and she's nurturing, like Paige. Both my saints are tender and strong. Erzulie has her knife, and Paige has her scissors so they can defend themselves."

Laughter rimmed the room. "I hear we're all in accord on Millienne's saints," Beka said. "How about you, Hope?"

"I pass for now," Hope murmured, swiping a hand across her forehead. A hectic red colored her cheeks; sweat beaded the hairline below her white perm.

"You okay there?" Beka asked, peering hard.

"Just a bit out of breath." Hope's hands were splayed across her upper chest. "Need a little time to catch my breath."

"Take your time, my friend. We'll come back to you at the end." Beka's tone was reassuring. "Reverend Ruth, you're next."

"Well, I name Saint Anna, too." She narrowed her eyes at Beka and raised her voice in an effort to re-establish her ministerial authority. "I name the real Saint Anna, the one in the Gospel of Luke. She was a prophetess, even older than me. She fasted and prayed to be a pure channel for the Holy Spirit. The real Saint Anna was first to recognize baby Jesus as the Messiah." She ended on an oratorical note, glaring.

The silence among them was like a held breath. Millienne broke it with conciliatory words. "Not all saints are alike. True saints may be involved in fighting. Sometimes holiness gets tarnished. "

Rev Ruth's chin came up, pupils wide and brows lifted. "What?"

"Saints like the two Annas. They both fought shame with love. No fists, no guns. They fought with love."

This time the silence was light with relief. Millienne had made Beka and Rev Ruth both right. She was a peacemaker and everyone in the room felt warmed by understanding. Softened by empathy.

"So Dot, what say you?" asked Beka with a smile.

The hefty African American shifted her weight. Her folding chair creaked. "My saint is the woman that bugged Jesus until he helped her child. I don't know her name."

"Nobody does," Rev Ruth responded quickly. "You mean the woman who protested that even the dogs got crumbs from the master's table?"

"That's the one." Dot firmed her jaw. "That girl would not give up. She's my saint 'cause she gives me strength when I have to give them people at the welfare office a hard time."

"Yay, Dot!" Beka pumped her fist in the air. Everyone followed, except the priest.

"There are different kinds of saints," Rev Ruth cleared her throat. "Saint Paul says there are different gifts but the same Spirit. Different ways of serving, but the same God is served."

"Thank you," said Beka, "but here in Circle we don't preach or teach. We're here to listen." She did not look at Rev Ruth. Neither did anyone else. "Hope, you're last. Ready to name your saint?

"It's not easy to be saintly." Hope's voice was barely audible.

"Not even great saints were saintly all the time," said Beka, "but none of us can carry on without help. Who helps you the most?"

"That would be my grandmother. She's with the angels now, but she usually comes after the sun sets behind Twin Peaks and before sunup over Hunter's Point."

"So, tell us her name," Beka prompted.

"Susanna. Susanna Merritt Nelson. She had bones to pick with God and so do I." Hope's voice caught as if she might be choking on a piece of old bone right now.

"Tell us more," Beka encouraged.

"Grandmother Susanna tried to set the record straight for me. I was innocent and she knew it, but men made the rules in those days. Men broke the rules, then ruled about the rules and by their rules labeled me a loose woman." Hope's tone and face were both heated. Her voice broke and she swallowed hard. "Even my brother didn't believe me, didn't speak up for me." Her eyes blazed. "But Susanna did."

TRIGGERS

Beka fretted most of the night.

In her head, Beka went over a long list of things that troubled her. Rev Ruth's judgmental attitude toward Lydia Circle. Beka's awkwardness in trying to explain what they did and why Circle was so important. Even when the Head Beacon wanted to think about something else, she couldn't stop hearing Rev Ruth arguing over which ancient woman was the real Saint Anna. She couldn't stop worrying about Hope's flaming face and labored breath. The smallest details lurked in her mind. She could not even stop the picture of everyone but Rev Ruth pumping fists in the air for Dot.

Beka wanted to speak about this to Rev Ruth but didn't know what she would say. Things were still too confusing. Too humiliating. She was afraid she'd look bad no matter what she said. Stupid. Beka could not bear the thought of being made to feel stupid. Her pulse beat against her throat so fast she feared it was a heart attack.

The next night was worse. She couldn't understand how anyone slept. Beka lay very still, praying for unconsciousness. Sometimes a moment of blankness would steal over her for a moment, then she'd be awake and remembering again.

How could I have been so wrong about Rev Ruth?

BLUSTERY

"I don't like her!" Beka hit the table with the side of her fist. "And I don't trust her. How did we get such a pushy priest?"

"Well, you headed the search committee." Dot pulled the crust from her egg-salad sandwich and bit into the soft part.

"That's the problem. I'm kicking myself for pushing to bring Rev Ruth to Saint Lydia's. And now I'm too mad to eat!" She pushed away her pastrami on rye. "Have you noticed how often she butts in when she's with a group?"

"I have. I also see how you rein her in without getting hot under your own collar. Sometimes, anyway. Good work, Beka. Maybe you should be our pastor instead of her."

Beka's chin came up fast. Her gray eyes flashed and met Dot's brown ones across the small table. Their gazes locked until Beka dropped her head. Her long, dark hair fell forward, curtaining her expression.

A small smile crossed Dot's strong black face. The Gospel of John came to mind. *You shall know the truth, and the truth will set you free.* She didn't say it. Instead, she chewed slowly, nodding her head.

"Well, I still don't like her!"

"All right then, we can talk about our interim priest instead, but I've got your number, girl, and we both know it."

Beka picked up her iced tea and sucked noisily through the straw.

Half a dozen UCSF medical students pushed in from Irving Street, crowding the small café with animated chatter. Beka glared in their direction. Annoyance wrinkled the skin around her eyes.

"Back to Rev Ruth," Dot said. "What did you think she'd be like?" Her tone was level, her expression friendly.

"I thought she'd be sweet." Spit flew from her lips. Beka quickly dabbed her mouth with a napkin. "A nice little old lady." She grabbed her sandwich and took a big bite. "Sweet," she said, chewing forcefully.

"Tractable, you mean? Someone you could push around?" This time Dot's tone had an edge to it.

Beka raised her brows and flicked her eyes at Dot. Her posture went rigid and the cords in her neck twanged visibly. "That question has a painfully obvious answer."

"Which is?" Dot's fingers tapped the tabletop.

"Stop that. You don't usually act like this."

Dot opened her mouth to protest, then stopped short. She held up five fingers and stiffened them into a short push toward Beka, then folded her hands into a gesture of prayer and lowered them—very slowly—into her lap. "You were saying." Her voice was honeyed with politeness.

Swatting the air, then clenching both hands, Beka let out a blustery sound. "Yes. You are right." She aimed a forced smile at her friend. "Which I hate."

"Right about what? Say it," snapped Dot.

"Right about me wanting to be in charge at Saint Lydia's. Right about the way I handle difficult situations."

"Which is?"

"Right!" Beka exploded. "I do things right at our church. I know it and you know it. But the Reverend Ruth Salter does not know it. She could care less." Beka dropped her head into her hands.

Dot rose with surprising lightness for a big woman. On the way to Beka, she bumped butts with a slender student at the next table, murmured "sorry" and moved behind her friend. She placed two warm hands at the base of Beka's neck and massaged gently. "You are a good woman," she murmured. "A good pastor. And I've got your back."

TROUBLE

A three-year-old set off the trouble. Early in the Beacons Meeting, Rev Ruth let them know how outraged she'd been when a little girl caused a commotion during worship. "Who allowed that child to climb up on the pew and stamp her feet? She made such a racket nobody could hear my sermon. Why wasn't she in the nursery?" demanded the interim pastor.

The Beacons gave each other a look and exhaled in unison. Beka went over it again, the open-door policy of their historic church. "At Saint Lydia's," she repeated, "all people are welcome, including Sissy and her mother."

"Both are mentally...ummm...defective," added Hope. "But Sissy was so proud of her shiny new Mary Janes, she just wanted people to admire them." Hope directed a conciliatory smile toward Rev Ruth.

"Reverend, I trust that you remember," said Dot, "how Saint Lydia's was founded in the post-war Forties to combat racism in San Francisco." She spoke with exaggerated patience, slowly and a bit too loudly.

"Don't patronize me," snarled Rev Ruth. "You sound like a kindergarten teacher talking to an idiot child."

Everyone knew Sissy and her mother were black.

The women avoided looking directly at each other. A long awkward silence followed. Millienne stepped into it, in her sturdy low-heeled black shoes. She wore old-fashioned shoes because, to her, fashion did not matter a bit. She was known for wearing whatever made her comfortable. Now she smoothed the collar of a soft cotton turtleneck, worn beneath a mannish Argyle sweater. She arranged her large, strong-boned face into a neutral expression. "In this city," she said quietly, "this church has a well-deserved reputation for welcoming people of all languages, all races and all nations. Mentally retarded children are welcome here. So are disturbed kids who don't play well with others."

Rev Ruth eyed Millienne the way a tiger might view a baby elephant. "How far does this open-door policy go? Will every kid be in the pews next week, acting up like she did?" There was no softness in her gaze.

Nobody met her eyes. None of the Beacons tried to interrupt. They'd seen Rev Ruth in action long enough to know how quickly the old dear could get on a roll. It was best to ride out the storm. Everyone met her tirade with silence.

That's when Rev Ruth went ballistic, voice heated with indignation. "You'd even let robbers worship at Saint Lydia's? Rapists? You'd even welcome Patty Hearst and the bloody Symbionese Army, is that what you're telling me?"

Hope and Paige looked toward Beka, who sat with shoulders squared, hands flat on the thighs of her gabardine slacks. Her face had hardened. But before Beka could speak, Rev Ruth lashed out again. "You people would let Charles Manson and his deranged females into this sanctuary?" Her voice ascended to a shriek.

The Beacons took in lungs full of air. They gaped at Rev Ruth as if she was clueless. She ignored them, staring straight ahead in self-righteous fury.

At least she's paying attention to San Francisco's crime beat, thought Dot. She had often wondered what was going on in that gray head.

Rev Ruth wasn't done. "The Zodiac killer! The Zebra murderer! You'd even welcome assassins like those?"

The Beacons kept speechless, faces empty of expression. They could sense Dot preparing to counter-attack. They avoided eye contact until Hope shot a glance at the Head Beacon. What the hell do we do?

Beka forced a smile then gazed down at her caramel-colored Candie's. They were totally impractical shoes, but so fashionable.

Dot gave a loud, metallic bark of laughter. Ebony hair framed a furious face. Hard eyes challenged Rev Ruth's. "What is your point?"

For an instant Rev Ruth's raggedy brows drew down, then she willed away her frown. She curved her lips into a tight smile and lifted her chin with an imperious look, showing these women how forcefully she could escalate the tension. Ignoring Dot, Rev Ruth scanned the faces of the other Beacons. "If you keep the church doors this wide open, Pastor Peacock could walk right in and take over."

This time her remark struck their ears like an obscenity. Even Millienne lost her good manners in the melee that followed.

STANDING LIKE A TREE

Millienne Guillernos did her best to blend in. Wherever she went, she drew silence around her like a shield. Or better yet, a shawl. Born and raised in Haiti's mild Caribbean climate, prone to chills in San Francisco, she always carried a shawl. Two shawls, actually; one of wool and one of stillness.

She still felt like an outsider although she'd lived in the Golden State for twenty-two years. In the beginning she'd worked as a waitress, then a hospital aide, and now as a licensed vocational nurse. Some days, she wished someone would say, "Okay, Millienne, you have followed America's rules long enough. You are now free to be your own true self," but no one ever did.

She did not judge others so much as hold a kaleidoscopic view. She looked at others from a variety of angles and perspectives, which had its charms. And if she sometimes wondered whether the opportunity for romance had passed her by, she never thought of herself as a tragic figure. Wherever she went in her adopted city by the Bay, she sought connection with others even as she did her best to avoid confrontation.

She approached the innate loveliness of creation directly, absorbed it through her pores. Millienne carried herself like a Hispaniolan pine, though she never put this into words for herself or anyone else. Bodily intuitions pulsed up through the soles of her size ten feet, ancient knowings more suited to Creole, more sensate than the language of English could capture.

Rooted in shadow—like trees that sheltered her ancestors—memories of Grandfather's secret rituals gave her strength. He had showed her ways of loving as certain dark things are to be loved, without knowing where, or how or when.

Standing like a tree through seasons of darkness and light reminded Millienne that she belonged to something bigger. That's why she often went to the Arboretum in Golden Gate Park to lean quietly against the dark trunk of a pine and wait for guidance. There was something religious about gazing into the high, open crown of a tree, absorbing sunlight and insight. It gave her a sense of belonging to watch birds settle onto the high branches. Grandfather's spirit came near as she leaned against a pine. He said nothing, but his silence told her he was listening.

QUEEN TUT

"That new priest treated me like a servant." Mattie Henderson stamped her size twelve foot. "Here I am, measuring coffee and filling the urn like I've been doing every Sunday for twenty-some years, always making sure folks get treated right at Saint Lydia's." The sputter in her voice turned into a nervous, dry cough.

"You do make fine coffee." Dolly Mason filled the small silence.

Mattie went on as if she hadn't heard. "Never had anyone complain until Her Majesty strutted into my kitchen. She picked up the Folger's can, squinted at it and said 'Is this the best you can do?' Imagine!" Mattie lifted an age-spotted hand and brushed her bodice as if shooing flies from white lilies woven into the lavender polyester.

Three women stood at the long counter, pulling waxed paper from casseroles brought from home, stepping around each other to slide dishes into the warm oven. They were here for the noon potluck on the first Wednesday of each month. Lunch Bunch was a treasured social occasion among the older ladies. The menu was rich in desserts but today some came with a sour taste in their mouths.

"The new reverend asked me to bring her a glass of milk during Coffee Hour," added Millienne Guillernos. "When I told her we used powdered creamer, she said 'You mean to tell me you do not keep four percent homogenized milk in the refrigerator here?'"

"How bossy," said Dolly Mason.

Gossip about the interim pastor continued as they ate. Lunch Bunch ladies had strong opinions, seldom agreed on politics or economics but all contributed criticisms of Rev Ruth.

Queen Tut is how Mattie Henderson dubbed her, pairing the pastor's royal air with Egypt's King Tut whose golden masks and jeweled goblets were drawing crowds at the DeYoung Museum. The Lunch Bunch was getting carried away with Queen Tut jokes when Hope Hudson spoke up. "I had a bad impression, too, the first time she came to Circle." Her voice was calm. "I thought the new pastor was wrong to bully Beka, so when Rev Ruth phoned to say she'd like to visit, I almost told her I wouldn't be home."

"Why, Hope," blurted Mattie, "I've never known you to lie."

"You're right, I didn't lie, but I will confess something." Hope paused and looked around the table. The women stopped chewing. All eyes were fixed on her. "The truth is, I did not want to let the new priest into my house. There, I've said it." She refilled her teacup. "But, ladies, I changed my opinion during Rev Ruth's visit." She forked in a bite of scalloped potatoes and took her time chewing.

"So, tell us. What happened?" Mattie could be impatient.

"She's a widow, too."

"We know that. It was in her papers," Millienne's tone was dismissive.

"But did you know she was married to a twin, too, just like me?" Hope went on as if she'd not been interrupted. "Well, not exactly. My Hank was a fraternal twin and her Nolan was an identical twin."

"Ooohhh," mouthed three women in unison.

"Imagine that!" murmured Dolly.

'Twins. No kidding!" exclaimed Mattie.

"Rev Ruth does act like a tough cookie," she concluded, "but I think she's got a soft center." Hope thoughtfully rubbed two fingertips across the brown mole beneath her jaw. "In fact, she and I may be more alike than I first imagined. And speaking of cookies, who brought dessert?"

JEALOUS

Dot Davis's piercing gaze rankled Rev Ruth, reminded her of Mother whose scowl across the dinner table could make her feel it was wrong to be alive. *You were part of a matched set. Why did you let your twin sister die?* Little Ruthie saw each sharp shake of Mother's finger as an accusation. *I gave birth to two identical little girls, and you're not enough all by yourself.* When she thought about Dot Davis, which she had been doing a lot lately, Ruth felt ashamed and guilty, like a sinful child who deserved punishment.

But Dot Davis was not Mother. She was just one of five Beacons in charge of the pastor's future. Dot had her good points. She'd shown Ruth the alley in North Beach where they trapped Reverend Petersen. Gave her a guided tour of the Fillmore where they'd shared a few laughs with two old men. So why did Dot make her so uneasy?

What's the worst that could happen with Dot? The *worst?* Ruth didn't know where to start. Her imagination had become as morbid as Mother's. 'You can charm the pants off anyone if you set your mind to it,' Mother used to tell her, but Ruth did not care to charm the pants off Dot. A pantless Dot Davis was the last thing she wanted to contemplate.

During adolescence, Ruth had been frightened when she had to speak to powerful men. Father coached her "Remember, your teacher's bark is worse than his bite." The thought passed through Ruth's mind that Dot had gotten her teeth into the Head Beacon. Beka Ash was pretty and competent; smart enough to earn a degree from the University of California, but Ruth suspected the girl of ministerial pretensions since she'd stepped right into the pulpit after Reverend Petersen flew the coop. She figured Beka was susceptible to Dot's influence.

The reverend leaned back in the faded wing chair to mentally rehearse her views of Dot. The tall black woman was just too confident. She had made a name for herself in San Francisco as a provocative, and effective, child-welfare advocate. At church, she was an opinion-former. And she was the only Beacon with a husband.

The past three Sundays, Rev Ruth had stood at the door of Saint Lydia's greeting parishioners after worship when she heard the rumble of a motorcycle. She'd sneaked long, appreciative glances at the muscular Dick Davis and watched enviously as Dot hopped onto the bike and laid her cheek against her husband's leathered back. Jealousy seared the pastor's throat. It had been too long since a man had touched her. Ruth fiercely missed Nolan; she ached for their once-active sex life. Her head rolled back against the plaid upholstery. Imagination took her into Dot and Dick's bedroom where cries of ecstasy and sweat-soaked passion made her throat go dry with yearning.

One leg jumped with muscle contractions, jerking her back to reality. "Stop it," she commanded herself, but her voice came out barely above a whisper. She stared out the window where the buildings of Russian Hill glinted in the moonlight.

Stop it. Mother's voice. *Stop thinking about Dot's sex life.* Ruth suddenly saw herself as Mother would see her, a grumpy old widow trying to ease her loneliness by fantasizing about parishioners passionately embracing.

"Stop it," she said aloud, this time to Mother. "Stop it. Stop it. Stop it!"

A feeling of doom lurked in her gut. If Beka and Dot ganged up on her, the next Beacons meeting could be a car crash waiting to happen. There was every chance she'd end up in the wreckage.

BELONGING

Dot Delilah Davis was used to that sharp jab in the ribs that meant you don't belong, not here among sober, decent people. All her young life she'd heard her mother's heart drumming a single beat: drugs, drugs, drugs. Sunny Davis had lived to get high. Until addiction killed her. Dot vowed she would never use drugs, but still she had become all too familiar with the kind of forgetting her mother sought in heroin.

It was not until she took a first tentative step through the door of Saint Lydia's, greeted by the woman whose nametag read "Hope," that Dot tasted of the kind of hope that had eluded her for so long. Hope Hudson welcomed her with genuine warmth, then asked her to stay after worship and sort rummage. She could see Fellowship Hall heaped with boxes and bags of donated stuff; all hands were needed to sort and price everything before the big sale. Dot knew rummage, so she pitched in. This was somewhere she could belong. Saint Lydia's had been her refuge for twenty-some years, but now her church had come under threat. By a woman priest, for Christ's sake!

Instead of the anger Dot hoped to access when she thought about Rev Ruth, a hot ache throbbed at the base of her throat and quickly turned into a persistent ache down deep in her chest. She wanted to shake it off like a dog shook off rain. The only way she knew to do that was to get up and keep busy. If she didn't move, she'd be in danger of shivering to bits. Dot steeled herself by thinking of the one gift her drug-addicted mother had given her. *You are here for something better.* Sunny had repeated these words so often, they got permanently stuck in Dot's mind, like a sort of mantra. She was not ready to forgive either Rev Ruth or her long-departed mother, but Sunny's words could warm her like hot tea on a chilly day. *You are here for something better.*

Dot had a kind of seriousness about her, a reserve unlike anyone in her family, or for that matter, her whole neighborhood. Beka told her she looked at life more closely than most people. Millienne's eyes conveyed appreciation that Dot, too, could hold herself half a step above the fray. And everyone knew she was a hard worker, more dedicated than they were. Until Dick came into her life, Dot could lose herself in the mission of saving kids like her brothers from swirling down the drain and getting lost in San Francisco's fetid foster homes and juvenile halls. It was only when Dick made love to her in his tiny studio apartment that her natural reserve dropped away and she felt a fierceness that made her catch her breath.

Afterward, curled in bed, he'd ruffle her sticky hair and draw her close. For those hours, Dot was totally at one with herself and with Dick. His fingertips left a trail of goose-bumps across her shoulders. She loved that he could make her feel so treasured. She could sometimes calm the pulsing bruises of life by letting her memory follow the curve of his back, so that's what she did now. To ease her upset over the ways Rev Ruth was upsetting people at Saint Lydia's, Dot concentrated on recalling the muscles of Dick's thighs. The dark sweep of his hair. The Cointreau scent of his breath.

FAME

"I don't trust celebrities." Dot pinched the bridge of her nose.

"Talking about anyone I know?" Hope bit into a wedge of pepperoni pizza. "Rev Ruth, of course. She wants us to bend and bow because she says she is famous." Dot grimaced, grabbed a slice of pizza and chewed vigorously.

"Well, she did tell us she was well-known back in the Forties when she invented some new chemical compound, but why hold it against her now?"

"Because she expects to be treated like a celebrity at Saint Lydia's and that rankles me." Dot flicked fingers in front of her nose, as if waving away a bad smell.

"Your scorn is showing, my friend." Hope made a scowly face in Dot's direction. "I've heard it said that a celebrity is someone who is famous for being well known."

"And she expects us to be fascinated because of that." Dot applauded in a deliberately false fashion.

"Like how?"

"Like autographs. Last Sunday I saw young Tina Washington hold out her worship bulletin and ask Rev Ruth for an autograph." Dot narrowed her eyes.

Hope widened hers. "So what's wrong with that?"

"Do you know what our interim pastor did?" Dot slowed down her speech to emphasize the point. "She wrote her name at the very top of the worship bulletin, right at the top edge."

"Why?'

"Tina asked the same question. And do you know what the answer was?" Dot twisted her mouth and went on. "When one is famous, she said in that imperious tone of hers, one must always make sure she signs her name at the very top of the page."

"Why?" Hope asked again, wrinkling her nose.

"So nobody can write anything above her signature."

Hope gave her friend a puzzled look.

"Don't you get it!" Dot's volume caused two people in the next booth to look their way. "That's what's wrong with society today. The more we fan the flames of fanfare, the less attention people will pay to ordinary folks."

"Okay, Dot. You object to Rev Ruth feeding the fires of fame when she should be teaching young Tina to be humble. Is that your point?"

"Not humble, exactly. I just think it's wrong to encourage kids to admire celebrities instead of focusing on churchly things. Our religious leader shouldn't be kidnapping the kids' attention from matters of faith. It just isn't right."

"Last slice of pizza. Want to split it?" asked Hope.

"Nope, I'm full. But here's another thing. Have you seen how she carries her Vassar diploma in a pink silk handkerchief?" Dot rolled her eyes and blew out a breath that rattled her lips.

"Yes," said Hope. "She showed it to me soon after she arrived. 'This is to show I am a member of the elite,' she told me."

"Didn't it just make you sick?" Dot gave a quick, disgusted snort.

'No, it made me laugh. Reminded me of an old-time stage magician, pulling out a silk handkerchief and flourishing it open to reveal her fancy diploma."

"That's what I mean. Rev Ruth puts on a famous act. It's just not the right way for a priest to behave."

"She told me she's from the aristocracy," said Hope. "Her father was a famous politician in Cleveland."

"I hadn't heard that," said Dot, forming her fingers into a steeple.

"Rev Ruth does come equipped with upper-class tastes," said Hope, "but she's also quite thrifty. Ever notice how she goes around turning off lights? I made a hit with her last Sunday when I flicked off the lights in the kitchen while the coffee was perking."

"So, okay, she's thrifty with electricity." Dot's gaze came back into focus, including Hope in the moment.

"And she carries a Swiss Army knife so she can pare her own apple. I like that in a woman." Hope's lips twitched with amusement.

"She told Millienne that she thinks like a man and prefers to act like a man."

"What do you suppose she meant by that?" Hope straightened her posture and opened her wallet to pay the bill.

"When Millienne asked what she meant, Rev Ruth said it means she lets other people do her cooking and cleaning and sewing."

"Well, I won't be doing any of that stuff," sniffed Dot. "Not for her, not on your life.

CHAPTER 5

THE PRESIDIO

Traipsing

ROMANCE

When Dot got stressed, she took refuge in memories of her first night with Dick. She couldn't resist the man, even though sex was expressly against the rules she'd set for herself, even though she was fairly certain only one person was falling in love. But she was hungry for him and you never knew, never could tell about these things.

She wondered about him every time Dick showed up at IHOP driving a Harley but wearing a Muni bus driver's uniform. It got so she could hear him coming, would stop what she was doing to watch him park the gleaming silver and black bike at the curb. She would break into a sweat, watching him swing his leg over the bar and stride in.

And then it got so he would scan the room and head straight for her section. At first all he talked about was the Harley, and she loved listening. "My cycle means the world to me, everything," he said. "It takes every part of me to ride it fast at night. On the Harley, that's the only time I can catch up with the fire inside me."

She wanted a taste of that fire, someday, but first she was hungry for him. Hunger was the byword now. Nothing else mattered.

Time had the power to alter everything, even love. Even though her days were full of work and college responsibilities, it was worth burning the candle at both ends to ride behind him in the wind. Making love with Dick was hot and intense. It took her beyond the Western Addition, beyond the Fillmore. His hands made her feel things she hadn't expected, do things she hadn't even known about. With him, Dot found parts of herself she'd never known; deep, urgent, mysterious parts. She figured he'd probably been with a lot of women, but she didn't care because she was the one in bed with him now, and it wasn't one kiss but thousands.

The next morning, she was dreamy. Dot overslept and had to slip out of Dick's bed, run back to her own place and get ready for the morning shift. It wasn't easy being up half the night, doing things you shouldn't be doing, and then report to IHOP on time.

She poured black coffee at the counter and sipped it, standing beside Tillie. "I worry about things," she murmured, but her co-worker wasn't listening. Dot walked away fretting about venereal disease, the risks a girl could run sleeping with a man she'd just met. A stranger. She was thinking she proba-bly hadn't been so smart.

When her shift was over, she walked to the Panhandle and sat on a bench in the park, smoking cigarettes. It was mid-af-ternoon and cool. The city felt damp and gray. Most of the golden leaves had already shaken off the trees. She pulled in smoke and held it as long as she could.

One night when her mother was dying, she'd made Dot promise to never smoke. Emphysema was the worst thing she had ever seen. Dot was nineteen years old. Her mother, pale in the hospital bed, struggled for air. "Save me," she'd whis-pered, so Dot ran for a nurse who slipped an oxygen mask over Sunny's mouth. That was when Dot realized there are people you can't rescue, no matter how hard you tried.

Sunny was fickle about men and Dot had been too, until she married Dick. Early on, she decided to keep her husband to herself. Truth was, Dot did not want anyone at Saint Lydia's getting a whiff of him, so she made up a story about Dick being shy and preferring to stay in the background. She definitely did not want anyone speculating about what they did in the dark. On Saturday nights they stayed up 'til the wee hours, but she made sure to be on time, spruced up and in her pew by ten o'clock on the dot.

HERESY

"Do you smell something?" Mattie Henderson's nose tilted skyward. Agnes Bascombe followed her lead. "Smells like heresy to me." The Lunch Bunch ladies nodded in unison as they ate casseroles and gossiped about Dot Davis.

"Call me old-fashioned," sniffed Mattie, "but when I took the Lord Jesus Christ as my personal savior, I did not sign up for no cannibalism."

"Can you imagine such a thing?" Agnes again.

Hope didn't dare catch Paige's eye for fear of uncontrollable smirking.

"Oh well…" Paige struggled for something to say. "I can see how…so it's sort of a question of …"

She was floundering pitifully, so Rev Ruth helped in her usual way, by interrupting. "I know what you mean. When you belong to a non-denominational church, you expect to be given the purest version of the sacraments."

"Thank you!" Mattie and Agnes spoke in unison. "I told Dot we want to be with Jesus all the time, too," added Mattie, "but I can't imagine saying I eat him."

Just then, Rev Ruth pulled from her bag a communion set crafted of Regency sterling silver. Why she carried it to Lunch Bunch, Hope could not imagine, but there it was, wrapped in an ivory silk scarf, the kind a bigwig would wear to the opera.

"This," declared Rev Ruth, "is the pure and only way to receive the sacrament of Holy Eucharist." She held the engraved chalice aloft in one hand and the shiny round paten in the other. "The body and blood of our dear savior must be blessed by a duly ordained priest." She tilted the chalice toward her own heart and modestly ducked her chin. "And consumed in a liturgically appropriate place."

A dumbfounded silence overtook the Lunch Bunch, or maybe it was a reverential silence. Hope attempted to lighten the mood. "You may not get everlasting life from this, but do take another helping of my chicken tetrazzini. The recipe was invented right here in North Beach in 1908, in honor of a famous opera singer "—long pause—"whose name I have forgotten."

She meant it to be funny, so the ladies laughed, grateful for a moment of levity to release them from the unwelcome and overbearing solemnity of their new interim pastor.

THORNS

How had things gone so wrong? The ladies of Lunch Bunch, chattering happily in the kitchen, had left her alone at the table. Rev Ruth had expected to be happy in San Francisco, but she was not happy.

Carefully rewrapping her precious Regency chalice and paten in Father's silk scarf, she felt their bad attitudes tearing into her like a thorn in the flesh. Dot Davis was certainly a troublemaker. Beka Ash, too. Did the Apostle Paul have women like this in mind when he wrote about being tortured by a thorn in the flesh?

The best defense is a good offense. Father's voice. Adopting an offensive strategy worked well for the distinguished Doctor James Salter. It helped him gain respect in Cleveland's medical community, and gain traction with local and national politicians of the Republican variety.

Maybe she needed to needle people the way Father did. Maybe a good old-fashioned brawl would clear the air at Saint Lydia's.

Rev Ruth left the church, head bowed against the wind, imagining ways to blast the Beacons out of their self-righteousness.

Half an hour later, she realized she'd been so busy plotting revenge that she had taken off in the wrong direction. There was no option but to retrace her steps.

WIDOWS

By God, Rev Ruth was determined to succeed in San Francisco, even if it meant making pastoral visits when she would much rather write sermons. Listening to complaints about arthritis bored her, but the importance of pastoral care had been drilled into her during seminary. "Do not build your church upon the sand!" Professor Dobbs could shout like an evangelist. "Every priest must build his church upon the solid rock of pastoral visitation."

It was slow going with her bum knee, climbing the grade to Hope Hudson's house in the Upper Haight. Halfway up, she plopped down on a bench to catch her breath. She was no spring chicken, after all. And nobody had warned her the whole city was vertical.

Professor Dobbs' stentorian voice came to mind as she rested. "Pop quiz!" he would shout. "What IS the rock of ministry?" He had trained the divinity students—all men, except Ruth—to shout *Pastoral Visitation* in unison, as if they were kindergarten kids. Dobbs' silly strategy must have worked, she thought. It got me away from my desk to climb the steps of a small stucco house and knock on a parishioner's door.

Hope's greeting was cordial but restrained. She motioned Rev Ruth to sit in one of two matching brown leather La-Z-boys facing a wide television console. The TV was on, an audience-participation show, but soon Hope snapped off the power and murmured, "Take Hank's chair."

"Will he be joining us?" Ruth eyed a tweed couch with crocheted doilies covering the armrests.

"No, he's....not here." Hope swallowed. "Won't be back." She swallowed again. "He died last year."

"Oh, I am so sorry. I know how hard that is. I'm a widow, too."

"How long has your husband been gone?"

"Nearly a decade. Nolan was much older. Died at home, beside me in bed, just before dawn on his seventy-ninth birthday."

"Oh, I'm sorry." Hope's voice was barely audible.

Ruth went on as if no one had spoken. "My husband was an identical twin. His brother Neils died earlier that year, and Nolan missed him terribly. When I realized my husband had stopped breathing, I called my son Timothy, who came right away. "Papa couldn't face a birthday without his twin, he told me. I think he was right."

"Hank was a twin, too. Fraternal. His brother Chuck is still alive. In Montana." Hope's voice cracked.

Two white-haired women sat in quiet remembrance, twisting golden bands on knotted fingers, lost in their own thoughts. When the Hummel clock on the mantel chimed eleven, Rev Ruth fingered a gold cross on a fine chain resting in a canyon of wrinkles at her throat. "Tell me about your loss, if you wish."

Hope cleared her throat. "Hank and I wanted happy endings but neither of us necessarily believed in them." She rubbed her nose, already reddened, and nervously rubbed two fingers over the brown mole beneath her jaw.

"The night I found him burning with fever, I called the ambulance. Doctors thought he might have TB, so everyone had to wear masks in his hospital room. Those masks! Hank told me he knew it was bad news when the nurses stopped wearing masks and started treating him with excruciating kindness. He always did tell dumb jokes, clear up to the end."

"And how did the end come?"

"Awful. Cancer metastasized to liver and brain. Inoperable. Necrotic. 'We can make him more comfortable.' The end came in ten days." Hope's voice went ragged and petered out.

Rev Ruth's legs were weak as she hobbled to the bus stop. There was more to say about her own loss, and more to hear about Hope's, but on this day, neither widow had the strength to say more.

OPTIONAL

Rev Ruth was mad and she let the Beacons know it. "The communion table should be in the CENTER of the sanctuary, in the place of greatest honor! Yours is pushed over to one side and that is just not right!"

"You also objected because the pulpit is not in the center," said Beka heatedly. "Communion table and pulpit are on opposite sides of the chancel because the sacraments and the sermons are equally valid ways to focus attention on the love of God."

Rev Ruth was on her feet, waving her cane at Beka like a sword. "You couldn't speak with more satisfaction if you'd come up with that parallel yourself." Her voice was metallic with irony.

Cheeks flushed to plum, Beka rose and stepped closer to Rev Ruth. With fists clenched against hips like a warrior, she spoke slowly and loudly. "At Saint Lydia's we welcome every person who walks through our doors. Each is unique." She enunciated each word clearly. "Each is beloved of God."

Rev Ruth opened her mouth but Beka stopped her with the glare of a prophet. "Some members hold a traditional view. Others come from Unitarian or Buddhist backgrounds. That is why communion is optional here."

"Surely," shrieked Rev Ruth, "you are not telling me the Sacrament of Holy Eucharist is optional in this Christian church." Her pitch and volume continued to ascend, prompting Millienne to reflexively cover her ears.

Beka, still face to face with the pastor, pulled up her spine and dropped her jaw to reply. Too late. Rev Ruth was in full exhortation mode.

"No Christian church worthy of its name would allow parishioners to go to Coffee Hour instead of Holy Communion. I cannot believe you practice such apostasy here. I will not have it. As your designated priest I insist that each and every member regularly receive the consecrated body of Christ and drink from the cup of salvation!"

Paige stared at the top left corner of the ceiling with a fixed expression.

Beka glanced up, too, in case the brown crack was widening in the melee, threatening to bring the roof down on their heads.

Millienne kept both hands over her ears as Rev Ruth's plosives singed the air.

Hope rubbed her knuckles so vigorously the skin turned pink as a peony.

Dot shook her head side to side so fast the beads on the end of her braided cornrows clacked like castanets. Planting both hands on the conference table with such force that her tangerine nail beds turned white, she bellowed STOP!

Rev Ruth stopped. Her cane clattered to the floor like an exclamation mark.

"You do not listen, Miz Salter." Dot spoke in molten steel. "Have you have heard nothing? The ways of this congregation were formed long before you arrived, and for very good reasons."

"Please, Dot, sit down." Beka's voice shook and her cheeks flamed. "Beacons and pastors will not yell at each other as long as I am Head Beacon." She lowered into a chair. Dot and Rev Ruth sat down, too.

Beka took one long, uneven breath and audibly let it out. "Let's all do the same. Please breathe with me."

When order was restored, Beka mopped her face with her napkin, prompting Hope to reach over and flick brownie crumbs off her friend's cheek. The shouts of laughter that followed released a lot of energy and eased a little of the tension.

Beka cleared her throat. "I remind you, Rev Ruth, that not all members of Saint Lydia's consider themselves Christian. Our congregation includes a healthy number of Unitarians, a handful of Buddhists and many members who grew up in the AME Zion Church. This is why some choose to enjoy coffee hour while others take communion."

"That still doesn't make it right," spluttered Rev Ruth.

"It may not be right in your eyes," interrupted Dot, "but it is right among the people of Saint Lydia's Church in San Francisco."

"She's right," Hope said quickly. "On Communion Sundays, about half of us come downstairs for coffee and doughnuts after the benediction while the other half stay in the sanctuary for bread and grape juice."

"Yes, that is the way we do it here," confirmed Paige.

"Sorry our ways upset you, Rev Ruth." Millienne's tone was conciliatory. "This tradition was established by our esteemed founder, Reverend Howard Thurman."

"That still doesn't —" said Rev Ruth.

"Like it or leave us," snapped Millienne, squinting her eyes at the pastor.

Everyone took a sharp intake of breath. Millienne, the consummate peacemaker, just said what the other Beacons were secretly thinking.

BEACONS KNOW BEST

Five Beacons were already seated, staring up at the six-foot wooden cross on the west wall when Rev Ruth came into the room. Sensing a problem, she glanced around at five closed faces. She took the chair nearest to Hope.

Paige shot a glance at Beka as if to say get on with it. The Head Beacon gulped, mustered her voice and spoke. "Rev Ruth, perhaps you can guess why we asked you here tonight. The people of Saint Lydia's are having problems with your leadership."

"Huummph!"

Hope thought she sounded like a character from Dickens.

Rev Ruth stared at her palms as if they held the answer. A long moment passed. Beneath the table, shoes scuffed against linoleum. Knees clasped tight. Overhead, the long fluorescent tubes buzzed.

A fire engine screamed past the church. Rev Ruth put a hand to her heart.

The silence stretched thin. Beka inhaled through her nose and charged into it. "Things are not working out as we had hoped. The Beacons think it is time for you to leave Saint Lydia's."

Rev Ruth bunched her eyebrows and glowered. She growled something that sounded like "damned shenanigans" and tugged so hard at her gold cross that Paige expected the slender chain to break.

Hope saw muscles quivering around the pastor's mouth and made a small moan of empathy. Hearing this, Rev Ruth firmed her face, making it as unreadable as granite. The last thing she wanted was sympathy, even from this kindly widow.

"We are not expecting our leaders here at Saint Lydia's to be perfect." Dot waded into the tense silence. "And nobody's saying you're a wrong-doer, but...."

Rev Ruth's chin came up fast. The rims of her eyes ignited. "Who are you to judge me, you self-righteous hypocritical workaholic. You are not nearly as principled as you pretend to be. And God knows, it's a sin, what you and that man of yours do behind closed doors!"

The tirade left them stunned. Dot made a gagging noise, as if throwing up. Turning toward Beka, she spat "Get rid of her. We need a new one."

Dot raised both palms and scooted her chair back with a mercurial screech. "I refuse to listen to such crap, especially from someone who calls herself a *pastor.*" With a fiery glare at Rev Ruth, Dot grabbed her jacket and stalked out.

Hope half-stood as if to follow then sat with a thump when Beka motioned down.

"Let us pray," Millienne said firmly. "Our Father who art in heaven…

But Rev Ruth was already on her feet, the staccato thud of her cane marking her passage to the door.

The Beacons stuttered to a stop before anybody got as far as "forgive us our trespasses."

A GOOD OFFENSE

Cradling her purse against her heart like a football, Rev Ruth muttered *The best defense is a good offense* as she stomped to the bus shelter where she stepped out of the wind and waited for her heart to stop banging against her ribs.

Stuff blew around her feet. A Wonder bread bag, a flurry of waxed-paper squares from a packet of Kraft sliced cheese, and a circle of plastic that once held bologna swirled in the bus shelter. She felt an insane impulse to pick up the litter.

Priorities, she told herself. She'd just made a fool of herself by insulting a church leader. Had very nearly been fired, would have been canned for sure if she had not walked out when she did. Time was of the essence, but the compulsion was too great.

Ruth dropped her purse to the sidewalk and bent to pick up the trash. Just as she was shoving the wad of plastic debris into her pocket, a whirlwind of boys burst into the bus shelter and out again. By the time she recovered her wits, her purse was nowhere to be seen, swept up in the welter of adolescent commotion.

When the reverend rose to make her way home, her face was wet, whether from fright or sorrow, she did not know. In this strange new city there seemed to be no difference between the two.

FAILED

Beka chewed on her thumb and her troubles, peering into gray morning light through hair fallen around her face. A restless night had not lifted the film of despair from her visage nor had it erased the vengeful thoughts from her mind.

Plan A had gone awry. She had to face the truth. The Head Beacon had failed at training the old woman to get along with strong female leaders. And now she had failed at getting rid of Rev Ruth.

Faintly, Beka heard—or thought she heard—a man clearing his throat.

Shut the fuck up. Dad's voice.

Her face dimpled slightly, the precursor to a smile.

Flat on her back, Beka stared at the ceiling through dim light. True, she had not managed to fire the troublesome Rev Ruth, but was that any reason to get mad at herself? She'd been half-afraid of failure from the beginning. She waited for her mind to kick into gear, to come up with another plan.

Tilting at windmills. Patty's voice.

Beka glanced around, blinking with confusion. For a moment her fatigued brain couldn't make sense of it.

Never mind, we'll make do. Patty again.

Then she remembered, eons ago, a conversation with the lamp switched off, Patty coaxing her through some crisis or other.

Beka felt a smile plucking at the corners of her lips. Very faintly, to her left and behind, she could hear something. Not the wind; more like the uneven sounds of human laughter.

Ahhh, it was the Beacons. Laughing.

DANGER

Millienne's thoughts had stalled midway through the Beacons meeting, until the moment she told Rev Ruth love us or leave us. Outdoors again, pictures ran freely through her mind. She felt more free and clear walking beneath trees. Ideas chattered in her imagination, ways to restore peace among the people of her church. Hopefully, this also included bringing peace to the new priest. As wild possibilities played in her head she no longer noticed time passing on her wristwatch. In the Arboretum, Millienne measured time with visioning and remembering.

A broken bird's egg on the ground beneath a bent pine reminded her with splintering tenderness of the skull of her eldest patient. Miz Jackson was one hundred and four years old, blind and dear, with skin so thin that every vein showed blue. Millienne had carefully printed a sign on pale pink paper and posted it above the patient's bed: *Fragile SKIN. Do Not Touch.* This detail was as real as the earth beneath her feet.

In her imagination, she could see the worry lines on Rev Ruth's forehead, the folds of loose skin against the tiny gold cross she wore on a chain at her throat. Our new priest is in danger, she thought. Rev Ruth's tense face and short breaths frightened her. As a licensed vocational nurse, Millienne tended plenty of patients who'd been struck down with strokes and heart attacks. Saint Lydia's pastor could be heading for a catastrophic event, and the newest Beacon wanted to do whatever she could to prevent a medical tragedy.

Just then, sunlight broke through the trees. Buoyed by the shimmer of an evanescent beam of light, she knew she was on the right track.

FIREWORKS

Dot was still chewing fireworks, though time had passed since the reverend had attacked her. How could a so-called woman of the cloth spout such filth, that's what Dot didn't get. Ministers were supposed to comfort the afflicted. Hah! What a crock of crap!

Her moods flashed between fury, resentment and revenge. Each day she woke with sulphur on her tongue, like she'd been spitting nails all night. Gargling with Listerine erased the metallic debris for only a few minutes. If she didn't rinse often enough, her breath smelled like she'd been chewing aluminum foil. She began to carry mouthwash to work in a little nutmeg jar and slosh it around in her mouth every time she used the restroom.

Dot had managed to keep her jaw clamped during the last Beacons meeting. She did get some sympathy for being Rev Ruth's victim, but Dot was not about to tell others what her inner critic had to say about her own shortcomings. She was far harder on herself than any minister could be, though nobody else knew it.

"We Beacons are here to bring light to the work of the church," Millienne had reminded them, but Dot was mad as hell and not about to be some kind of phony light bearer. She could not imagine doing what the others had agreed to do, and told them so. Nobody pushed her. Beka said she could take as long as she needed to decide, but the rest of them would go forward with the plan. Dot was making plans of her own, plans to take scalding revenge on the mean-tongued pastor, but had to admit her secret plans had no muscle to them.

On Sunday she scrubbed the hell out of her floors and windows. Sorted through dressers and closets. Tossed out whatever she hadn't worn in a year. Scoured sinks and tub. Swabbed baseboards. Sorted papers littering her desk. Shredded old utility bills. Tossed old Christmas cards. Hauled bottles and cans to the recycling center.

Dick had seen her in such moods before. Every so often he would put a warm hand on her shoulder and give her a grin. The rest of the time he stayed out of her way.

Dot had every intention of going to church the following Sunday. She wanted to be cleansed. Remembered when Sunny forced her to sit through Mass, and even though she spent her time figuring out ways to beat the boys in pickup games of H-O-R-S-E on the projects' basketball court, she did leave worship feeling a little lighter, breathing a little easier. As a kid, she saw the church as a Doctor Seuss machine, the kind where you walk in one end and pop out the other with a whole different set of beliefs. So Dot had put on her tangerine jacket and her mid-heel shoes, combed her hair and painted her nails, but she just couldn't do it.

ANGELS

Paige loved to stroll through her house in morning light, noon light and moonlight, cradling a mug of tea, gazing at her angels and humming her theme song.

All night, all day, Angels watchin' over me, my Lord. Yes, Paige loved her band of angels—Juliana. Pentimentio. Ventiuno. Celestia. Prudencia. Narcissia—each one a uniquely beautiful creation. She felt safe and happy in their celestial company.

Long before her birth, Paige's pale moth-wing of a mother had been a smoker. Cigarettes seemed to preserve what little vitality she had, until they killed her. From a tender young age, the child feared tobacco poisoning and drew crayon angels for protection. Mother's nervous uncertainty made little Paul feel flighty, so he drew angels to combat the demons. Grownup Paige still did this; every bout of anxiety sent her to work designing another angel.

Paige was not nuts. She understood she had to do something with her hands; physical activity compensated for an over-active imagination. During adolescence, when art-making steadied her nerves, she also realized that something as ordinary as knitting bored her to tears. Angels, now, were never boring. She loved to design and craft celestial companions. Any material would do. And Paige was not only proud of her creations—paper-cut angels, beaded angels, wire sculpture angels, ceramic angels, wood-sculpted angels, satin angels and denim angels—she absolutely loved them.

When a visitor expressed admiration for her art, Paige was not the sort to puff out her chest and brag, but her small, radiant smile could quickly turn cocky. "It's a pleasure to introduce you to my Gabrieleno," she would announce with a cocked eyebrow and a look that said, *See? See what I have created?* She would lean back, at ease and in control, take deep satisfied breaths, then casually anchor a hand on her hip and gesture upward. She would lift her chin and proudly pronounce each name—Magisterio, Annuncio—giving a crisp nod to each. She would survey them with a satisfied expression, extend her arms to include the visitor of the moment and bask in the company of her merry band of angels.

A HUNCH

The Beacons gathered in Hope's living room for the second meeting in one week. Millienne touched the embroidered Tree of Life on her way to the couch, letting her fingers linger on its symbolic roots.

"How can we fire Rev Ruth if we can't find her?" Beka sounded cross. "It is time to put that woman on probation."

"I don't think she knew what she was up against when she came to us." Millienne spoke softly. "Saint Lydia's isn't just any old run-of-the-mill church."

"And what does that mean?" Beka turned petulant.

"I know what she means," asserted Dot. "We are a solid group of lay leaders. Especially you, Beka. You are a religious force to be reckoned with. We all remember how courageously you counseled Helga at the end of her life."

"Amen, sister," murmured Millienne.

Beka liked their praise. It made her feel like the star she wanted to be, not the dull-witted Head Beacon who had failed to fire the interim pastor. And not the jerk who'd been unable to protect Dot from attack. For Beka, it was vital to look good in the eyes of others, but her status was slipping. She could hardly bear it.

"Rev Ruth sees us as a bunch of working-class ladies who haven't been to seminary." Dot puckered her lips as if sucking a lemon. "Putting her on probation would get her to respect us."

"I agree," said Paige softly. "Probation is necessary. But I also think we need an additional strategy, because Rev Ruth is a woman who hates being told what to do."

"Well, duh, so do I," said Hope. "So does every other woman I know."

"She is so damn argumentative!" Bits of spit watered Beka's words.

"I imagine she had to be tough, and persistent, to get where she is in life." Millienne's tone was quiet, even confident.

"I hate her attitude of *me versus them*," protested Dot. "Rev Ruth versus US."

"Don't forget how short-tempered she is." Beka again. "Always has to be right."

Millienne held up a wide hand. "Paige, I want to go back to something you said earlier. What kind of additional strategy are you talking about?"

"Total support," said Paige. "Unconditional love."

CONNOISSEUR OF PAIN

Paige shaved carefully, curving the razor beneath her cheekbone and down the length of her jaw. Whatever made me blurt out *total support and unconditional love?* What in the world did I mean? The Beacons must think I've gone nuts.

A yearning sort of love throbbed beneath her Adams apple but she could not figure out what unconditional love would look like in real life, especially at Saint Lydia's. The answer to the Rev Ruth dilemma must be hidden in there somewhere, down in her deepest feelings, but today it eluded her.

Reaching up to touch a wire-sculpted angel dangling above the sink, Paige gave thanks to God for finally getting to live alone. Since Mother died, nobody intruded on her fantasies. Father dismissed her as melodramatic, once accused her of being in love with darkness, but Paige adored her inner life and could now indulge in pondering, wondering and fantasizing as much as she liked.

She puzzled over what she'd said at the Beacons meeting. What in the world did I mean about total support and unconditional love? How can any form of love solve our conflicts with the troublesome Rev Ruth? Paige's flamboyant imagination came up with no workable solution.

As she leaned against the sink, scraping whiskers, her thoughts took a melancholy turn. I bet they're going to kick me out of Beacons. After my silly suggestion, Beka and Dot will know I'm too stupid to be a church leader.

Millienne is so calm and wise. I've envied her qualities all my life but never found them. What's wrong with me?

Paige turned away from the mirror to gaze at a dead bee on the windowsill, its yellow body barred in black and feathered with dust. The bee's little head is tucked in so neatly. Why isn't human death this neat? The sweet little bee reminded her of Hope, so kind and generous. Why didn't Hank's death swamp her boat? How come I'm drowning in confusion?

She wandered into the bedroom where dead flies scattered the windowsill, lying on their sides as if a quick nap would revive them to be up and about their business. The scene reminded her of Dot. Bigger problems than mine, but she also has a better job than mine. Why can't I save damaged kids from harm? Why was I born defective?

Returning to the bathroom, the mirror reflected a flush of shame darkening her tender skin. The solution came as she wiped off remnants of Colgate shaving cream and dropped her face into a damp towel.

I must be the one to leave Saint Lydia's, not the one who is left. The only way to keep my self-respect is to drop out before they kick me out.

Pull back. Stop going to Circle and Lunch Bunch.

Stop attending Beacons meetings.

Don't tell anyone why.

If nobody misses me, then I'll know I'm not worthy to be a Beacon.

The next evening Paige sat brooding in dusky light, stitching embroidery threads on linen to create a woeful angel kneeling at a gravestone. The rustling caused her to notice how hard her hands were trembling. She stopped sewing to concentrate on developing her higher self. Ordinary people do not understand what it is like to cultivate pain. This thought made her shiver. Maybe God wants me to become a connoisseur of pain. A glow suffused her face and she placed fingertips on her warm cheeks.

Becoming a connoisseur of pain would not be easy, but it was a higher calling. Jesus and Paul learned to cultivate their pain. Her breathing quickened. Some of the saints went to their death in pain. So can I.

But how?

Anna Karenina came to mind. Paige rose and plucked Tolstoy's worn book from the shelf. A length of purple ribbon marked page 109. Her heart sped up at the thrilling words. An eavesdropper would have heard melodrama in her tone, but Paige did not as she read aloud, theatrically:

"She was frightened by this, and gladdened...The state of tension that had tormented her at first was not only renewed but heightened to a point where she was afraid that something in her that was stretched too far would break any minute. She did not sleep all night. But there was nothing gloomy or disagreeable in this tension, or in the visions which filled her imagination: on the contrary, they had something joyful, glowing, and exciting."

I don't need Saint Lydia's Church, she decided. I can follow the higher calling of pain with Anna Karenina as my guide. First, I need to work on falling in love with my own suffering. Yes, I must make pain into my spiritual practice.

When it gets so bad I think I can't go on, I shall try to make it worse.

When I am certain I can't stand it, I shall go one moment more.

When I can bear anything, I shall know I have become a true connoisseur of pain.

CHAPTER 6

THE BRIDGES

Connecting

GROUNDING

While Ruth was brewing strong tea and girding her loins to get through the probation period imposed by the Beacons, Millienne picked up the shawl Hope had knitted for her and wrapped its rainbow warmth around her shoulders. She boarded the 5:40 AM bus to Golden Gate Park, arrived just past six, slipped into the Arboretum through the gardener's gate and walked through the California wildflower meadow to reach the Hispaniola Pines. San Francisco had only three pines from her island home, but three was enough.

After the heated upset between Rev Ruth, Dot and Beka, Millienne definitely needed the company of her first people. *Mamman. Gran-papa. Fre' Guilloteau.* In rhythmic Creole chant, she called forth their souls. *Mother energy. Grandfather energy. Big brother energy. Be with me today. Ground me in your love.*

Grounding was how Millienne called herself back to herself. Given the sheer pace of life in San Francisco, all the stuff coming at her, it was easy to get unbalanced. Conflicts unsettled her, as did patients' troubles. Memories threw her into the past; daydreams spun her into the future. Millienne had learned that her doorway to the present was to drop fully into her body and connect with humble energies of Earth. Grounding was a spiritual practice that took full imagination, full attention and full intention. She could do it anywhere outdoors, but the ancient grounding practice she'd learned from *Gran-Pere* worked best near the strong trees from Haiti.

She put the rainbow shawl over her head, took off her shoes and placed her broad feet as far apart as her shoulders. She stood tall yet relaxed on the layer of pine needles, wiggling to find the right balance between the pine-root knuckles. She pointed her feet straight ahead, turned her toes inward a bit, bent her knees and put equal weight on the balls of her feet, between the second and third toes, which was where she felt most rooted to Mother Earth.

Grounding started by keeping eyes slightly open, looking down with an unmoving gaze. Once her eye muscles came to rest, her mind also quieted. Earth-touch relaxed her body into spaciousness, gradually uniting with the taproot of the great pine. Keeping attention on the balls of her feet, she sensed the connection going down, straight to the pulsing core of magma at the center of the planet. Mother Earth seemed to sense the connection, too, and return it, swelling Millienne's feet with power. The primal force of creation pulsed up through her ankles, calves, thighs and hips, lighting up her joints. Her body seemed to grow huge as she connected energetically with earth, air, water, rocks, plants, animals and sun.

Grounded in the embrace of Life, an idea took shape, a way to bring Rev Ruth into closer connection with the people of Saint Lydia's, put Paige's idea into action by connecting with unconditional love and expressing it. Millienne dedicated every bit of her attention and intention until the plan formed fully in her mind. Afterwards, too light-headed to remain on her feet, she knelt on the pine needles, placed her broad forehead on the cool dirt and breathed countless prayers of thanks into the good earth.

GRIEVING

On Beka's bedroom wall, within easy view of her pillow, was a large print of women asleep in a field. Some had the tops of their dresses undone to reveal smooth white breasts. Some lay flat; others were on their sides, resting heads on rounded arms. Gazing at the sleeping women, Beka could feel the sun warming bare shoulders and soft stomachs. She could smell the hay, feel the breeze and sense the vitality of these women who slept in her room every night.

Patty bought the print on one of their early dates. They'd been strolling down Telegraph Avenue in Berkeley when they caught sight of it in the window of a small shop near Cody's Bookstore. Patty thought it would cure Beka's insomnia so she rolled the print into a cardboard tube, carried it home on BART and had it framed. The first night they slept together, they hung it on the wall. This was Beka's favorite piece of art, a vision of future shared with Patty. Neither knew, of course, that the vision would be fulfilled for only one.

I want Patty, she moaned to the pillow. God, I just want Patty back. She raised her eyes to the women asleep in the field. You understand, don't you.

Beka's eyes filled; she pushed the heels of her hands into them, then bent double and wept, bowed by the kind of grief that would not let her stand straight.

SAUNTERING

Paige's diet was casual. She sometimes gorged on sweets. There was nothing outwardly strong about her; she did not have a robust body but inwardly she carried an intractable belief in herself. Her only exercise was walking, in all kinds of weather; walking set her thoughts at peace. She had not yet made time to walk with the conflicts brewing between the Beacons and the Rev, but Paige had a mystical trust in the guidance of spiritual mentors. Mid-morning, when Henry David Thoreau's voice

interrupted her work—*I wish to speak a word for Nature*—
Paige turned off her transcription machine and covered her
typewriter. Never mind that this was a work day; it was time
to take her worries for a walk so she laced her high-top Keds.

Back when she was a sophomore in high school, Thoreau's
essay on "Walking" inspired her to become a "saunterer." She
wanted to be like folks in the Middle Ages who roved the coun-
tryside on their way to the Holy Land. As Thoreau described
the origin of sauntering, children would call out "There goes a
Sainte-Terrer." This story convinced Paige to develop 'a genius
for sauntering. '

Today she decided to saunter in the Presidio, along trails
shaded by groves of pine, cypress and eucalyptus. A century ago, the northwest corner of San Francisco was covered
by barren dunes, until Army men planted the now-tower-
ing groves. A thorough pacifist, Paige nevertheless breathed
prayers of thanks for soldiers of old, the men who'd converted
a dreary landscape into this lovely parkland.

Sauntering through the Presidio Pet Cemetery, her mind
went back ten thousand years to the native Ohlones who'd
hunted deer where the remains of Army officers' dogs and cats
now rested. Sensing the presence of long-dead elk, Indians and
soldiers, Paige knelt and stretched her arms wide, angel-like,
to honor each creature who once left footprints in this soil.

Spiritually restored, she walked on, skirting the Presidio
Nursery where gardeners were tending beds of native plants
which, she'd heard, would soon be placed in restoration projects around the city. If laborers, then and now, could convert
an historic military base into a place of such peace and beauty,
surely she and the Beacons could find a way to bring peace
among the warring factions of Saint Lydia's.

PRAYING

Paige invited the Beacons to her home to figure out what to do
during the six-month probation period they'd imposed upon

the new interim pastor. Surrounded by hand-crafted angelic host, she began with some carefully crafted thoughts. "We are not the first Christians to welcome the stranger. Rev Ruth has some strange ways, but how can we support her while also setting limits on behaviors we cannot tolerate?"

Paige's pale eyes seemed innocent, but they were always noticing and analyzing. Her muted gaze lifted to the imposing Dominico hovering above them. "The Apostle Paul preached basic equality between men and women, slave and free," she went on. "Since Rev Ruth views Paul as her biblical hero, how can we use Paul's teachings to guide her in creating more meaningful sermons?" Her tone was carefully uninflected; she might have been reciting a recipe for sugar cookies, but her probing questions opened the way for a fruitful discussion.

Hope swabbed sweat from her face and audibly cleared her throat. "At Saint Lydia's, we do have a tradition of praying for the wound-ers as well as the wounded."

"And for the powerful as well as the powerless," added Beka, brushing back stray hairs from her untidy mop.

"Well…" Dot sounded tentative. "Praying for others does make divine love visible in human relationships." Her face revealed the strain of trying to be nice. Even though Rev Ruth was not in the room, Dot pressed her lips so hard the pink turned white.

"Dot's right." With effort, Beka made her voice agreeable. "God needs us to do the praying. I trust our prayers can actually make a difference in what Rev Ruth is able to do in our troubled congregation."

Dot grimaced. "She gets very stubborn when crossed. I should know."

Millienne nodded knowingly. "Rev Ruth needs more than our prayers. Her temper goes up when she feels misunderstood."

"Or rejected," ventured Paige, glancing at Admiratio swaying overhead. "How can we convince Rev Ruth we're here to work with her, not against her?"

"Pray for her," declared Hope, "starting right now."

After a heartbeat or two, Dot made eye contact with each Beacon around the circle. "Sincere prayer for our enemies is not for the faint of heart," she insisted, "but thank God we've got the guts to do it."

They joined hands beneath the Angel Admiratio and offered a variety of intercessory prayers on behalf of Saint Lydia's and their troubled pastor.

"Dear God, "said Millienne, "we close tonight by offering all we've been given back to you, our Creator, to use for the divine purposes of love and justice. Amen."

"Now, let's get to work" said Beka. "We've got a lot of details to work out if this pending peace plan has any chance to succeed."

By the end of a very long evening, the Beacons had outlined a two-part strategy to restore the peace at Saint Lydia's. The first step was for Beka and Paige to collaborate with Rev Ruth in composing sermons based upon the Pauline Epistles. The four-week series would begin with Romans 7:14: *The good thing I want to do, I never do. The bad thing which I do not want, this is what I do!*

BRISKET

"It smells great in here!" Rev Ruth's gusto was layered with bravado as she stood in the doorway of Beka's apartment on the dot of six. They were taking the first step in the peace plan. The Beacons had offered to shorten her probation by two months if Rev Ruth would agree to meet with each member of Saint Lydia's, face to face, for solely social purposes. No talk of church people; no talk of church politics. Only personal interactions were allowed. Rev Ruth agreed. So here they were.

If Beka was nervous, she didn't show it. "Brisket. I hope you eat meat."

"I love meat. Know I shouldn't, they say its not good for you, but I've eaten meat all my life. When I was your age, I weighed one hundred and sixty-two; now, at seventy, I weigh the same so I must be doing something right."

"It's ready. Let's eat."

"You're doing something right, too. I like my meals served right on time."

"Where'd you learn to be so timely?" asked Beka.

"In Cleveland. Every day, promptly at six, a maid in a white apron rang a tiny silver bell and I had to appear promptly at the table, formally dressed."

"Well, we aren't so formal here in San Francisco. I don't even wear shoes." Beka playfully wiggled bare toes tipped with maroon nail polish.

"Dinners were four-course affairs in my family. Every day. Appetizer, salad, meat and potatoes. Dessert. I had to dress formally. Shoes shined, hair combed. Every day."

"Sounds elegant, but..." Beka scrunched up her face.

"But tiresome," Ruth nodded. "I would usually ask to be excused when the grownups were ready for coffee and liqueur. Once in a while I could talk Mother into letting me eat in the kitchen with Cook. But I did love my meat."

"I know brisket comes from helpless creatures," Beka admitted, "but I saw a funny bumper sticker on a VW van. 'If God didn't want us to eat animals, then why did He make them out of meat?'"

Rev Ruth laughed. "That must come directly from the Torah."

"I'm sure it does."

"Why do you serve brisket on Friday? Seems an odd thing to do, for a Christian."

"Grandmother Ash cooked brisket. I'm named after her. Rebekah."

"So, is this your Shabbat tradition?" Rev Ruth looked confused.

"No. I don't exactly know how Shabbat is celebrated. My parents ignored our Jewish lineage and brought me up atheist. Or maybe agnostic."

"So, what brought on tonight's brisket? Which is, by the way, superb." Rev Ruth took another bite.

Beka hesitated, then rose and took a framed photo from a shelf. "This is Patty, my true love. She died seven years ago today. The first time I invited Patty home to dinner, I served brisket and…"

"Oh my dear, I am so sorry." Ruth reached out as if to touch Beka, then drew her hand back and studied the photo instead. "Lovely girl. Tell me about her."

"I got the impression she was Jewish and since I wanted to make a good first impression, I cooked Grandmother's brisket. Turns out Patty was Christian and I was nothing, so she took me to Saint Lydia's and I've been there ever since. Sorry, I talk too fast when I'm upset."

Beka stood abruptly to clear the table, clattering plates onto the tile counter.

All of a sudden, Rev Ruth sensed Caro's bright spirit filling the room. She fervently wished Beka could meet her granddaughter. A vision of the two lovely lesbians softened the pastor's heart and she was on her feet before she planned it, wrapping her arms around her hostess, who shook with big wrenching wet sobs.

There they stood, enfolded in the fragrance of brisket, as the tragic story poured out. After a wildly happy anniversary celebration at Disneyland, they'd been driving home up 101, near Salinas, when a farm truck smashed into the passenger side of Beka's little Triumph. The ambulance screamed through the night, but Patty died just before reaching the Monterey hospital.

When Beka was cried out, they had chocolate gelato and Constant Comment tea.

"I used to have nightmares about disasters, when I was a kid in Los Alamos," she said. "They were always testing bombs in the desert and I was afraid the whole town would blow up. I didn't go to church, but I did pray to God to keep everyone safe."

Rev Ruth nodded and licked her spoon, savoring the last of her gelato.

"Praying made me feel powerful, I guess." Beka paused. "I liked to think my worried whispers got to God's ear and protected us."

"You were God's helper."

"I guess so. Things turned out fine every time I prayed, so I figured God had swooped in and taken care of us. By the time I turned fifteen, I figured my prayers had prevented dozens of atomic disasters."

"Perhaps they had. Wasn't an early atomic bomb called Trinity?"

"Yes. Why?"

"Trinity is a theological name for the divine. Father, Son and Holy Ghost."

"The scientists must have known that."

"Humans playing God."

"My morbid fears imagined atomic disasters but not car crashes." Beka sounded hoarse "It never occurred to me to pray for protection so Patty wouldn't be crushed by a speeding truck."

CONSOLATION

After folding laundry and neatly stacking clean linens on the shelf, Hope moved restlessly through her house, tightening the belt on the butter-yellow quilted bathrobe Hank had given her the day she became a grandmother. The day Cody and Shirley adopted little Rex. She hated all the heartaches that came later, and still needed to talk things over with Hank. And she hated him for not being here, beside her in his recliner, right where he was supposed to be.

Oh what a terrible thing to think. Hating Hank made her nervous. Guilty. Afraid of God's punishment. She shook her head, knowing she would pay—sooner or later—for such bad thoughts. But for now, Hope decided to pamper herself. She quick-thawed a filet mignon under running water, hoping it wasn't sacrilegious to Shake n'Bake the steak in a skillet. She stirred half a cube of butter and a full cup of sour cream into a bowlful of Betty Crocker's instant mashed potatoes. But she was out of green vegetables so she scanned the spice rack, found a jar of Schilling chives and shook a healthy dose of dried greens on her spuds.

Hope spread an embroidered cloth over a TV tray next to her recliner. She lit a rose-scented candle. Loneliness is no excuse for sloppiness. She dusted off her wedding china, and filled the ceramic creamer shaped like a cow. Lawrence Welk provided dinner music on the phonograph.

After rocky road ice cream topped with Hershey's syrup, and coffee pale with half and half, she decided to give herself a facial. Using a recipe clipped from the *Parade* section of the *Sunday Chronicle*, Hope cooked up a mixture of oatmeal, dried prunes and paprika. While it cooled she ran a bath, poured in a capful of Avon Skin-So-Soft, smeared the sticky goop on her face and slid into the silky tub.

Hope still wanted to talk to her husband. For decades, she had talked to Hank about all the business of daily life. When he got sick and couldn't talk any more, neither did she. Through all those hours beside his hospital bed, did Hank even know she was there? Was he suffering? She hoped the morphine spared him pain but didn't know for sure. At the end, silence became their bond.

Tears came then. Hope dropped her chin and cried. The funeral. She didn't think she could get through it. "Can you make it to the door of the church?" Cody had asked. But she couldn't. Her son and his wife had to hold her up.

"The dead protect us," Millienne said later, after Hope told of feeling Hank's arm around her during the funeral. *Thou art with me*, Hope had prayed at the time, not sure whether she meant God or Hank.

And now Hank was here, perched on the rim of the tub, grinning at how silly she looked with oatmeal goop on her face.

Oh my God, she realized, it was you that caught me during my crash course in grief, wasn't it? My knees would go out from under without warning and I'd land in a soft chair or couch. Never once fell to the floor. It was you that kept me from breaking bones when I fell, wasn't it?

He chuckled in his soft, knowing way, amused by how slow she was to see the obvious.

After her bath, stretched out on Hank's side of the too-big bed, memories careened like pinballs. The hospital chaplain had urged her to tell Hank everything she hadn't already said. There's nothing, she'd replied. I've already told him everything.

One thing they don't tell you about mourning, she realized midway through the night, is we only fret about the living. She still worried about her son and his son, but she did not worry about Hank. Not any more. That was a relief.

As light touched the eastern rim of San Francisco Bay, Hope made a list in her head of the things she wanted to do before she died.

Visit cousin Louise in Duluth.

Find somebody besides Hank to talk to, someone nearby.

Find something useful to do.

Make a new friend.

And, oh—get right with God.

Not a very long list.

CONSTERNATION

"C'mon in, " called Hope when she heard the doorbell. "I'm in the kitchen, taking cinnamon rolls out of the oven."

"Thank you for inviting me over for coffee," said Rev Ruth. "I wasn't sure I'd be welcome in anyone's home again after the way I conducted myself at the last Beacons meeting…" She let her words trail off.

Hope interrupted. "Oh, don't fuss at yourself about that. Most people under the influence of Genesis believe in some version of the fall from grace."

"What a remarkable thing to say!" Rev Ruth's brows lifted in astonishment. "That is a great way to begin a sermon. May I quote you?"

"That'd be a first," puffed Hope, gesturing her guest toward a place at the table. "Never been quoted in a sermon, but why not start at sixty-eight."

Both remembered the peace-plan crafted by the Beacons, the agreement to stay away from church matters, though neither mentioned it. Grandkids became their first topic of discussion, followed by the weather. Neither took long.

Hope noticed Rev Ruth glancing at the clock on the kitchen wall, which marked each second with a tiny tick. "Can you stay for a few more minutes? Have another cup of coffee?" The genial grandmother usually kept her emotions concealed behind a happy face, but today her hands moved in jerks and she picked at the skin on her knuckles, a sure sign she was agitated about something.

"Of course. I can stay for as long as it takes." Rev Ruth quickly cast her memory back to seminary, recalling tips for pastoral counseling. "Let's begin with prayer. Is that okay with you?"

Hope's nod was quick, her hands restless. After the amen she abruptly stood. "I need a candle. Need the Light of the World here with us."

Rev Ruth watched as she rummaged in a cupboard, located a tall white pillar candle, put it on a saucer and lit it. "So, my dear, tell me what's wrong."

"It's Cody. My son. He called last night. Said he had something important to tell me but not now, he'd talk about it next weekend when he comes. I told him I have too much on my mind to play guessing games. It's easy to get impatient with Cody; he can beat around the bush forever. So I said I'm too busy to wait around for him to finally tell me what's going on." Hope's voice wavered and stalled. She ducked her head, turned away and choked back a sob.

Ruth picked up a box of Kleenex and extended it. "Is Cody ill?"

"No. Yes. Maybe." Hope flapped her reddened hands around her cheeks. "Oh, he told me he's bisexual." She burst into tears.

Rev Ruth fanned herself. Sipped her coffee. Waited for the storm to pass.

"Bisexual." Ruth kept her voice level, without inflection.

"He said, Mom I have a boyfriend. Just like that."

The pastor could see Hope reliving the moment. There was a shocked expression on her face, a faraway look in her eyes. Rev Ruth kept still.

'Where did I go wrong?" Hope blew her nose and avoided eye contact. "I keep asking myself what did I do wrong?"

"What makes you think you did anything wrong?"

"I had to do something wrong, otherwise he wouldn't be..."

"Did you have any inkling Cody might be gay when he was growing up?"

"Well, no, that's the problem. He wasn't, not that I could tell. He married Shirley, they adopted little Rex who has so many problems..." She looked up, met Rev Ruth's eyes, firmed her voice and went on. "You met my grandson when I brought him to church a few weeks back. You can see how troubled he is, what a handful he can be."

"Rex is what now, about five?"

"Nearly six. And Cody is a good dad even though the marriage was never good. He and Shirley split up when Rex was two, so I never dreamed..."

"Bisexual, you said." Rev Ruth brought things back to the crux.

"That's it. My son says it didn't work out with women so he's dating men. Is that normal? That's not normal, is it?" Beads of sweat popped out across Hope's upper lip, adding poignancy to the pleading look in her eyes.

"One of my grandkids is lesbian," said Rev Ruth, "so I know a bit about the subject. You've had a shock, Hope. I was shocked, too, at first. It took my family a while to get used to it, because my eldest granddaughter dated men for years before she settled down with a woman."

"Really!" Hope narrowed her eyes and rubbed the back of her neck.

"You look skeptical."

Hope gave a condescending smile.

"Science has shown that most people are at least potentially bisexual, and many animal species, too." Rev Ruth paused, realizing she might sound like a professor. She could get on a roll, but this wasn't the time to teach a distressed grandmother everything she knew about homosexuality

"The way I see it, you raised a son who is confident enough with his own sexuality to be true to himself."

Hope looked aghast, as if her pastor had turned into a witch doctor. "But what about God?" she squeaked. "What about what God wants?"

"What do you think God wants?"

"The Bible forbids it!"

"True, there are some troublesome texts in scripture, but there are other ways to look at those passages. We can hold a Bible study, if you'd like..."

"No, no, no. I couldn't bear that. How can I face the Beacons? How can I ever go back to Lydia Circle?" Hope punched both fists against her thighs.

"Calm down. This isn't about your reputation. It is about loving your son."

Hope reared back, but Rev Ruth's stern tone brought her back to the moment. She shook her head as if clearing it. "What can I do?"

"What do you want for Cody?"

"Well, I want him to be a good Christian man."

"Hope, I've only been at Saint Lydia's for a short time, but I already know several gay men and lesbian women in the congregation—Paige, for instance. Don't you think she manages to be a good Christian?"

"Yes," Hope wailed, "but she's not my son!" She wept again, more softly this time. When she was done blowing her nose and tossing a wad of Kleenex into the trash, Rev Ruth spoke.

'Hope, listen to me. God has large family. Christ's love is big enough to embrace many kinds of people, and it does."

Hope nodded weakly, not trusting her voice.

"Does Cody go to church?"

"He did when he lived with Shirley, but I'm not sure if he goes now."

"Your son may walk away from Christianity if you judge him or turn away from him. Since you want Cody to be a good Christian, why not give him the benefit of the doubt and treat him like one?" Rev Ruth paused to let the idea sink in.

"You mean...?" Hope frowned in concentration.

"As I hear it, you're the one struggling with your son's bisexuality, not Cody. And probably not God. Since Cody and God have their own relationship, and both are grownups, I suggest we leave them to it."

Rev Ruth had been right to stop watching the clock. It took much more than the hour she'd intended to spend. By the time Hope tossed her last damp Kleenex, she was ready to offer goodwill to her bisexual son. She was even willing to invite his new boyfriend to come along next weekend and be a guest in her home.

FRIENDING

In Hope's mind, Hank hadn't died; he was just outdoors with pruning shears in his work-worn hands, trimming the oleander hedge, his pale eyes watching her as she moved past the window, tucking in the sheets on his side of the bed.

She would go out at dusk and sit where the kitchen window threw a soft square of light into the garden. Listen to sparrows settling into rest in the branches of the plum tree. Remember dreams she'd had the spring before he died, traveling to Norway where they'd never been. Tracing down cousins on her mother's side and looking up kinfolk on Hank's side. But she wouldn't go now. No matter how often she'd imagined it, she could never go to Norway alone. Instead of the world traveler she had hoped to be at this age, she was the lone widow sitting under a plum tree at nightfall, jacket collar upturned against the damp, trying to accept her loss.

On the mantel beside the Hummel clock sat a framed wedding photo of Hope and Hank Hudson. "When were you married?" asked Rev Ruth during another pastoral visit.

"Nineteen forty-five. Right after Hank came home from Japan."

"Where?"

"In the chapel at The Presidio. On the twentieth of October."

"There is a tragedy in every wedding picture," mused Rev Ruth. "Not simply love growing old, or even the threat of divorce, but the fact that one of these two happy people will die before the other. That's the tragedy, isn't it?"

"It is," said Hope. "I still draw breath to call out to him— Hank, I'm home— every time I open the front door, then I have to let it go, his name uncalled."

"One of us had to die first, and I'm glad it was him." Rev Ruth had a faraway look in her eyes. "Glad my Nolan didn't have to suffer any longer. Glad he wasn't left alone to grieve my death."

"I know what you mean." Hope's sigh gusted with such force it blew back the white hairs at her temples.

So they left it there, no longer needing to discuss their losses.

Rev Ruth was a woman for rapid friendships and sudden discardings, so the speed with which she grew close to Hope seemed natural to her. Things were different for Hope. She was one for long-term friendships and never lost touch with someone once the bond was formed, so she found the rate at which Rev Ruth befriended her to be pleasant but also quite surprising.

Valentine's Day. Hope's birthday in April. Fourth of July. These occasions had hurt without Hank, but Rev Ruth's almost daily visits eased the pain of their wedding anniversary in October and Hank's birthday in November. The pastor's quick wit cheered Hope and the fact that she could still be essential to someone—to Rev Ruth—solaced her somewhat for her lost occupation as Hank's wife. The new pastor was vociferous and scattered, which brought out Hope's calmness and competence. Both, it seemed, drew strength from each other.

SCARS

Dot had always wondered about Millienne's history with men, but she'd never asked because her only language for sex was ribaldry, and that did not seem fitting. Dot imagined sexual intimacy had long been over in her friend's life, but when Millienne invited her to meet at Swensen's, it sounded like maybe it was a going concern.

As they sucked milkshakes through wide straws, Millienne described Benet back in Haiti, such a creature of habit. Sex with him had been very straightforward, but she'd been chaste since immigrating to San Francisco. Too busy earning her LVN certificate and getting established in a steady job.

She alluded to one awful night in the parking lot behind Mission Hospital. She'd been raped. Blood pounded visibly in Millienne's temples as she spoke, tracing the still-pulsing routes of fear.

Dot kept her gaze steady, her voice calm. "Having a healed wound that still hurts is different from having an unhealed wound," she said quietly.

"What's the difference?" Millienne's gaze was on the marble tabletop.

"If it's unhealed it could have pus. Could infect a partner."
Millienne shook her head, eyes downcast.

"But if you have a healed wound that's still tender, then you're like an old shaman whose scars still throb when the east wind blows," Dot added.

Millienne nodded and raised her gaze. Their eyes met. "That's it, the second thing. It's been too long since I was with a man. Telling you gives me some relief. And now I think maybe I'm healed enough to risk romance."

"Okay, so Caleb Jones is a person of interest." Dot decided to be blunt. "Is he the kind of man you can imagine taking your clothes off?"

"No, the whole point is, that he isn't," groaned Millienne. "He may be the man of my dreams but I'm afraid he's too shy to make the first move."

Dot gave her friend a long, measuring look. "Shall I stand guard at your door, then, and push the rascal away?"

"No, it's okay." Millienne grinned into her peach milkshake. "But don't tell anyone at Saint Lydia's, or they might try to take Caleb away from me."

After they hugged goodbye, Dot watched until Millienne turned the corner. She admired her friend's long stride. Hearing her troubles had brightened a dull day for Dot. She hoped Caleb Jones was worthy. She didn't think she could bear it if something bad happened to her good friend.

FREE AS A BIRD

Ruth lay rigid in the narrow bed, her body so taut with listening that she felt composed more of silence than of flesh. She ached straight to her core, yearning to be sheltered in the girl's kindness.

Replaying the scene from her dream, the pastry smell was strong, a thick combination of baking dough and sweat, half pleasant, half not. Half asleep, she rose to embrace a girl so vivid she seemed to be in the room, the dream girl who'd rested her arm across Ruth's shoulder. *Free as a bird*, the girl had said. Her pretty face was full of life.

Ruth had to shove her fingernails into the crook of her elbows to wake herself up. There was no girl in the room, yet the old widow felt happy.

Was this girl, this stranger, an angel?

If you can be unaware of angels, can you also be unaware of love?

Was she love?

Tears spilled. Ruth prayed to be worthy, prayed to belong to this lovely girl.

A little later, though, she could hardly move. What had changed? She couldn't figure it out. Every time she tried to rise from the wine-dark chair, spasms shot from throat to ribs. Earlier, she'd done her usual morning routines—showered, made tea, ate toast—but then the spasms came.

Ruth tried to distract herself from the pain by puzzling over Paige Palmer. Something about her wasn't quite right. She couldn't put her finger on it. What was off? She should make a pastoral call on Paige, but even thinking about that was like climbing a steep hill. She wished she felt stronger. Even the flat stretches of Ruth's day had an upward slant.

Glancing out the east window, she watched a cloud rip open and a low spangle of polished light break through. She saw the mass of gray split again, revealing new colors. Peach. Molasses. Cinnamon. Beautiful, but she still could not move.

The light spilling onto the city was as vivid as her dream. Even her skin was warm with it. The air still smelled of fresh bread dusted with cinnamon, full of promise. Ruth was so stiff she could barely lift her feet, yet she felt a giddy bolt of hope. Focusing on a vision larger than her troubles, that's what she'd have to do to succeed as Saint Lydia's pastor.

She waited for the rain to stop before setting off to visit Paige. A brief downpour had smudged the colors of the sky. As Rev Ruth walked toward the bus stop, she spotted a crow on a power pole, head bowed, wet feathers shining like tar.

She stopped, waited, wished the bird would fly, but there it sat, sodden and alone. Homesickness stabbed her, pierced with longing to be back in her native Cleveland. How long before San Francisco would stop feeling as alien as the moon?

Move along. Mother's voice in her head. *Going back is not permitted. Walk on into your future, my dear. Best foot forward.*

ADMIRATIO

Last Sunday, Paige felt a kind of electric hum when Rev Ruth quoted Saint Thomas Aquinas. *"We must love them all, those whose opinions we share and those whose opinions we reject,"* she'd preached, *"for both have labored in the search for truth and both have helped us in the finding of it."* Paige trembled with the wonder of this coincidence. She'd always been alone in her ardor for Aquinas. If anyone at Saint Lydia's had ever heard of him, they didn't care, so she was delighted to hear that the troublesome priest shared an affinity for her favorite ancient scholar. The possibilities of connection suddenly seemed endless.

Paige, always oversensitive, grew up in a bickering household where she grew suspicious of people with big egos. In adolescence, she found guidance in John's Gospel: *I no longer call you servants. I have called you friends.* Jesus' words took root in her heart, laying the groundwork for a real and intimate friendship with God and his Son. Paige was twenty-seven years old when she first seriously read the work of Saint Thomas Aquinas. By the time she opened *Summae Theologiae*, composed near the end of his life in 1274, she was already struggling to understand how spirituality and theology could work together in what philosophers called "the good life."

Make yourself familiar with the angels and behold them frequently in spirit, for without being seen, they are present with you. Paige lived by these words penned by another of her spiritual guides, Saint Francis de Sales. Desire for God and *admi-*

ratio for all creation permeated her heart and soul: attraction to goodness led her—as Aquinas put it—*to deal with all things in the light of God.* For the medieval philosopher, everyone and everything deserves our *admiratio:* the English translation that most delighted Paige was *gobsmacked wonder.* Soon after the egotistical pastor preached about *admiratio,* she phoned to arrange a pastoral visit. Perhaps, thought Paige, the angels had prompted Reverend Ruth Salter's call.

"Welcome to my *poustinia.* Please come in." Paige beckoned Rev Ruth inside, gestured with one hand toward a desk covered with medical records and transcription equipment and lifted the other toward an alcove filled with angels. "This is where I work, and that is where I pray."

Paige was slim and looked to be in her forties. She wore a plain white T-shirt tucked into sharply creased chino slacks. Her face was narrow and pale; her dust-colored hair was so thin Rev Ruth could see her skull. Eyeglasses sat astride her nose at a slight angle; she gave the impression of being extremely focused, which put Rev Ruth off a bit.

The pastor turned toward an open window and inhaled the clean, salty air flowing in from the Pacific. She heaved a theatrical sigh. "Very refreshing. We don't get sea air like this in Cleveland."

"I'd be pleased if you took the chair by the window," said Paige.

When Rev Ruth sat, the chair leaned back with her weight and raised her legs up onto a supportive cushion. "What a smart chair," she said approvingly. "Very comforting to these old bones." She gazed around while the hostess brewed tea. The house was small and modestly furnished. Straw angels dangled from doorways and chandeliers. Angels sat and stood on every flat surface. Ceramic angels. Carved wooden angels. Stone angels. Blown-glass angels. Plastic angels. A half-completed embroidery angel lay on the table beside the lounge chair.

Paige returned with a tea tray. She moved with grace and appeared more feminine than masculine, except for pale whiskers sprinkling her upper lip and chin.

"By this time, you know a good many things about me." Rev Ruth smiled encouragingly. "Tell me about yourself."

Paige returned the smile. As much as she wanted to converse about Saint Thomas Aquinas, she had to get something out of the way. "To begin at the beginning, I was born a hermaphrodite with predominately male organs."

Rev Ruth gulped audibly, as Paige knew she would. For two decades she had practiced telling the story in a soft, pleasant voice until she could do it without hesitation or embarrassment. "My parents already had a daughter, so they thought it would be nice to have a son. Shortly after my birth, they instructed the doctors to perform the necessary surgery."

It took every bit of Rev Ruth's willpower to keep her jaw from dropping, but she managed to stutter "Which means?"

"I still have the male equipment." A heavy sigh. "I knew you'd be wondering. Everyone does."

"So you grew up a boy and ..." Ruth's voice got stuck in her throat.

"Yes. They named me Paul. I played with my older sister. Played with Angela's dolls, dressed in her clothes. There I am in my sister's prom dress." She gestured toward a framed photo and laughed. Her tone was bubbly.

"Pink is definitely your color," Rev Ruth managed. It was the right thing to say. Paige's relaxed grin set them both at ease.

"What happened at school?"

"Torment. Gym class was the worst. Guys jeered at me in the shower, called me fag and queer. Something was wrong with me, but I didn't think I was queer. I simply wasn't interested in sex with boys. Or girls. Only with God."

"Sex with God," Ruth repeated, too dumbfounded to say more.

"I'd sneak into the Orthodox Church on Union to gaze at the icons and listen to priests chant in Greek. I adored the

Orthodox liturgy. That's where I fell in love with God." Tiny lights of gladness sparked in her eyes.

"Orthodox," mused Rev Ruth. "What did your parents think about that?"

"I never told them. Mom was passive; she pretty much let me do whatever I wanted. Dad mostly ignored me, until the day he left and never came back."

"Ouch." Rev Ruth mirrored the pained expression that flashed across Paige's fine-boned face. They both went quiet, gazing out the open window.

"I'm not gay." Paige shook her head from side to side. "During the Summer of Love, when the flower children streamed into San Francisco, I put on Angela's long skirt and walked through the Haight Ashbury to see what was going on. A long-haired hippie guy offered me a joint, so we sat on the grass. He read poetry while we smoked, then started petting. When he discovered my penis he grabbed his backpack and ran off without a word. That escapade made me think if I could be a real woman–sexually, you know –I'd have a chance at happiness, so I went back to the doctor who delivered me."

"My goodness, that took a lot of courage." Rev Ruth patted her heart.

Paige nodded and plunged on. "Doctor Bennett was very understanding. He said it was possible to reverse the surgery he'd done when I was an infant but it would be very costly. And painful. And uncertain."

Ruth grimaced in sympathy, but held her tongue.

"The one thing he could be certain about was I would never bear a child."

"God help you," murmured Ruth.

"God did help me." Paige's voice was firm. "And still does. Without God's help, the bullies and beatings would have killed me. Or I'd have killed myself."

A beam of sunlight filtered through the dissipating fog, illuminating the curve of her cheek with its blond stubble.

Rev Ruth pressed her hands to her stomach and peered at Paige. "So you decided not to have reconstructive surgery?"

"Right. I can't say I'm living happily ever after, but I have made peace with myself, thanks to therapy and huge helpings of God's mercy." Paige hesitated, taking a breath that was deeper than usual. She let it out slowly as she rubbed fingertips across the stubble on her jaw.

"There's more, isn't there?" Puzzlement wrinkled Rev Ruth's brow.

"Yes. Now that we've gotten gender out of the way, what I really want to talk about is my favorite spiritual guide."

Paige plucked a leather-bound book from the shelf and extended her well-worn copy of *Summa Theologiae*. "How well versed are you in Aquinas?"

They had a satisfying conversation about the medieval scholar, but later, alone in the cool of evening, Paige felt unsettled. She recalled words attributed to Queen Elizabeth the First: *Do not tell secrets to those whose faith and silence you have not already tested.* Paige memorized those lines in college but hadn't thought about them in ages. Why now? What was the Queen trying to tell her? *Was it a mistake to tell?*

Paige did view Rev Ruth as queenly—or more accurately, kingly—because her strong suit was telling people what to believe and while she did admire the pastor's scholarly mind, the Beacon was not convinced she belonged at Saint Lydia's. Rev Ruth had iron in her spine, but didn't show much soul. Their interim priest seemed better suited to teaching in a school of theology than pastoring a modest church.

Was I too hasty, spilling my gender beans to an untested pastor?

Can I trust her with my most private secret?

AMICABLE CONFIDENCES

"Rev Ruth," said Hope, "why didn't you tell me this earlier?" Surprise was all over her rosy face. One fuzzy pink slipper slid off as she heaved out of the La-Z-Boy to sling a rounded arm around her pastor's bony shoulders. "This is so exciting. It makes me lightheaded, hearing such confidences from a woman of your stature." Her tone was flattering. "Now tell me more about your boys."

"That was a difficult time in my life," stammered Rev Ruth. "I rarely talk about it." She pulled at her clerical collar and rubbed the back of her neck. "Motherhood was a great challenge for me." She fiddled with her sleeves, too emotional to say more.

"Well, I can't tell you how glad I am to hear that," grinned Hope. "But wait. Let me refill our tea and bring more banana bread."

They both settled, the hostess comfy in her Hawaiian muumuu. The pastor undid the top button of her black clergy shirt and snapped off her stiff white collar. Rev Ruth was feeling stimulated in spite of herself. "Our honeymoon was short," she said. "I got pregnant right away, and all three boys came within four years."

Hope gave a sympathetic sigh but did not interrupt.

"When I was on track as a good mother, I felt benevolent, even triumphant, but those times were rare. My boys were too rowdy and my temper was too short. The constant demands of three young sons drove me to bouts of crossness. You have no idea how often I prayed for patience." Rev Ruth twisted her mouth into a sour expression.

"Did your prayers work?"

"Not often enough." She stared down at the floor. "When I slapped a boy, or shouted, I'd confess to my priest and do whatever acts of atonement he gave me." She pressed her lips tight.

"Mothering was a spiritual practice, then... for you?" Hope tilted it up into a question, not wanting to sound too certain.

"My mind worked full time, assessing how I was doing as a mother. Since I was not immune to sudden explosions, I tracked myself in terms of spiritual morale." Rev Ruth flashed a fake smile, trying to laugh it off.

Hope did not return the smile. "They were very active little boys," she said reassuringly. "I only raised one, but my Cody was a corker." She lifted and dropped her shoulders for emphasis. "So I can see why bouts of crossness would give you a sense of urgency in prayer."

"Yes! Once I got my temper up, God alone could stem the tide of my anger." Rev Ruth swiped a hand across her brow.

Hope curled both hands around her ample middle and remained attentive, but still. She cast a glance at the mantel where the Hummel boy held his fiddle, a gift from Hank early in their courtship. The little figurine remained quiet, too. The clock chimed three.

"I used to think, in some ways rightly, that I was a very accommodating person," mused Rev Ruth, "until our third son arrived. Timothy was a sickly baby, allergic to everything but yogurt and honey." She shot a too-quick smile at Hope. "Thank God my health was good, but it nearly killed me to keep the baby alive while keeping two toddlers safe. My mother had a crew of cooks and nannies to raise her children, but I had to do everything myself." She pushed back her shoulders and stiffened her spine.

Hope cleared her throat. "No help from their father?"

"Rarely." Rev Ruth shook her head. "Nolan was a good man, a scientist...but he often had his head in the clouds." Her voice stalled.

Hope inhaled deeply through her nose and exhaled through her mouth. "I am going to change the subject," she announced. "How did you meet Nolan?"

"That's quite a switch." Rev Ruth uncrossed her legs and straightened them out. "What brought this on?"

"You've heard about my marriage. Now I'd like to hear about yours."

The pastor's focus went so far away that she jumped when the doorbell pealed. By the time Hope got rid of two tidy

Jehovah Witnesses and made a fresh pot of Lady Grey, Rev Ruth was ready to talk. "I was in my late twenties when I enrolled at the University of Chicago to study organic chemistry. It wasn't long before I fell madly in love with my professor. Nolan Salter was enamored of me, too, but far too shy to make the first move. So I invited him on a picnic."

"A picnic? What time of year was it?"

"Indian Summer. I packed Swiss cheese sandwiches, a thermos of tea and a red plaid blanket, and took him to the Lake Michigan shore. He was very awkward so I decided to do something silly to loosen him up." She gave a snort through her nose.

"Something silly?" Hope's curiosity was up.

"Yes, I climbed a tree, shimmied out on a branch and hung upside down by my knees." Ruth's face reddened at the memory. "My skirt fell over my face and my bloomers gleamed in the sun." She swallowed her laughter and turned away to collect herself.

"What did he do?"

"Nolan was such a gallant man, quick to rush to my assistance. He'd been trained as an engineer, so he quickly figured out how to get me out of the tree without cracking my skull. Once he had my feet on the ground, he held me in his arms for a long time. And that's how our courtship began."

"What a good story! And it must have been a feather in your cap, a student adored by her professor."

"Yes, our romance made me a star among the student body. When Doctor Salter finally got up the courage to propose, I said yes immediately. By then, most faculty members, even the Dean, were cheering for us."

"Did you finish your studies?"

"Oh, yes. I graduated one week and married the next. Mother always insisted that holy matrimony was a solemn vow, but I could not be solemn about marrying Nolan. I was nearly thirty, you know, and in a great hurry to be wed."

DREAM DAUGHTER

Four in the morning and Ruth's blurry brain said *labor*. She was dreaming but her back hurt, which it never did in dreams. An odd strangled sound erupted from her throat, yelps punctuated with low, guttural breathing— panting, really. She sniffed, a rough sniff thick with saliva and pushed out a small bloody thing, such a thrill she forgot to be frightened. Childbirth noises from her, but no wail from the infant. The silence thrust her into fear. She listened hard but heard no baby sounds.

Bumping up out of sleep, she said "Nolan! Did you hear? I just had a daughter."

"There's no baby. It's a dream." His familiar voice was rough with reality.

She sent one courageous hand out into the dark to find the pull chain on the lamp. "I know that," she whispered.

Awake now, she knew there could be no baby. Her husband died years ago. So did their only daughter.

Stillborn.

Ruth's fault.

Lord, have mercy.

A moment later, she awakened to another sensation, a new one; a sense of extravagant consequence. Ruth wanted to pay careful attention to it, and did. She sensed something coming to meet her—some one, actually—a young girl, or anyway a warm temperature whose pulsing presence produced an odd bubble in her chest.

The room was quiet. So were the streets of San Francisco. Ruth pressed at the tenderness in her chest, the bony plate between her breasts; it throbbed with a puzzling familiarity. She rose from bed and crossed to the window, glimpsing the white blur of her feet on the thin carpet. She opened the curtains with a dramatic gesture. Larkin Street below looked exactly as it did at four every morning. A pool of amber light spilled from the corner streetlight onto trashcans clustered in front of the darkened dry cleaners.

"Hello?" she called. No one answered, yet she felt the girl nearby, dressed in her best clothes. Waiting for Ruth's forgiveness.

Rev Ruth brewed tea. She sat in the upholstered wing chair, the one chair in this dumpy apartment that her sore hip could endure for any length of time. She sipped Oolong. The sipping was dreamlike. The labor, the sensations of birthing felt like a diminishing dream. She took her time steeping in the extravagant warmth of the dark-haired girl.

By lunchtime she might have totally forgotten it, but for the presence of the girl. The daughter. Her shape remained clear. She came forth with a vitality that was both thrilling and terrifying. There was something urgent about the girl, something dark yet appealing. Something that Ruth—who still longed to be a good mother—was reluctant to give up. She had been granted three living sons, with whom she had rather fractious relationships. She had buried a stillborn daughter, spent years wishing for a living one and thought she'd finally given up that hope.

The warmth of the girl's brown skin and the sheen of her black hair produced uncontrollable shivers that made Ruth's hand jerk; tea spilled into the saucer.

"Do I know you?" she asked in a shaky voice. She meant this sincerely. Possibly she did know the girl, although this dream daughter was far too young and dusky to be Ruth's stillborn daughter.

And she was waiting for forgiveness.

If Ruth had been told at twenty-five that it would take half a century to have a girl look at her like this, she would have been heartbroken. Now she was only a little sad. Today's distress was both bearable and tender.

Ruth was ready for something more to happen, but the room remained quiet. Her readiness had a pendulate quality, almost avian.

Keep fluttering, little bird.

Ruth flinched, recalling Mother's clipped tone.

Just then a pigeon landed on the windowsill. An omen.

Ruth's heart jumped and suddenly she was desperate for more certainties. She struggled hard to become the pastor she wanted to be, without notable success.

What if she was mistaken in believing Christ had died for her sins?

She vibrated with the possibility then cringed from the heresy of it.

Stop. That. Mother again, as clear as if she was speaking on the radio. Her voice carried divine fury. *What Are You Doing, Thinking Such a Thing?* Mother enunciated each word with a capital letter. *Do. You. Hear. Me.*

Ruth might have wept, or at least cussed, but for the serene presence of the girl with the shining eyes. She closed her old eyes and rested her head on the nubby tweed, feeling an unshakable gratitude towards the girl whose dark head rested beside hers.

"It's all right about last night," said Ruth. "What I mean is I forgive you."

CHAPTER 7

THE TENDERLOIN

Lures

KISSES FOR CASH

The story of Rev Ruth and the Beacons of Saint Lydia's can be told another way, and this one is also true. The city of dreams dazzled the eyes of a girl who'd just come from a dusty village south of the border. To Luz Rivera, hunched at the corner of Market and Mason, San Francisco's heavenly body of light came down like flaming arrows, so bright it could set her hair afire. She was proud of her bounteous black hair, styled by dear *Abuela* the night she left Hermosillo. It was her crowning glory, thousands of silky strands moving all together when she turned her head. Luz had a lovely body, too; one man told her she was shaped like a Stradivarius. She didn't know what he meant, but liked the pretty word.

Luz was a perfect girl, except for one fact. She was not free.

She stood on Market Street and rubbed her eyes. Soft hairs covered her bare arms, brown hairs the tawny tan of a newborn goat. She rubbed her cold arms and moved closer to the flickering neon lights of an all-night eatery, but found no warmth there. Men looked her up and down as they walked past. Luz felt lonely. She knew it was *stupido* to feel lonely because her boyfriend was leaning against a wall, just across the street. She could see the jut of Juan's jaw and the glisten of his lip in the flare of a match as he lit another cigarillo.

Yes, Juan was right there, watching. Gesturing. Pointing toward a soldier in a brown uniform. Luz didn't want to be standing here alone. She wanted to go dancing with her sweetheart. Juan had promised music and dancing and marriage, once they got to the glittering city. But first, he said, we need money. It's up to you, baby. You've got to give some kisses and get some cash. We need American dollars to buy tacos, rent a bed. She shivered in the night air, remembering those terrible words. *You've got to give some kisses to get some cash.*

When Juan said she had to come with him to America, there was nothing to do but go. Give goodbye kisses to her grandmother and sisters. Follow her handsome Juan. Bump along on top of a train, teeth knocking under the cold stars, waiting to be told what to do next.

Family, then no family. Soft dust, then concrete sidewalks. Adobe hut, then dark doorways. Everything felt strange as Luz shivered on Market Street in a place called The Tenderloin. She smelled boiled coffee and remembered the coconut milk candies Juan bought her in the *zocalo*, where long lines of electric bulbs fenced out a bright piece of night just above her head.

A pack of sailors strode toward her, white arms swinging. She caressed the lace blouse across her bosom, straightened her skirt and froze in place, waiting. There was nothing left to do but take a breath and say what Juan told her. "Hello, Mister. Want a good time?"

HEARTS

Everyone in San Francisco knew where Tony Bennett left his heart because the famed singer performed nightly at the Top of the Mark on Nob Hill, where the city's glitterati sipped martinis and swayed on the dance floor. But no one had a clue about Luz Rivera's heart, the heart of a girl who worked nights at Market and Eddy where addicts shot heroin in doorways and drunks staggered from bar to bar. Luz could not read much English, had never seen *The Chronicle* in which columnist Herb Caen described the Tenderloin as "a place of broken dreams and frozen screams."

The Mexican girl's reality was a million miles from Tony Bennett's idyllic San Francisco where tiny cable cars climbed halfway to the stars. Luz had, in fact, left her heart in the state of Sonora, in the town of Hermosillo. A restless girl, her head was filled with dreams of the grand adventures promised by Juan before he smuggled her into California and forced her into prostitution. Since then, her pretty brown eyes had seen only nightmares. As Tony Bennett crooned on Nob Hill, Luz shivered in the summer chill. Hugging a flimsy jacket around her shoulders, she did her best at womankind's oldest profession. "Want a little fun, sailor?"

That night, Hope Hudson's wild young heart was in North Dakota astride Pal, a palomino gelding with blonde mane. Hope could gallop for hours beneath the wide sky, blonde hair flying, only the heaped clouds for company. One fateful summer afternoon, Hope reined in to let Pal drink from a pond in the copse, and there was Chuck Adams with his cropped blond hair and sizzling gaze. Her heart kicked like a colt when she spotted her brother's buddy leaning against a cottonwood, arms folded across a well-muscled chest. She slid from the saddle right into his manly arms.

Mother had warned her. She'd seen how their eyes met over the meatloaf whenever Nash brought his buddy home for supper after football practice. Mother had also told her she was pretty, but when Hope looked in the mirror (she'd been much slimmer then) all she saw was a fifteen-year-old with a plain face, fair hair and blue eyes. She didn't believe Mother about prettiness, so why believe her warnings about trouble?

How Chuck knew she'd be at the pond, he would never say but Hope was thrilled that he showed up. Not scared, though she should have been. Nash trusted Chuck to treat his sister like a lady, but Hope wanted romance. It started with one nearly chaste kiss but she wanted deeper kisses, more exciting touches. Nobody knew about their secret meeting place except Pal, and he wasn't telling. Mother didn't suspect and, as long as Hope was home in time to set the table for supper, there was no trouble. Until she started going clammy at the smell of fried chicken, and throwing up before breakfast.

The Beacons of Saint Lydia's enjoyed a modest nightlife near their church on lower Russian Hill; movies at the exotic Alhambra Theatre, chocolate sodas at Swensen's Sweet Shoppe on Pacific, but none of them dared venture into San Francisco's rough Tenderloin, at least not after dark.

Beka might buy a Reuben at Sam's German Hofbrau during daylight hours.

Hope and Millienne might order tortellini and sangria at Paoli's.

Paige might splurge on a delicate honeyed baklava at Minerva's after studying at Central Library, but not one of the Beacons went into Luz Rivera's neighborhood after dark. San Francisco's Tenderloin was simply not a safe place to be female.

In 1976, the Tenderloin, with its bums and crime, was said to contain some fifty thousand people crowded into forty-five square blocks. Luz Rivera slept during the day in a flea-trap motel and worked nights surrounded by massage parlors and X-rated movie houses, a world away from Saint Lydia's Church. While Christian ladies sipped tea and talked about saints in Hope Hudson's lovely home in the Upper Haight, Luz tried to attract paying customers on Market Street.

The night a strong hand landed on her lower back, she shrieked.

"Keep quiet," growled a low voice, "or I'll hurt you."

Luz believed him.

A hefty man propelled her toward a black Mercedes Benz idling at the curb. Another man, face hidden in shadow beneath the bill of a Giants baseball cap, demanded "Get in."

Heart thudding, bare legs shaking, she got in.

NIGHT MINISTER

The San Francisco Night Minister leaned against the grimy wall of the Greyhound depot, keeping an eye on three guys loitering at the curb. He recognized them as gay prostitutes, but did not judge. Sexual preference was not Reverend Don Stuart's concern: his mission was to protect the innocent. He came to the terminal every night in an effort to intercept young runaways as they stepped off the bus. It was his mission to guide them toward the YMCA before hustlers could lure them into the sex trade with promises of free housing, food and drugs.

The Night Minister's beat was the armpit of the city. The Tenderloin could take on a warm glow after dark, attractive to naïve youth eager to explore its seductive glitter. It was a place of whispers and shadows, hilarity and misery. Smoke and perfume. Punches and promises. Anything could happen in the Tenderloin.

Reverend Don Stuart straightened up and adjusted his white clerical collar. Ordained in the liberal Protestant United Church of Christ, he was neither Catholic nor Anglican but wore the priestly collar because it was a sign that he was a man of the cloth. His scowl wasn't just an act to show the pimps he meant business. He fretted over news of San Francisco's latest sex scandal; Reverend Perry Petersen had disgraced himself and sullied their noble profession. Reverend Don's wife would kill him if he ever did that, broke his marriage vows, or God help him, his ordination vows, though the Night Minister had plenty of opportunities. He was propositioned regularly on his nightly rounds of bars, clubs and coffee shops.

Waiting for the Chicago bus to pull in, he had time to wonder about the leaders of Saint Lydia's. They caught their pastor with a hooker. Who were those ladies, anyway?

PERISHING

Walking the streets a few foggy nights later, the Night Minister spotted a heap of humanity in a doorway on Sixth. Was that a woman? He crossed Howard to get a better look. At first it looked like a decapitated corpse, one leg bent under, one shoe missing. When he flicked on his flashlight, the beam caught a gleam of forehead beneath tangled black hair.

He moved closer. It was a woman, covered with a man's wool coat, chin folded against her chest, one ear on the grimy brick. Her breath came in ragged huffs and hacks. The stench enveloping her was awful. Acrid. Strong enough to make Reverend Don hold his breath. Familiar, though he couldn't quite identify the smell. One leg twitched, startling him.

"Lady," he whispered, "lady can you hear me?" But she was out cold. In the shock of the moment, Reverend Don forgot to pray.

"Let's get you some help," he said more loudly than usual, hoping she could hear his voice. "I'll try to flag down a police car. Don't move. I'll be right back."

By the time he returned a small crowd had gathered and the young woman had begun to cough. "Help is on the way," he said, bending near. Grimacing at the fumes – sharp, sour, dangerous – he suddenly realized it was kerosene. The wool coat covering her small body had been drenched in kerosene.

"Nobody light a match," he shouted. "No cigarettes. This girl is flammable."

SF GENERAL

At San Francisco General Hospital, a bombardment of noise made the patient duck. A strange pounding on the roof made her cover her ears. Men crowding into the doorway made her curl into a tight ball. Clashing knives made her repeat the Hail Mary. She braced against the threats and curses, raised one hand and made the sign of the cross on her forehead.

Stop! cried Abuela, glaring like a general. Grandmother filled the doorway, hefty arms crossed over pendulous breasts. Two glossy braids fell over her shoulders. *Alto, alto, alto,* she shouted and the men went quiet.

Her three sisters appeared in the doorway, whispering *adios, adios, adios.* Consuela wet her finger with spit and made the sign of a cross on Florencia's brow. They faded from view.

A white-haired woman leaned over the bed. Her wrinkled face said she had worked hard all her life. Her voice said we cannot let this girl live her last days in loneliness. The old woman smelled warm, like fresh-ground masa.

Grasshoppers and crickets droned in the dry grass. The sweet spermy smell of juniper came to the girl's nostrils. A strange, low singing filled her ears, the chant of owls. Nightjars and bats whirred overhead as the setting sun passed from orange to gray. Then all the creatures rested. And Luz rested.

A few days later Luz asked the hospital chaplain to bring her a woman priest. "Not a man. I don't trust no men, especially with white collars."

The founding director of Safe House lifted her blonde eyebrows. "You know the Roman Catholic Church ordains only men, don't you, Luz?"

"Yes, ma'am, but I need a woman priest, understand?"

Reverend Glenda Hope did understand, all too well. She knew far too many Catholic girls caught in the sex trade. Perhaps Luz had been abused by more than one man of the Catholic persuasion while working the streets of San Francisco.

Reverend Glenda had established Safe House to care for women like Luz Rivera. She hired only female staff, and referred clients only to female doctors, social workers and therapists, but this was the first time one had insisted on seeing a woman priest.

"I need to talk to a woman priest," Luz repeated.

"Will I do?" Glenda teased. "I'm a Presbyterian minister although I wear a priestly collar."

"Why?"

"So people will recognize me as a Christian when I make hospital visits. I also wear the collar during court appearances, memorial services, protest marches. For the same reason."

"Sorry, ma'am." Luz stared over Reverend Hope's shoulder, mouth set, teeth clamped. "You seem like a good woman. I'm glad you came to see me and all, but I got to have a woman priest hear what I got to say."

"Of course you do, Luz. I respect you for being clear about what you need. I'll do my best to find someone to visit you."

LUNATIC LADY

"Jesus doesn't need your money, but I do!" A woman with a tangled mane of maroon hair kept shouting as they passed. Her face was contorted, her stare insistent through the afternoon mist. Insanity mottled her dusty black throat.

Rev Ruth and Beka flicked eyes at each other, mouths pinched as they registered needle tracks on her thin, bare arms.

"Give me all your money, ladies," she harangued aggressively, "because I need a lotta help today. And it's way too late to help Jesus."

Beka bit her lip, feeling the full force of the woman's pissed-off hopelessness. She should look up but just couldn't meet the crazed eyes. Instead she gave a swallow that smacked of impotence and muttered "I'm sorry" in a barely audible voice.

Rev Ruth drew herself up tall and fumbled for words, but there weren't any. The sudden lift of her shoulders showed uneasiness, though she did not voice it.

They hurried toward the Tenderloin Interfaith Self Help Center, passing two hookers leaning against the wall of a defunct sandwich shop. "Lunatic Lady's really on a roll today," they heard one say.

"Yeah, " replied the other, "she don't watch it, I gonna get on a roll too and then she wish she'da talked nicer 'bout Jesus."

The Beacon and the Rev nodded at the hookers, confirming their sentiments with small dips of the chin. Anxiety nibbled at Rev Ruth; she resisted letting it in. Fear was her lifelong companion, the only force that made her come fully alive.

The block where Golden Gate and Taylor intersected Market was in transition, downscale hotels giving way to upscale, a café under construction. Rev Ruth stopped to eavesdrop on three refugee children arguing in what sounded like Vietnamese. Beka was forced to step aside by three half-grown boys zipping past on skateboards.

The lobby of the Interfaith Self Help Center had once been a burlesque theatre. The air was dim and cold, tinged with stale cigarette smoke. A bored security guard switched on a light, revealing tired red carpet and a wall of marbleized mirrors. Things had clearly not been upgraded since the Interfaith Council took over the lease.

"We are here from Saint Lydia's Church," Rev Ruth told the guard. "I am the pastor, and we would like to speak to the director."

"We're here about Luz Rivera," Beka added.

NO ROOM IN THE INN

"What a messy city," the Rev complained to the colleague who'd offered to help find Luz a place. She waved a hand past her nose to clear the exhaust fumes spurted by a departing Muni bus. Pigeons winged overhead, dropping splats on the sidewalk. Rev Ruth moved just in time, but Reverend Don Stuart took a direct hit on the shoulder.

He rubbed at the chalky spot with his handkerchief and said "Just goes to show you what a complicated city this is, what can happen to a guy here." The Night Minister grinned to show he was just kidding. "I'll tell you more as we walk to the cable car stop. It'll take us to Mary Elizabeth Inn, halfway up Nob Hill."

Bankers brushed by as they hurried along Montgomery Street; clerks disappeared into gleaming marble buildings. Rev Ruth dropped a dollar into the grubby hand of a whiskered man huddled in a doorway. Pigeons pecked at donut crumbs scattered around his blanket.

"Do you think this inn will take Luz Rivera?"

"I know Kae Lewis, the director. I'll do my best to convince her," said Reverend Don. "The founder, Lizzie Glide, was a lifelong Methodist; she named Mary Elizabeth Inn for her daughters. They're all long gone, of course, but her estate has provided safe, affordable housing for women since 1916 and young Luz Rivera certainly needs a safe place to live in San Francisco."

"I'd much rather see her among good Christian women than in that dingy room at the Union Gospel Mission." Rev Ruth stopped to catch her breath. "Wait, that street sign says Maiden Lane. What kind of a name is that?"

"San Francisco was founded by gold rushers, and the madams weren't far behind. A few enterprising women set up bordellos right here." He patted a wall and gave a phony leer. "Railroad magnates and lumber tycoons found many pleasures here on Maiden Lane, though Chinese laundrymen and Italian fishermen were not welcomed."

"Humpff," she snorted, smacking her cane on the cobbled street in protest. "Where do we catch the cable car?" she wheezed. "I'm tuckered out."

"Just one more block. Here, take my arm." His tone was encouraging. Walking the streets of the Tenderloin as he did every night, Reverend Don encountered a lot of folks who were tuckered out. He was practiced at encouraging them to do what was in their best interest.

The Night Minister was able to keep Rev Ruth moving along to the Inn, but their combined charm was not able to secure a room for the battered Mexican girl. Director Kae Lewis reminded them that Mary Elizabeth Inn only accepted women over the age of eighteen. Luz Rivera was barely seventeen.

NIGHT SHIFT

"What does a Night Minister do, anyway?" asked Rev Ruth. "What is a typical night for you?"

"There isn't one," said Reverend Don. "Every night is an adventure. You never know what might happen on the streets of San Francisco."

"Do you give money?"

"Never. I'll help any other way, mostly by listening and making referrals, but our Night Ministry policy is to not give cash. I give plenty of attention, though, and sometimes prayers or blessings."

"Out on the street?" The tremor of her hand on the cane showed her uneasiness.

"Or in the bars. Folks may be high or holding a can of beer while we pray. God loves them just as they are, and I want them to know that."

"Bars!" Rev Ruth's judgment showed in her face and voice.

"But I only pray when someone asks for prayer. I always check. Do you want a simple churchy prayer, I'll ask, or something from the bottom of my heart? Do you want to pray here, now? If they say yes, we hold hands and pray right where we are."

"Well, I never heard of such a thing," she snorted.

"I've performed marriages in bars for people who'd never be welcome in a church because they were broke, or too stinky. Twice I've held funerals in bars, too." Reverend Don's grin had a touch of challenge in it.

"Aren't you offended by dirty drunks?"

"Occasionally afraid, but never offended. I view people as valuable and lovable whether they're well dressed or tattered, sober or drunk. I can listen to addicts talk about lost love, to hookers telling tales of abuse. I can watch a schizophrenic on Polk Street shoot arrows at aliens and pick up an imaginary bow of my own to help him keep San Francisco safe from alien invasions."

"Well then, you're a lot more like Jesus than I am."

"Night Ministry isn't about evangelizing," he shrugged. "Half the people I meet on the streets of The Tenderloin don't believe in Jesus. Many have been called sinners. No, I'm not out to convert anyone. Tenderloin folks are no different than us except when they're begging or being noisy."

"Frankly, my dear, I prefer my parish ministry to your street ministry."

"And that is where you're needed, Rev Ruth. As for me, I choose to be out here with the unwashed, the angry and the mentally ill. Some are also sweet. Many are sick and vulnerable. My big challenge is not to get furious with Christians who insist on 'saving' people by arguing or saying they're going to hell. That makes my belly ache." He placed both hands at his waist for emphasis.

"Judging our Christian brothers and sisters, are you?" She couldn't resist giving him a wicked look.

"Got me." His grin was lopsided. "I shouldn't judge, but I can't always stop."

"Would ice cream soothe your bellyache? My treat." She gestured toward a nearby O'Farrell's.

"Sure."

They stepped inside. "Make mine mint chocolate chip."

"I'm glad you're on the church's night shift, Don," she said between bites of almond mocha fudge. "You are a helluva lot more loving than most ministers I know, including myself. You actually do love your neighbor, even if he stinks."

SAFE HOUSE

Beka had been looking for someplace to volunteer. Before Rev Ruth came, she'd had both hands full with work and ministry at Saint Lydia's, but now she had energy to spare. Hope advised her to get involved in a worthy cause. Dot suggested Safe House.

On her way to check it out Beka strolled along Valencia, gazing at the odd mixture of stucco row houses, small apartment buildings, frame cottages and classic Victorians. She stopped to admire tidy front-yard gardens, smelled more than one illegal chicken coop, and wondered how many aging hippies grew marijuana in their backyards. She smiled at children running errands to corner markets and held doors open for young mothers pushing baby strollers into tacquerias.

Beka appreciated San Francisco's constantly evolving character and its wide range of characters. Inner Mission residents lived in a different day-to-day world than the middle-class professionals near Beka's apartment. In the Castro, gay couples wearing Red Wing boots and short shorts strolled hand-in-hand, crowded into bars and kissed under the portico of the historic Castro Theatre.

Here in the Mission district, she saw Asian produce shops scattered among small bodegas and sushi bars beside Vietnamese restaurants. Posters for Spanish language videos covered the windows of a rental shop which shared an awning with a Filipino travel agency. A Zen meditation center was under construction next to a karate studio. Beka liked it here. The neighborhood vibrated with global complexity.

Safe House occupied a storefront in the grubby heart of the Inner Mission, in a building that once housed a bookstore café. The rear of the space had been divided into cubicles for counselors and administrators. She found the Director in one cubicle.

Shirley Wendt was a tall, vigorous woman with stylishly short gray hair. She wore a soft chambray shirt with black jeans tucked into black boots. When Beka stepped in, she was on the phone, jabbing the air for emphasis. Shirley nodded and waved her into a wooden chair wedged between the desk and the flimsy wall-divider.

"Why?" the Director of Safe House hollered into the phone. "Because we're trying to turn these disadvantaged young women into outstanding citizens and leaders. Thursday at four? She'll be there."

"Now, what can I do for you?" She pointed a nicotine-stained finger at Beka who took a breath and began to respond. Ms. Wendt interrupted after six words. "You bet we need volunteers. Be here Friday at six. I'll get Graciela Martinez to show you the ropes."

The elderly priest groaned as she limped down the steps of the shabby Victorian, an anonymous three-story structure that housed women trying to get out of the sex trade. The pair from Saint Lydia's had just visited Luz Rivera, a lovely girl who reminded Rev Ruth of the daughter she never got to know.

"My knees are too old for this," she complained. "Why didn't you tell me that everything in San Francisco is vertical."

Beka took her arm." One step at a time. We'll go down slowly, the same way we went up."

The interim priest of St. Lydia's Church had recently been introduced at the San Francisco Clergy Women's Council; there were only five members. Reverend Glenda Hope had asked her to make a pastoral call at San Francisco General Hospital. When she wanted to visit Luz at Safe House, Rev Ruth asked Beka to go along. "I don't know my way around your hilly city. Any chance you could drive me to Valencia Street?"

"Of course," Beka said. "I even know where to find parking. I met Luz Rivera when I started volunteering at Safe House. Ready when you are."

On their way to Beka's Subaru, she said "While you were talking to Luz, I helped Elsa study for her GED. I like Luz. What did you learn?"

"A sad tale." Rev Ruth grimaced. "Rough sex. Abuse. Alcohol." She whacked her cane against a parking meter. "Enough sins to sink a battleship, and more shame than most creatures could bear."

Beka had no reply to this. She'd heard plenty of tragic stories during Wednesday evening volunteer shifts at Safe House. Most residents weren't far from the gutter. "What got Luz into recovery?"

"Being stabbed in the neck. Getting sober in San Francisco General."

"Ouch."

"Luz and her caseworker tell me she needs a sponsor."

"Which means?" Beka's eyes were half-closed with concentration, not good for someone driving through city traffic.

"A church home among women who won't judge her," said Rev Ruth, "and a pastor who won't hold her past livelihood against her."

"St. Lydia's sounds like a good fit. What would it take to sponsor her?"

"First we need to find someone willing to take her in." Rev Ruth spoke slowly, thoughtfully. "Luz has nearly completed the program at Safe House and will soon need somewhere else to live."

"You know, Hope has a guest room on the ground level of her home," exclaimed Beka. "I wonder how she'd feel about having a former prostitute in the basement."

GETTING ACQUAINTED

Luz stubbed out her cigarette in the sand-filled Folger's can squatting between her wicker chair and Rev Ruth's on the porch of Safe House. She had already declared her refusal to go back to the Union Gospel Mission. Luz had a particular look when she was defiant, not unlike the expression frequently adopted by Rev Ruth's rebel granddaughter.

Today, Luz's hair was charged with electricity. A green light sparked in her eyes. Her mouth was pink, her lips pursed. Her breath was fresh with mint toothpaste. A slight tremor pulsed beneath her left eye, like a bomb set to explode.

"You're aren't going to mess up, are you?" Rev Ruth braced her chin. "We are trying to work out housing for you at Saint Lydia's Church. It could be your one chance to have a real future with a nice, normal congregation."

Luz glared and looked away, then sneaked a look back. The priest's face was thin, bloodless. Almost saintly. With someone this old—Luz pictured dear Abuela—a little wisdom might leak out.

Rev Ruth kept her eyes fixed on the girl, her mind spinning a series of what-ifs. What if she explodes at me? What if she isn't ready to behave? What if she hurts Hope Hudson? What if this whole idea is a mistake? What if our plan is doomed to failure?

Luz cast about, looking for something to say. She stretched her arms high, wiggled her fingers in the air, grabbed one wrist and stretched. She brought her hands down and pressed a thumb to her throat as if trying to take her pulse, or contain a sudden burst of energy. She opened her handbag. Rev Ruth figured she was getting another cigarette. Instead she pulled out a pair of scissors and aimed the sharp end at her visitor.

The sight of a weapon jolted the priest out of her chair. "Put that away!"

Luz fired off a wicked smile. "I'm ready for anything now." She shaped her lips into a kiss and made a loud smack.

Though the girl was small, there was a dark assurance about her. Rev Ruth felt a sudden wave of sympathy, a tidal surge that almost wrecked her. All of a sudden she was afraid of losing her power. Losing her priestly objectivity.

The priest rose and stepped toward Luz in her careful and unsteady way. She kept her eyes on the girl. She reached for the scissors. Luz handed them over. Rev Ruth received the cool metal in her open palm the way she received the consecrated host during Holy Eucharist. Their eyes held. A lucid sweetness flooded over her. The silence between them was a relief.

A HOPE AND A FUTURE

"Tell me about yourself." Beka was on duty at Safe House. She wanted Luz to remember the good parts of her life in Mexico, the good parts of her self. "Who were you before you got hurt?" This question was part of the strategy for counseling staff.

Luz stood with one hip cocked and a skeptical expression on her face. Her skin was the color of café-au-lait. A double cleft at the right corner of her mouth gave her an impish smile. A thin horizontal scar trailed from her hairline to her eyebrow. A wide, vivid scar marred the left side of her neck. Her left ear had a nicked lobe. A pink flip-flop dangled from one small foot.

"Who loved you before you came to San Francisco?"

"Abuela." The answer came quickly, sweetly. "Her hands made my hair pretty. She loved my little toes," Luz said, wiggling five toes, "and I loved her square old feet and cracked sandals."

"Who else loved you when you were small?" Beka kept her tone level.

"Miguelito. My big brother touched me in the night, made me feel good."

Beka flinched with dismay.

Luz didn't notice. "But I could not save him from drugs. Miguelito. Knifed in the back. Buried in Hermosillo." She squeezed her eyes shut.

"I am so sorry." Beka touched the girl's shoulder. "You mentioned sisters. Tell me about them."

"Si. Three sisters. Consuelo, Florencia, Maria. I miss them. I think most of Consuelo, the slow music of her voice, how sweet to sing with her on warm nights."

"Your medical records say you couldn't speak for a while after you got stabbed," ventured Beka. "I was afraid you might never get your voice back."

"Me, too. That was a terrible time. I am so glad to talk again."

"What do you want to do next?" This was the last question on Beka's list.

"Do kind things for sad people. Be a big sister to girls like me, show them a better way. Make people happy."

"I like you, Luz. I want you to be happy so you can make others happy, so I'll do my best to find the right place for you. Meanwhile I want you to do something for me."

Luz squinted, not sure where this would lead. At last she said "What?"

"Make me happy."

This led to a mutual grin. One was topped with a lifted eyebrow.

"If you would memorize a few lines from this," Beka held out a small black leather Bible, "it will make me very happy."

Luz jerked away as if it might bite. "Oh no! Only the priest can touch *La Bibla*."

"Not here. In the Golden State, people have their own Bibles. This Bible is mine, and I want to give it to you."

Looking doubtful, Luz let Beka place the Bible in her lap.

"I've put a red ribbon to mark Jeremiah 29:11. This is the verse I want you to memorize. *For I know the plans I have for you, plans to prosper you and not harm you, plans to give you a hope and a future.*"

"Is that true?

"Yes, Luz. God loves you and wants to help you. So do I."

MATCHMAKER

Beka woke up feeling guilty about having asked Hope Hudson to shelter the troubled Mexican girl. Just a little guilty, though. Not guilty enough to cancel the plan. Hope was enjoying leisure for the first time in her hard-working life. She sometimes complained of fatigue; she was sixty-eight, after all. And Beka could see, especially as her problem of finding a place for Luz was mostly solved, that in less than an hour she had altered Hope's life, and not necessarily for the better. At the same time, Beka was certain her friend could no more refuse to take Luz Rivera into her home than water could refuse to run downhill.

It wouldn't have happened if Hank were still alive. If he had picked up the phone he would have said "Look, don't do this to my wife. Hope isn't young, you know. She gets tired." So, yes, Beka was relieved Hank hadn't answered.

Hope did take the call and she did say yes. Eventually.

And yes, Beka had flagrantly manipulated Hope's goodwill and generosity. She admitted this to herself in the cold light of dawn. But was it wrong? Surely the girl would be good for her. Think of the zest that would come into her friend's narrow, uneventful existence. Luz might become a ray of sunshine in Hope's dull life, even if she would add to the strain of it. Her name did mean *Light*. It could make Hope happy to have a bright seventeen-year-old in the house. It could stop the depression from coming back. It could even make her feel young again.

Beka liked the feeling of being a benefactor. Surely, she thought as she spooned yogurt on granola, it was doubly beneficial of her to broker an arrangement that would be good for her friend and good for the homeless immigrant. She imagined Hope and Luz at the breakfast table. Hope had qualities that were good for Luz. One was generosity, general goodwill toward all. Another quality was how Hope routinely rooted for the underdog, a category into which Luz definitely fell. Don't forget Hope's sturdy common sense. When Beka'd been young she had mocked these qualities in the adults around her but now she was grateful for them.

Beka reviewed her list of good qualities; she added Hope's itch for variety. Surely she would benefit from having something new going on at home, something beyond the ordinary. And finally, there was Hope's tendency to switch off her attention. If she had the television on, or knitting needles in hand, the presence of a prostitute in the basement would scarcely enter her awareness at all. And whenever she was paying attention to Luz, she could teach the girl how to be socially appropriate.

By the end of their conversation Hope sounded more intrigued than burdened. She had agreed, of course, and they fixed a time. Today at two.

Hope lived in a modest stand-alone two-story on Stanyan Street in the Upper Haight-Ashbury. Beka parked in the driveway, directly in front of the garage door. She and Luz climbed ceramic-tile steps to the porch. The front door featured a stained-glass sunrise spreading yellow rays across a bright blue bay.

Beka knocked twice, lightly. Footsteps sounded and the door swung wide and they were looking at a rounded woman, arms crossed over ample breasts. She wore a homemade cotton shirt with big, square pockets at hip level. Her shirt hid the elastic waistband of her blue nylon slacks. Her feet were clad in fuzzy pink slippers.

The Head Beacon gave Hope an idiotic grin and bounced in with the exuberance of a Jewish yenta, singing *Match-maker, match-maker, make me a match.* The tune from *Fiddler on the Roof* had been running through her mind, though she didn't sing it aloud because of Luz. Not that a Mexican girl would understand a Jewish song, but still.

Beka wrinkled her nose like a rabbit. "You mean you don't have cookies in the oven?" She was doing her best—with teasing affection—to bridge the gulf between the homeless immigrant she'd just fetched from a shelter and the generous homeowner who'd agreed to take her in. The differences between them were vast.

"Hope, it is my pleasure to introduce you to Luz Rivera." Beka spoke brightly, turning toward the girl.

Luz stood behind her, frozen in the doorway.

"Come in, come in," beckoned Hope, her smile fake as paste rubies.

Luz took one short step and stopped, as if she'd been told to walk on ice.

Beneath her calm demeanor, Hope was doing her best to subdue the swells of uncertainty roiling her belly. *What have I gotten myself into?*

Cheerily trying to shape an awkward moment into a welcoming one, Beka kept up a line of chatter. She took Luz by one arm, pulled her toward the couch and pressed her down. The girl perched on the edge of a cushion as if it might be a sleeping panther, ready to eat her alive.

Luz studied things while the grownups were in the kitchen. *Will this lady keep me?* The house had a pulse that made her knees quiver. Colors vibrated. Her leg muscles bunched into spasms. Fear of expulsion exploded bitterly in her mouth. *This lady won't keep me if she knows what I've done.*

Hope's eyes, skewed by a heightened awareness of the void between them, blurred when she glanced in the girl's direction. *Too late to back out?*

Luz' shoulders jerked when the china teapot rattled against a fragile cup. *The lady is trying to pour tea. Why's her hand shaking? Is she about to make me go away?*

"I could just hop with happiness," exclaimed Beka, bunny-hopping toward the couch. She slid a plate of cinnamon cookies onto the coffee table and playfully flapped both hands overhead like floppy ears. "I am so happy to be your matchmaker. You two are really going to like each other. And remember," she said, voice oozing with vitality, "the Beacons of Saint Lydia's want the best for both of you."

With contagious enthusiasm, Beka tried to save the day by being true to herself. "I am confident you will get along great. I can tell."

And the sun beamed in, shining on all three.

Humming happily, the matchmaker took her leave

ABUELA

Luz liked Hope right away, although she'd not expected her to be so old. She liked the looks of her hostess' neat white hair, round arms and soft tummy. She liked Hope's lovely smile and primrose blue eyes. "You remind me of my *abuela*," said Luz, "and she's still going strong in Hermosillo."

"Good," said Hope cautiously. "That's a good start."

"Thank you," said Luz. "I could cry, but I won't." She wiped her fingers across one cheek. "Your home is lovely. *Muchas gracias* for taking me in."

"Would you like to see your room? It's small, but has its own bathroom. Here, follow me through the kitchen door and down the basement stairs. Your room is on the ground floor. We'll go through the garage, just past the washer and dryer."

"I hope you don't mind having me here." Luz stopped on the threshold and bit her lip, as if afraid to step toward her new bed.

"What I do mind," said Hope, "is feeling terrified that I may not be able to help you enough."

Luz dropped her face into the crook of her arm and shivered.

Hope moved quickly for a woman with belly fat the size of a truck tire. She circled an arm around the girl's shaking shoulders, the first step in bridging a wide cultural abyss.

Morning. Luz crept up the stairs without a sound. The kitchen door stood ajar. She held her breath and peeked around the doorjamb. Her hostess wore a half-smile and a roomy print blouse, faded as if from repeated washing. Her ankles were swollen. One slippered foot tapped rhythmically to a song hummed under her breath. One hand rested on the red-checked cloth covering a small table. Light from a lamp mounted on the wall above transformed her hair into a halo of white. She had her head bent over a small black leather-bound book. *La Bibla*. One finger, knotted with arthritis, moved in a slow, straight line across the page.

The girl knelt quietly on the threshold and bowed her head. Lustrous black hair spilled across clean squares of linoleum. The kitchen was fragrant with perking coffee perking and cinnamon rolls in the oven.

CHAPTER 8

THE VALLEYS

Shadows

BOOK OF CREATION

After Beka told about Luz being tortured, Paige's nightmares started up again. Granddad forcing her down the cellar steps. Granddad telling Mother, 'Paul's skinny, but he'll do.'

Her figure had always been based on straight lines. Back in the Sixties, when girls tried to achieve "the Twiggy look," Paige could never pull it off, even if she had been a girl then. You had to be pretty to carry off skinny, and nobody ever called her pretty. Granddad liked skinny, though. He liked her hair, straight as a twig, light brown. It was just like his. Friends told Paige that her fine hair softens her features. Her face is naturally plain; she doesn't fuss with blush or mascara. Granddad liked the natural look.

Oh God, memories of Granddad gave her a stomachache. She patted her pocket for the pills; she'd get the runs if she didn't get Imodium down the hatch. The pills tasted foul but made her feel better.

The Beacon had to get outdoors—read The Book of Creation, find God in nature. She checked with her gut. The Imodium was working; safe to leave the house. She grabbed her jacket and headed out.

'Thomas Aquinas, come with me,' she whispered, and heard the saint's rusty voice in her inner ear. "*Nature is the primary revelation of the Divine. Creation is our first and final cathedral.*"

Paige had memorized lines from *The Summa Theologie* for times such as these. Intonations of the ancient sage continued as she walked toward Golden Gate Park. "*Nature is the one song of praise that never stops singing. Matter is the outer lovely form, but Spirit is the inner source of everything we know and see.*"

Once in the park, she wanted to close her eyes, but that was dangerous because the cobwebby cellar was engraved on her eyelids; memories of the moldy smell made her gag. Grandad's hands on her ten-year-old body made her heart bang away in her chest. A stomach cramp got her and she doubled up. Repulsion jangled her skin.

She limped toward a skinny pine sapling. "Hello," she whispered to it. "I need a friend. May I sit with you a while?"

After a few minutes, her irritable bowel calmed down. Nature had that effect. She looked around and confirmed she was alone in the wooded glade. "I need to tell you something," she said to the sapling. Her voice was thin, vulnerable. "Need to tell you the whole truth."

Afterward, emotionally spent, Paige rested her forehead against the slender trunk. "Thank you for listening." She slipped Granddad's curved flask from the pocket of her chinos. "Here's something for your thirst," she said, patting the rough bark. Placing the silver flask near the pine's roots, she tipped the last of her drinking water into the soil.

BREAD OF LIFE

Dot Davis was a friendly, fast-talking woman. She brought lively leadership to Saint Lydia's, along with a knack for controversy. The Beacons noted how quickly she could contradict herself from one remark to the next. This gave them plenty to chew on when they talked about her, which they did frequently.

Jesus first came to Dot when she was in her twenties, with no family to help her through the tragedies and the traumas. Nearly wrecked by a suicidal addiction to whiskey, she finally stumbled into a church basement where a bunch of drunks were testifying to a higher power. Hungry for something she couldn't name, she decided to risk going up the stairs. Dot figured the people of Saint Lydia's Church would disappoint, because people always disappointed her, but she had to get closer to Jesus so—heart pounding—she went upstairs on a Sunday morning and that's where it happened.

Jesus lodged in me like a crumb. Dot repeated the phrase to herself. She couldn't explain how Jesus had lodged in her like a crumb, had no idea how that happened. The first time she took communion with the people of Saint Lydia's, the bread itself had been ordinary—dense, wheaty, slightly sour— but when she opened her mouth and took it in, chewed and swallowed it, these simple human acts made Dot felt more alive ever before.

The first time she received the sacrament it left her physically unbalanced, as if she'd stepped off a curb into a place without gravity. Her reaction made no sense, yet she knew Jesus had actually entered her body. Jesus was as real as her blood and bones. As real as bread made from flour, yeast and water.

When she was young, her mother Sunny, a lapsed Catholic, made Dot go to confirmation class, but for the longest time she wasn't sure how to think about Eucharist. At first she believed what the nuns taught, that the holy presence of Jesus was literally baked into the crisp little communion wafers that dissolved on her tongue. Then in her thirties, during an undefended moment, a new truth dawned on her: *O my God, I really am what I eat!* With that, propelled by the Bread of Life, she tossed out past doubts and began digesting new beliefs.

Fortified by dining on the sacred presence of Jesus during communion services at Saint Lydia's, Dot carried this holy power into the secular world of Child Protective Services, where the Bread of Life gave her formidable power to protect unwanted children. Dot didn't mind bristling at neglectful parents or challenging bored government workers. "Only a few people in the projects care about kids," she declared, "so I concentrate on them."

Church friends viewed Dot as she viewed herself, a fierce warrior in the war on poverty. The winds of good and evil blew sideways through the lives of kids in her neighborhood and Dot could never shake the feeling of being personally responsible for the wellbeing each little one. When she could not protect every child, the pain of impotence manifested in strange ways. When citizens thanked Dot for her service, she could not look them in the eye. At Saint Lydia's, her eyes leaked tears of empathy when she watched loving adults tend to the church kids. In the Fillmore, her eyes flashed with righteous anger when she saw ragtag kids playing in the littered streets.

Some things about Christianity made sense to Dot. She liked Bible stories of Jesus scattering the proud and rebuking the powerful. Jesus was a strong teacher, but he didn't keep her from getting crabby or feeling lonely. She had no idea where her intense longing for Jesus came from. All she knew was she had to put her longings in the hands of the Lord. She didn't pretend to understand, but she did need to eat Jesus every day.

At Saint Lydia's, they served communion only once a month, not enough for Dot. Eating Jesus was the only thing that made her strong enough to protect vulnerable kids. She had to take the bread of Jesus into her mouth and digest it into her body every day. Her hunger was there again the next day but the church communion table wasn't. It wasn't long before Dot took things into her own hands.

Why did eating Jesus move her so deeply? Words of an old hymn moved through her mind...*Mysterious, invisible, silent as light*...Dot could not explain it to herself, let alone explain to anyone else. All she knew was she had to have the bread of Jesus—the next day, and the next—because she was so hungry. It wasn't just physical; some mysterious spiritual hunger tugged at her, so Dot began to serve herself communion. Every day. When someone asked, Dot gave a big grin and announced "I chew on Jesus all the time, in church, at home and on the street. I am what I eat, you know."

At first, church friends thought she was joking but they couldn't deny there was something magnetic about Dot. She kept her hair pulled back and looked, in any weather, like someone just in from a brisk walk. "Jesus didn't say think about this," she announced with a straight face and a comic undertone. "He said eat this. So I do." They heard a hint of merriment, an exultant tone softening the message of her raised index finger.

Dot's unorthodox views were a source of endless conversation for the Beacons. When Hope was a girl, her Norwegian aunts and uncles had argued about the "how" of communion, whether it was magic or not.

When Paige was growing up, the big question at her Lutheran church was the "who" of the sacrament. Who could consecrate the bread and wine? Who had the power to turn ordinary bread into something holy?

But Dot had no time for such lofty questions. The children she served were stubbornly real entities, painfully kicked around by life. When she took a kid under her wing, he or she was not a symbol of anything, but a resonant living fact and Dot did her darnedest to return damaged boys and girls to their families in better shape than she found them.

Paige and Hope still hadn't figured it out. They supposed the source of Dot's power and passion must have something to do with eating the holy presence of Jesus. She claimed that her practice of personal communion fed her commitment to social change. It was, they thought, a sacred mystery. It was a paradox they never tired of exploring over countless cups of tea and assorted pastries.

GALLED

Surprise had given Dot Davis a powerful advantage. Rev Ruth had been on her way out of the room at the close of the Beacons meeting when she heard Dot announce that she ate Jesus for supper last night. Ruth was so dumbfounded she nearly fainted. How she made it home, she'd never know. Never had she heard such heresy. Eating Jesus all by her self! Without an ordained pastor to bless the bread!

Rev Ruth let out a noisy breath. Her apartment smelled of Lysol and loneliness. She stared into the emptiness and blinked once, twice, a third time. Angry tears glistened in the corners of her eyes. The priest was seething, could not contain her fury that a Beacon of the church—for God's sake—publicly insisted upon eating Jesus any damn time she pleased.

Lips tight, Rev Ruth anguished over this. What should I have done after she spoke out? Stood up and given her hell? Invited her for a drink at Little Shamrock, or whatever that pub is called? Could I convince Dot Davis of the sacramental truth about Holy Eucharist if we sat in a pub?

How could I have messed up something as vital as teaching my new congregants the truth about Holy Eucharist? The elderly pastor paced and fretted. *Have my ministerial instincts rusted to the point that a mere social worker—a woman who never once set foot in seminary—could put an ecclesiastical bullet through my eye? Shoot me dead before I even had a chance to blink?*

Too distraught to settle down and too ashamed to face a living soul, Rev Ruth breathed a little prayer of thanks that no one was here to witness her weakness. She tried to sleep, but heard the clock chime every hour. The night was torture.

Morning dawned gray. Rev Ruth had come to despise the fog banks that piled up over the city. For the past two days a high-pressure ridge over Northern California had kept the sky clear but today the looming wall of gray felt like a personal affront.

Rev Ruth rose to pace and fume. *The Lord's Supper is the core sacrament of Christianity, for God's sake.* She snorted like a sailor. *Everyone should call it Holy Eucharist.* And everyone in Christendom—everyone but Dot Davis, evidently—must know that the sacrament of Holy Eucharist requires an ordained priest to turn ordinary bread into the actual presence of Christ.

To make things worse, Ruth's troublesome sons were making their voices heard in her aching head. Stay home and tend to your knitting, Simon told her when she'd announced plans to pastor a church in San Francisco. So patronizing. James and Timothy, too: they'd insisted she stay put and take it easy. She'd scoffed, of course. Insisted on doing things her way, but now that she could not keep Dot Davis in line, her sons, her granddaughter, even old Bishop Tuttle were sure to find out that the Reverend Doctor Ruth Ridley Salter could not even convince a congregational leader that it was vital to honor the sanctity of The Lord's Supper by taking communion only within the sanctuary of Saint Lydia's Church.

If she couldn't handle such a vital part of church leadership, then retirement was clearly where she belonged. But God, it galled. It galled. She clenched both fists against her stomach, leaned forward and let out a moan. *Oh God, I am old, old, old.*

DOUBT

At three-thirty that afternoon, Beka—on a whim—phoned Rev Ruth at home. It turned out to be the day she'd decided to pack it all in and fly home to Cleveland.

"May I come by and pick you up?" Beka was thinking fast.

"Yes, please." Rev Ruth sounded morose.

An hour later, the pastor was on the sidewalk leaning on her cane, jawline as firm as her gaze. She wore creased navy slacks, a white turtleneck, a navy cardigan with gold buttons and a blue-and-white-striped scarf.

"You look very nautical," said Beka.

"I feel like a drowned rat," said Rev Ruth.

"Why did you decide to toss in the towel?" Beka pulled away from the curb and headed down Larkin toward the Bay.

Rev Ruth's teeth started clacking together. The weather was not that cold, but she was so thin. She teetered on the edge of the front seat and grabbed onto the dashboard; her knuckles went white.

Beka reached over and briskly rubbed her pastor's shoulder, as if warming a swimmer just out of the ocean. Neither spoke.

Without knowing where she was headed, Beka veered left on the Marina and followed traffic to the toll plaza. Before they knew it, the maroon Subaru was crossing the Golden Gate Bridge. Beka hadn't exactly planned to drive to Marin; it just seemed the right thing to do.

"So, tell me. When did you decide to leave Saint Lydia's and go back home?" Beka asked her question again.

Rev Ruth stuttered with genuine confusion. "I don't know. I think I need to live someplace small..." She stopped in mid-sentence.

"Someplace small?" Beka glanced over at her passenger.

"I need people nearby...to help... in case I fall," she stammered.

"Did you fall today?"

"No...its just...time to go..." Rev Ruth sounded very young.

"Couldn't you have talked with me first?"

No answer.

Without particularly meaning to, just before they got onto the Mount Tamalpais Road, Beka pulled off, parked in a bus zone and shut off the ignition. "Wait a minute. Let me ask you something. What do you want most? What does your heart say?"

After a long moment, the priest whispered, "It's time to leave Saint Lydia's."

This was shocking news to Beka. "Are you sure? The timing is just terrible."

"Yes, but I have to go because I've upset everyone enough." Her fingers fiddled with the gold buttons on her navy cardigan. She kept her gaze in her lap.

Neither spoke for a while. "But that's the worst reason to do something," Beka finally said. "You have the right to change your mind, you know."

"Really? Again?"

"Yep."

The air horn of an approaching bus made them both jump. Before she pulled out into traffic, the driver glanced at the pastor's face. She looked miserable.

Beka repeated herself. "You do have the right to change your mind."

Rev Ruth lifted one end of her striped scarf and touched it to the tears leaking from the corner of one eye.

"I'd like you to stay," said Beka. She put extra warmth into her voice.

Rev Ruth looked down at her chest, picked at the lint on her sweater.

Beka drove up the mountain toward Stinson Beach. "Let's eat by the sea tonight. It'll be a kind of last supper. We'll dine on fried oysters. I know just the place."

"Maybe I could stay," muttered Rev Ruth.

Beka smiled as she steered around another curve.

At The Sand Dollar they enjoyed a surprisingly good dinner, in a mood that was both giddy and gentle. Rev Ruth clinked her glass of Pinot Grigio against Beka's and murmured, "On a good day, old age is a dance with ministry."

Beka nodded and sipped.

"Once upon a time, I knew the right dance steps, but today I forgot them." Her voice went trembly.

"And on a bad day?" Beka's tone was tender.

"On a bad day, my thoughts don't go in the direction I think they should. When you called, I had no idea which way to turn. Why did you call me today, anyway?"

Beka brought her gaze back to Rev Ruth. The dark sea was topped with a star-sprinkled sky, blessedly free of fog. "I just spotted a flare of color," she said, widening her eyes. "At first I thought it was a plane heading for a landing at SFO, but now"—she flashed a grin at her pastor—"I think maybe it was a star being born."

ALLERGIC

It was a Saturday afternoon in early October. Autumn light spread like butter across the faces of four women who were cleaning candle wax off the altar and polishing the tall brass candlesticks. "As your reward for your labor," announced Hope, "I brought pumpkin-pecan bread, baked fresh this morning."

Conversational paths wandered, reminding Dot of sheep meandering through green pastures, but she had the good sense to keep this observation to herself. Eventually the topic turned, as it often did these days, to gossip about their interim pastor. It was mostly criticism, until Hope announced, "Well, I liked what she said last Sunday about communion."

"I played hooky, in case you didn't notice." Dot's tone was sour.

"I wondered where you were," said Hope. "Why do you skip church on communion Sundays, anyway?"

"I've been allergic to communion here ever since I caught Pastor Peacock leering down my neckline while I knelt at the communion rail."

"Did I ever tell you what I heard him say to the plumber?" asked Millienne.

"Yes," Hope spoke for the group, "but let's hear it again."

"Remember when the toilet in the women's restroom got plugged up? I was in the hall when I heard him talking to the plumber, so I eavesdropped. 'Man,' he said, "you should have my job. A woman's place is on her knees, and in my line of work I've got them kneeling at my feet all year long.'"

"Yuck," grimaced Beka, aiming a finger down her throat.

"Don't let our nasty priest ruin your appetite, ladies," said Hope. "Have more dessert, because I've got more to say about Rev Ruth and communion."

"Even if she does call it The Eucharist," interrupted Beka.

"That's just her language," Millienne was quick to add. "If you'd grown up Anglican, you'd call it Eucharist, too." The peacemaker spread her hands and gestured sideways, as if smoothing turbulent waters.

"Okay, okay," Beka conceded. "So, Hope, what did you like about her communion sermon? Tell us."

"Feeding. She said Eucharist is the sacrament of feeding."

"You would like that idea," laughed Millienne, patting her fleshy mid-section and gesturing toward Hope's. "You're always making sure we've got plenty."

Hope laughed cheerily. She was made for good meals, not modeling on Paris runways. She was constructed for happiness, and it had taken Hope a good long while to find it. To trust it. Even now, chatting and chewing with friends, part of Hope feared that her happiness could be taken away. A spiking fever. A stroke. Sudden death from cancer. Since Hank died, she'd been scanning the horizon for threats, real and imagined. Recently she'd begun to suspect the true threat to happiness came not from some dim disaster in the distance, but from expecting happiness. Waiting for it.

Her son jokingly accused Hope of living in the wreckage of her future. One day she'd looked straight into his blue eyes and saw he wasn't joking. Cody was warning her. But fear of loss was a hard habit to break, especially since the Beacons— and now the Rev—had become so dear.

Hope turned toward Dot, smelled her peppermint tea and heard her boot tapping against the linoleum. "Communion is about feeding." She spoke directly to Dot. "Rev Ruth says all

humans need to be fed, no matter what condition we're in."
Hope turned to Beka. "You heard it too, right? "

"Right. And I'd never thought of communion exactly that
way before."

"Pastor Peacock gave communion a weird sexual over-
tone," murmured Dot. "We're all survivors of the same church
wreck."

"Isn't that the truth," huffed Beka. "That predator gave
off the stink of sex even when he wore his clergy robe. Once
I told him an idea for the All Saints liturgy, but he turned
me down flat. When I asked why, he said, 'Since males take
initiative in the sex act, only males may take initiative in the
church.'"

The women groaned in unison. They'd heard the story
before.

"But Eucharist is not a sexual sacrament," blurted Hope.
"That's my whole point. Pastor Peacock defiled it, but Rev
Ruth is giving it back to us, giving it back in a womanly way."

Heads nodded. Bodies shifted. The furnace kicked on,
blowing warm air around their shoulders. Hope spoke
again. "That's why I liked it when Rev Ruth reminded us
how communion is primarily a sacrament of feeding people
who hunger." Her voice sounded sweet. Tender. Millienne
reached over and touched the back of her hand. The stillness
deepened.

"I can see your point," said Dot. "Bread and wine are
God's gifts to the people. The Bread of Life keeps us going
spiritually and you, my friend, keep us going physically." She
smiled at Hope.

"We all need to eat," murmured Millienne. "And not every
woman takes initiative in sex, although I'm thinking about it."

"What!" Beka's voice went up an octave. "Do you have a
guy on the string?"

"Maybe." Millienne lowered thick lashes and peeked out
beneath the fringe. "Too soon to say. But for now, please pass
the pecan-pumpkin bread. "

Hope did, and everyone took a slice. She refilled tea-cups, trying not to let her hand tremble. For some reason, the thought of Millienne getting sexual with some man gave her the shakes.

Five Beacons sipped and chewed without conversation. For four of the Beacons, the stillness was like a hum, a hymn, and they rested in it, grateful to be together in the comforting ritual of feeding and being fed. As for Hope, Millienne's startling announcement pierced like the sting of a wasp.

COMFORT

Millienne didn't mind waiting for people, didn't mind changing diapers for old folks at Laguna Honda Hospital, didn't mind cleaning up after someone barfed. She preferred things to stay in motion, stay unfinished, because finished meant over and done with. She liked things that kept moving. Sailboats on the Bay. Oceans. Clouds. Tree branches. Heartbeats.

It was a lovely evening, crisp as an apple. "I thought you'd never get here," she whispered when Caleb slid into bed beside her. She'd left the door of her apartment unlocked, even though she knew better. Crime was not as rampant in her Upper Market neighborhood as in some parts of the city, but she had taken a chance. Still, she wanted him to feel welcome. She'd taken off her clothes earlier, even though she didn't really believe he'd show up. And then he did.

Caleb wasn't the first man she'd been with, and that hadn't been Benet in Port-au-Prince, either. The first was a boy she'd met at a country torch dance on Fat Tuesday, back when she was fifteen. Millienne had decided it was time to have sex, the way an American girl might decide it was time to get a driver's license, and she'd gone ahead with it. Pragmatic, that's the way she'd always been.

But this was entirely different. It was as if she'd imagined Caleb Jones in her own mind before he showed up, that's how thoroughly she felt she knew the man. And now he was breathing next to her, stroking her thigh. The rest of the world was slipping away, which was exactly the way Millienne wanted it. So this was what happened when you fell in love, better than the first bite of an apple. Sweet and tart. She felt amazingly delicious.

In bed together, arms around each other, that's when she decided not to think about anything else. She wasn't going to worry, the way she sometimes did. She wasn't going to be responsible for anyone else. For now, no one else existed. She was just going to be with Caleb. With him she could be completely herself, Millienne Guillernos, totally her own true self here in her own bed. Nothing more, nothing less.

"Caleb comes by once or twice a week, " she told Hope as they sat on stools at Ruby's. "The guy from Jamaica who works in the hospital kitchen. Sometimes he takes me out after work, before we go back to my place."

"I suppose you drink now." Hope narrowed her eyes at her friend.

Millienne nodded once and spoke to the waitress. "I will have a Bud."

Hope ordered a Seven-Up.

"To Caleb," said Millienne, lifting her glass.

"I suppose you're about to tell me your heart beats faster at the sight of him." Hope knew she sounded crotchety, arms crossed over her aching heart.

"Perhaps a little faster," Millienne conceded generously, sidestepping the argument, suspecting she would not be able to explain her romantic notions.

"Love is more complicated than you might imagine." Hope's tone resembled the ice crackling in her glass. She sipped her soda and glared.

"Well, thanks for the warning." Millienne noticed the brass on the shelf behind the bar had not been polished. She concentrated on the tarnished bar as she sipped her beer, the brass with its lacy casings and leaded glass doors.

"Did you hear me?" Hope asked. "Drinking beer and not getting enough sleep is terrible for the dermis, you know." When her friend looked puzzled, she added "The skin. One day you'll wake up and your skin will be hanging off and you'll look like you're a century old. I can see the lines already."

"I'm fine," Millienne insisted. She could feel the echo of her pulse in her ears. She looked elegant with her dark hair wound up, wearing a pale pink blouse. "I hope you won't worry about me," she said to Hope. "I'll be fine. My plan is going strong."

"Well, mine isn't." Hope sounded cross. "I thought you and I would be going around together now that I don't have to get Hank's dinner on the table every night at six. But I'm not a complainer," she sniffed. Hope was startled by how jealous she felt, hearing Millienne's affection for Caleb. It shocked her, actually. It had been a very long time since she had wanted anything. Anyone.

Millienne stood up, high-heeled suede boots solid on the wooden floor. "You'll always be my buddy," she said, laughing a little. Then she bent down and kissed the top of Hope's white perm. She didn't do that often, in fact had never before kissed the top of anyone's head.

"Thank you," Hope said for no reason, clamping her hand on her chest as if her own frail heart might be ready to jump ship. There might have been a tear in one eye. "We all need a bit of comfort now and then."

CRUSH

Love. Hope was thinking about love.

A crush. I haven't had one of those since before I knew what age spots were.

She crossed her legs and swung her foot a little. She thought about Millienne taking off her clothes for some guy who was not her husband.

Jesus! The word sort of exploded out of her.

What? She imagined Millienne's placid voice in her head.

Thinking about love, sitting alone in her own recliner, Hope reacted viscerally. "Well, you can't just go around fucking everybody!" It came out as a plea.

Not everybody. Only Caleb.

Doesn't it make you nervous? Hope wasn't done with this inner dialogue.

No.

But an affair is so ... so intense. And you act like its normal.

It is normal. For me.

This imaginary exercise gave Hope no satisfaction. She washed her face and went to bed. Anger and confusion kept her awake. She stared up at the ceiling and practiced more ways to convince Millienne to change her ways.

How can you give yourself to someone you barely know?

How can you keep doing something so...so wrong?

Then: How can I keep on loving a woman I disapprove of?

And then, the aftershock:

How can I love a woman?

CHOCOLATE

"Meet me at Ghiradelli Square this afternoon?" asked Hope. Her voice went up an octave. "I need chocolate!"

"Is this about Saint Lydia's? What's the emergency?" Beka, ever responsible, was willing to don her Head Beacon hat, but only if absolutely necessary.

"No, it's not about church. It's about...me." Hope coughed in a phony way.

"Are you sick?"

"No, I'm not sick but...I've got a problem..." Her voice trailed off.

"And that's an emergency?" Beka was distracted, gazing at the muscle tone of her calves, turning an ankle to admire her spiffy new mid-heel pumps, blue suede.

"I've got a crush. It's got me all cattywompus."

"A crush. And you need chocolate?" Laughter lingered on the line.

"You're not taking me seriously," wailed Hope. "This is serious. I need to talk to someone right away, and I definitely need chocolate. Will you come?"

"So, you're saying fate brought you and Millienne together at the same time she was falling for a guy at work. Do I have that right?" Beka scooped fudge sauce from the top of her rocky-road sundae.

The Ghiradelli Chocolate Factory featured small, round white-painted tables, too dainty if you ask Beka. She had to keep shifting her rump on the little iron chair to stop her knees from bumping into Hope's knees.

Hope, who had already polished off her own triple chocolate-brownie sundae, dipped a spoon into Beka's. "His name is Caleb Jones." She bit off the words the same way she bit off a thread while sewing. "And it's not fate, exactly. It's more like I was once blind to Millienne's strength and beauty, but now that I see how gorgeous she is, I want to be with her all the time. More often than she wants to be with me." Her lips puckered into a pout.

"And how does that make you feel?" Beka's eyes were shiny with amusement. It took every bit of restraint to keep from wiggling her eyebrows.

"At first it felt like I was being drawn along into something wonderful, until..." Hope glanced toward San Francisco Bay. Beka followed her gaze. They watched the commuter ferry chug past Fort Mason toward Sausalito. "Until last night when Millienne told me she has started to spend nights with Caleb. It's not wonderful any more. It's more like... I'm on a sinking ferryboat."

Clamping her lips to keep from guffawing, Beka turned away to collect herself, then caught Hope's gaze. Eyes squinting with mischief, she asked "Why do you suppose love puts people into such comical situations?"

"Comical?" Hope squeezed her eyes shut.

"Eleanor Roosevelt said you have got to learn from the mistakes of others, because you can't live long enough to make them all yourself." Beka barked with laughter and took a playful swat at her friend.

Hope's rigid chest and neck muscles softened. "You may be right," she sighed. "Just when I think I have totally outgrown crushes, I go and fall for Millienne. I guess it is kind of comical." Hope dipped into Beka's bowl and licked fudge from her spoon.

"Especially since you get a crush on her the same week she falls for some new guy. " Beka gave such an innocent wide-eyed look they both dissolved into laughter.

"And she doesn't notice me any more," groaned Hope.

"So, now that the luscious Millienne is taken, you're free to start enjoying people who are only pretty good," whimpered Beka, nearly rocking off her tiny decorative chair. One of her suede pumps jiggled loose and she had to hold onto the wall for support to get it back on her foot.

"No wonder it feels like I'm on a sinking ferry boat," giggled Hope, drumming her beige orthopedic shoes against the floor. Her tiny chair tipped and she fell against Beka. "Just when I think I'm beyond crushes..." Hope plucked at the neckline of her blouse to cool down. Shoulder to shoulder, they gasped for air.

"A sinking ferry boat," repeated Beka, and off they sailed into a mirthful gale.

Holding her sides, Hope was finally able to wheeze "No more punch lines. You're giving me a pain in the ribs." Breathless and teary, the friends agreed that both were on the verge of losing bladder control, so they took a bathroom break.

Crossing Ghiradelli Square toward the parking lot, Hope gestured toward her ample midsection. "What you see before you, my friend," she intoned, "is the result of a lifetime of chocolate. Know who said that?"

"Missus Ghiradelli?"

"No, silly. Katharine Hepburn. In a movie on television last night."

"That is a good line," confirmed Beka. "Maybe you should adopt it as your motto aboard that sinking ferry boat."

"It's more fun getting silly with you than trying to get back into the garden with Millienne," grinned Hope. "You're more fun than a snake in the grass."

"And eating chocolate is smarter than biting into an apple," concluded Beka. "Sister Eve made a bad choice back in Eden. Shoulda snacked on chocolate instead."

AS IT IS

"I used to be incredibly lonely," said Paige, "after my sister Angela was murdered. I miss her every day."

"Death is cruel." Millienne was relieved to focus on Paige instead of herself.

"It is," Paige agreed, rising to turn on the gas under the kettle. There were hidden themes in this conversation that neither knew how to name, spiritual implications neither felt ready to unpack, so they talked about Millienne's job and Paige's work, the wet, messy human aspects of one and the technical, papery elements of the other. Then Millienne went back to worrying about whether she had cancer or not.

'I hate the idea of losing my hair." She buried long fingers in her thick tresses.

"You are you, with or without hair," Paige affirmed, "and always will be."

Millienne looked glum. No response to that.

"Here is some wisdom from Shakespeare, from *The Tempest*," Paige said brightly. *Do not infest your mind with beating on the strangeness of this business. Be cheerful and think of each thing well.*

Millienne was not interested in Shakespeare, and told her so. The matter of the tumor in her gut had a way of staining her thoughts, particularly when she tried to pray.

"Will you pray for me?" she blurted. Her eyes had a beseeching gleam. Her big square hands grasped Paige's small ones, squeezing the pale fingers adorned with tiny curls of hair.

"Of course. Prayer is a joint enterprise. Let's start with the one Jesus taught. Say it with me. Our Father who art in heaven…"

"As it is?" Millienne dropped hands. "Why'd you stop and repeat those words?"

"That's your line. AS IT IS," insisted Paige. "Your prayer phrase. Keep it close."

"Why?"

"Because God gave it to me, to give to you for times when you don't know how to pray. Those three words from the middle of The Lord's Prayer are yours. Repeat them whenever you start to worry about cancer."

Millienne nodded. "I will."

"And let me know what the doctor says. It may not be a tumor, but if it is, I'll sit with you through chemotherapy. You're not alone in this, sister."

VIOLET

Dorothy Delilah Davis had been told she was too softhearted for her own good because she could not bear to see a child flinch. A native San Franciscan, she had grown up in the projects where fistfights were as frequent as footsteps, gunshots as common as coughs,. Eldest daughter in a fatherless household, Dot grew up vigilant; did all she could to protect two younger brothers, but could not save Violet.

Dot was nineteen, a waitress at IHOP, when her drug-addicted mother delivered a frail baby, soon taken into custody by Child Protective Services. Violet died in foster care, under suspicious circumstances, just short of her second birthday.

Sunny and Dot managed to scrape together money for the funeral but not for a grave marker. Hours before her bereaved mother passed away, just a few months after Violet, Dot vowed

that she would put a stone on her sister's grave. Fourteen years
had passed, and she still hadn't come up with the funds.

The evening Lydia Circle focused on the theme *Sisters,* Dot
poured out the story; her baby sister's unmarked grave beneath
the low hum of high-voltage power lines. People walking in
the cemetery near the drainage ditch would never know a toddler lay beneath their feet. No one would know her name was
Violet or the sad fact that she had died a month before her
second birthday.

"A child's grave should bear eternal witness," wailed Dot.
"My baby sister's blood soaked into the body of the earth and
nobody knows she's there. Only the trees know about Violet."

The Beacons collected enough to purchase a simple stone.
A month later Millienne and Hope stood with Dot on the
withered grass as cemetery workers placed a marker on the
toddler's grave. Her name had been cut into dark polished
granite: Violet Vereen Harris. The dates were painful: February 11, 1961 to January 2, 1963. The kneeling angel with
"Beloved Sister" inscribed beneath its wings brought scant
comfort.

Violet's death, however, was what catapulted Dot out of a
waitress uniform and into child advocacy work. She found a
way to convert her angry grief into a lifelong mission. Though
she had only ten credits from City College, her focused intensity won an outreach worker internship with Child Protective Services. Eventually Dot worked her way up to a supervisory position, mentoring ghetto kids to look out for smaller
siblings. She was good at developing teams. She taught teen
advocates to be clever and resourceful in preventing younger
kids from getting hurt.

In memory of Violet, Dot dedicated her adult life to pro-
tecting innocent children. She was a fierce advocate who did
everything she could to prevent kids from getting lost in the
gap between parental limitations and the busy welfare workers
who supervised foster homes in the county of San Francisco.

NOBODY'S NOTHING

"How'd you get into this line of work, anyway?" Millienne hadn't yet heard Dot's history. They perched on red-vinyl stools and sipped Coke floats.

"At first I had no idea I would ever be part of something bigger," said Dot. "I was blind to how bad things had become in my neighborhood until I grew into my teens and started listening to conversations at the liquor store where I bought Cokes. It was all *'so-and so got thrown out, couldn't pay the rent,'* or *'Social Services took her kids after her water got turned off, 'cause she sent 'em to school dirty.'*

"Hard facts for a sensitive girl." Millienne scooted closer and pulled Dot into a side hug.

Dot pulled away. "You know what was even harder?" Her voice had a sharp edge. "The day I overheard two little girls in the aisle of the liquor store. 'They say if you live in the Western Addition, you're nothing,' said one, and the other said 'I know.' I'll tell you, hearing that from a pair of eight-year-olds about tore me up."

"What did you do?"

"I knelt down, stared right into their eyes and said *Nobody's Nothing.* Do not believe that, you hear. Repeat after me Nobody Is Nothing. And they did."

"Was that after Violet died?" Millienne's tone was soothing.

'Yes. Some fierce part of me came to life after my baby sister died. I made a list of everyone in my housing project who was on the skids. What were they supposed to do? You've gotta understand, my neighbors are not gonna fill out welfare paperwork even if they're hungry and cold. I figured they needed help even knowing where to call for help."

"I'd like to see how you do things." Millienne's hands floundered in the air. Fumbling for words, she said "I'd like to go with you, on your rounds."

Dot gave her friend a searching look, determined she was sincere, and nodded.

On the agreed-upon day, Millienne watched a six-year-old turn cartwheels on a lawn as scratchy as a hay bale. When the girl realized Dot was about to knock, she ran and placed herself between the visitors and her door. A bent woman answered.

"Hi, Consuelo, do you have enough food for the kids?" Dot held out a bag filled with surplus beans, cornmeal and dried milk.

The grandmother drew the child close and smoothed her hair, then took the bag. "Thank you," she said. "*Muchas gracias.*"

Dot wasn't finished. "Consuelo, please take these forms from the county." She held out a sheaf of papers. The wrinkled woman jerked back like they might be poison. "With the grandkids here now, you can apply for AFDC, you know. And I can help you fill out forms."

Ten-year-old Jorge edged past his grandmother, took the papers and glanced at the first page. "I can do it." Then he looked at Dot and asked "Are we multi-ethnicity?"

In the next apartment block, Manuel Ramirez didn't answer right away. "He's eighty-four, seldom goes out," Dot explained " so I holler yoo-hoo until he opens up."

A withered gentleman came to the door with a splintered guitar in hand, beckoned them in and sang Mexican waltzes until they had to go.

"Manuel says I'm loco to help these people, but he loves me," Dot said as they walked past the liquor store where her mission in life got its start.

"Nobody's nothing," Millienne repeated, tilting her head toward two skinny black girls skipping ahead of them on the sidewalk. "Wait up," she called.

The girls stopped and turned. Millienne hurried toward them. "Listen to this," she called merrily. "Doctor Seuss wants you to know something. *'Today you are You, that is truer than true. There is no one alive who is You-er than You.'* Got that?"

The taller girl nodded and bent toward her friend. The younger one shook her head, beaded braids clacking. As the girls went on, one asked "Who's doctor Zooos?"

"If they came to Sunday School at Saint Lydia's they'd know," said Millienne. "Those lines were part of Candace Wong's lesson last week."

"Nobody reads to these kids." Dot took Millienne's arm. "Maybe our next project here in the projects should be a Doctor Seuss reading club."

MIRRORING

In Hope's home, nobody could miss the mirrors. The one over the fireplace stretched the width of the living room and the dining room mirror covered a whole wall. The mirrors had been in place for decades; Hope hardly noticed them any more but she did notice something odd about Luz. The girl looked away each time she passed the mirrors, turned her shoulder and hurried past.

"Why would such a lovely girl avoid mirrors?" Hope asked Millienne.

"The problem with mirrors is, you can't turn them off."

"Luz is so pretty, though." Hope shook her head in confusion. "Why not appreciate her own reflection?"

"Ashamed, maybe?"

"Ashamed of not being a nice girl?" Hope was in the mood to probe this mystery.

"That's my guess." Millienne nodded.

"I was afraid it was something like that." Hope paused then plunged on. "Once I asked what she did before she came to San Francisco but she clammed up. Luz tries to be nice to me, but not when I ask questions like that."

"Does she act like a child trying to behave?"

"No, more like one who's been damaged…" Hope stuttered to a stop.

There was a long silence.

"Did you get to choose?" Millienne's brisk challenge made Hope jump.

"Choose what?" Hope braced her shoulders in case this was going where she thought it might be going.

"When to lose your virginity." Millienne parted her lips. "When and where to become sexually active. And with whom."

Hope hunched into her chair. She looked down and kept still as a turtle.

"Unless you look back at the past, Hope, the future never happens."

Was that a tinge of humor? Hope glanced up to see the glint in her friend's eye. They gave each other a look, then a few soft chuckles.

"I got to choose." Millienne glanced out the window in the direction of Haiti. "And my first time was very sweet."

"I did, too," confessed Hope, remembering a summer day under the cottonwoods, by the pond. Her cheeks reddened. The women locked eyes, nodded in unison.

"That's not the way it was for Luz." Millienne shook her head. "Loving sex can make a woman feel heroic, but when her virginity is stolen... "

"And sold!" exploded Hope. "Talk about evil! That damn Juan, pretending he loved her, then selling her sweet young body on the street." Hope picked up the tail of her shirt and wiped sweat from her hairline.

"I wish I'd known Luz in Mexico," said Millienne. "I'd have said stop. Don't go with that guy. Don't do it!"

"She probably wouldn't have listened," mused Hope. "Maybe her *abuela* did say that, but first love...well, you know how strong it is."

"Like the pull of the moon," murmured Millienne. "We've felt the lunar strength of it."

"What was his name?" asked Hope. "Your first love?"

"Benet," sighed Millienne. "And yours?"

"Chuck." Hope fluttered one hand in front of her eyes. "Such a handsome boy."

"You have good memories touching your Chuck and I have good memories caressing my Benet. Luz doesn't, though. Only shameful memories. With strangers."

Hope let out an uncontrolled moan. "Sweet touch with Chuck only lasted part of one summer. Then I got tossed out, into a cellar of shame."

Millienne placed palms up on her thighs. "God have mercy," she sighed.

"Do you suppose Luz was an unwed mother, too?" Her own question startled Hope. She'd read a magazine article that advised asking questions when you wanted to get someone thinking in a different direction. Or wanted to stall. Was she doing that?

"Possibly, but I don't think so." Millienne dismissed the idea.

"Luz does have a sad story," said Hope," but so far she keeps it clenched in her hand like a bullet."

"She may need to keep her secrets a while longer yet," said Millienne.

"Maybe." Hope did not sound convinced.

"I just want to hold her close." Millienne patted her broad bosom. "I want to tell her how dear she is to me, to the people of Saint Lydia's, and to God."

"How can we free her from shame?" Today Hope was interested in questions, not conclusions. "How can we change what Luz sees in the mirror?"

"That's the problem with mirrors," said Millienne. "You can't turn them off."

LOW STOOL

Millienne wished she had a carved pine stool like *Gran-Peres'*. Fearing she might have cancer, plus suffering over Luz's misfortunes, made her heavy and sad, body swollen with something inexpressible. In Haiti, she would've been able to sit on a low stool and wail, comforted by answering wails from leaf doctors in nearby huts.

But Millienne did not have a carved pine stool, so the toilet would have to do. She sat on the porcelain stool and rocked; she eventually shed a few tears that relieved nothing. So she rocked harder, knocking against the tank, then the sink, until her body was wracked with great coughing sobs that went on until whatever had built up inside her had been slightly released.

When her breathing eased, she rhythmically rocked back and forth for quite a while. Millienne looked at her bare feet; the nails of her big toes were ridged and yellowed with fungus. She blew her nose on a tissue, wiped her eyes with a hand towel, and went to phone Hope.

MULISH

Since immigrating to California in her twenties, Millienne had always been able to find work. Whatever else had gone wrong, she always got jobs, first in cafes then in hospitals. She had come to rely on her strength and good health. Yes, she smoked some, drank in secret and ate too much. Got fat because she exercised only enough to get from one place to another. Took her strong body for granted, like Gran-pere's mule, the one who plowed fields and reliably carried sugarcane to market.

Millienne assumed her body would always act like a mule, and so it had. Until now. But lately, her good body had let her down. Just like Caleb Jones.

All the while she figured her strong body would carry her mulishly toward seventy, it was secretly developing a carcinoma. She couldn't bear the thought.

Millienne sighed deeply, thinking bad thoughts. She lit another Virginia Slim, feeling sad betrayals. Surely she could not have drunk half a glass of rum already today.

This time when the phone rang, she was ready to spill her troubles.

"Did your appointment go all right?" asked Hope. They sat at a small table in the corner of Rosie's Café. She had offered to drive Millienne to the oncologist, wait for her during the appointment and have a cup of tea afterward. "I prayed for you while I was waiting," said Hope. They might not have gotten into this conversation except Hope had noticed a change in her friend and asked about it. Despite her natural and cultural reserve, Millienne was a truth-teller at the core.

It pleased Hope to help people, especially this friend. She had taken a liking to Millienne many years ago when they met at Saint Lydia's Church. They were about the same age. One had pinkish white skin and one had pinkish black skin, but their glimpse into a shared future was stronger than race. Each was delighted to recognize a sister-in-spirit, and to be recognized. Hope was more health-conscious, but neither could have guessed it would be Millienne's cancer scare that made them friends for life.

A decade earlier, Hope had been through a bout with colon cancer. A section of her intestine had been removed and stitched back together again. "Something I find odd," she said as they stirred brown sugar into their tea, "is how self-satisfied I feel whenever things are going well. When I'm digesting and eliminating the way a body is designed to do, I actually feel proud of myself."

Millienne nodded and bit into a chocolate éclair.

"But whenever I do get a pain in my gut," Hope went on, "even the least little twinge, I reach for God. Whenever something hurts, it kicks up my old fears. When I'm afraid the cancer is coming back, that's when I pray as if my life depends on it."

"Which it does." Millienne spoke with her mouth full, eyes wide as if she'd just discovered the same truth. They chewed in silence, each pursuing her private thoughts.

SUFFERING

Sometimes when light dawns it simply illuminates how dismal things have become. Each morning when Millienne awakened, she had half a minute of calm before despair crashed in. She didn't dream of *GranPere* any more; didn't dream of people at all. Now she dreamt of hobbling across rocky beaches, skirting stormy pools that reflected nothing but fog. Sometimes she climbed trees; often the branches cracked and fell. She knew these were pathetic dreams, warnings that something deadly was growing in her gut. She didn't need a doctor to explain them. Her dreams also confirmed that Caleb was not coming back to her bed. His abandonment had killed her trust in men. It's hard to live without trust, she thought, almost as bad as living without sleep. Eventually, she figured, distrust would kill her.

When Rev Ruth arrived for a pastoral visit, she did not notice Millienne's despair. She admired this tall, wide Beacon, saw her as immensely powerful in her flowing skirts, hair pulled back, primal curls tumbling down her back. Rev Ruth admired the dark skin that sucked in light and reflected it back, warm and somehow more alive than the elderly pastor felt herself to be. She saw teeth bright as stars, eyes flashing fire in the foggy light.

She heard Millienne speaking in tongues—Creole, or maybe voodoo—bringing forth mysterious words in some language the pastor could not understand. The Beacon was voicing something with intense force and it took every bit of Rev Ruth's concentration to respond. "What was it like when you learned you might have cancer?"

"I was horrified."

"Why?"

"My body has always been a hard-working mule but suddenly it's turned into a tiger. I can feel sharp teeth eating away at my organs." Millienne fell silent. After a while she asked "What about you?"

Rev Ruth jerked as if poked with a hot needle. "How did you know I've had cancer?" The question touched her. She looked down for a moment to hide wet eyes.

"Oh! Are you okay?" Millienne rose to pour tea, using the opportunity to peer closely at Rev Ruth, whom she loved by now. Something was disturbing the old lady. Her first instinct was ill health.

Rev Ruth proceeded steadily with the facts, putting out her cancer history. Millienne was riveted by the account; she stared steadily at her pastor's face.

"Goodness, I'm sorry for not having asked before." The pastor's cancer story brought the Beacon out of her troubling reverie. "Thank you so much for telling me."

"No trouble." Rev Ruth spoke huskily. "But cancer is cancer and mine's in remission. Who are you seeing for yours?"

"The GP." Millienne was factual.

"Yes, the GP would be the person at this stage."

After they parted, Millienne privately compared her symptoms with the ones Rev Ruth had reported and felt glad to have what she had. She also compared her kind of compassion with Rev Ruth's, a quality of realistic care and caution, free of pessimism. The parallels pleased her.

IR AL NORTE

Beka asked Luz to tutor her in Spanish. "Al Norte," she began. "Does that mean to go north to San Francisco?"

"No. We say *ir al norte*. My grandfather longed to see California, to live in this land of opportunity. *Ir al norte* was a beacon of hope for *mi Abuelo*."

"What else did you learn from him?"

" I once asked him what *macho* meant. He laughed and put an arm around me. He said *macho* means being strong enough to act kind and gentle."

"I like that definition," said Beka.

"But," Luz went on, "I asked him what about guys who treat girls badly and he said O Luz, they are just not strong enough yet."

"Did your *Abuelo* approve of Juan?" Beka sensed dangerous territory ahead, but she did want to unlock the girl's hidden story.

"My voice cracks." Luz lifted three fingertips to the scar on her throat. "I cannot make it tell that story."

"You have been quiet about it, but your voice will come when you're ready. You have so much strength and beauty, your story will probably make me dizzy." Beka flashed a dazzling smile.

Luz ducked from the intensity of it. "If my sisters were here they would squeeze it out of my throat."

"It hurts not to speak of difficult things," said Beka gently. "*Muy difícile.*"

"It would pain me more to say it." Luz shook her head, firmly.

Beka changed direction. "I bet you come from people with the patience of pyramid-builders. Tell me about your ancestors."

Luz brightened and sat taller. "I do have *mestizaje* power in my veins, *mulatez* blood under my skin. *La familia* gives me sugar-cane wisdom." A deep flush rose along her collarbone; Beka could see the pulse beat in her ravaged throat.

"*Aguante* is divine strength and energy, enough to keep me alive in the house of bad men..." she started, then suddenly moaned and dropped forward from the blackness washing over her.

Beka watched Luz go dizzy with the spent adrenalin of torturous memories. She was afraid to make things worse by touching the girl, so she took a deep breath and changed the subject. Luz needed the solid weight of Beka's voice to bring her back.

"Jesus suffered crucifixion for us," said the Head Beacon, "so something good can come out of suffering. Don't run from it, Luz. Faith in God will anchor you, along with the love of good, strong women."

"*Papacita Dios, Jesus, Maria y los santos,*" murmured Luz. Her prayer went nonstop for ten minutes, in words far beyond the range of Beka's rudimentary Spanish.

CHAPTER 9

THE AVENUES

Passages

PAN de MUERTO

The morning after Halloween, Hope's wild heartbeat shocked her awake. What was wrong with her? Why was her heart thudding like a pole-vaulter?

Just last night she stood in the doorway with Luz, handing out Snickers bars to witches and pirates, sharing a few laughs with ghosts and princesses. Hope had no idea what was causing today's turmoil.

With slow, cautious movements, she reached to the bedside table for her knitting. I must think of something pleasant, she told herself reasonably. Although she'd not yet had morning coffee, she propped her back against the pillows and went to work on the burnt-orange sweater she was knitting for Luz. Her heart still thumped against her ribs.

Hope made herself go back in time to find a happy memory. Baking, that was it. Her dry lips shaped whispering words—molasses cookies—as her hands remembered the pleasure of shaping soft dough into little ducklings for Cody.

She recalled July's hot sun and her son's giggles as he played on the floor with the cat he'd named Sweetie. Cody was three and totally adorable, tugging on one end of a length of yarn as his cat pulled on the other. Before the summer was over, Sweetie would deliver a litter and Cody would rub blue finger-paint into their soft tawny fur. Smells of kittens and finger paint, tastes of sugar and molasses, the combination of good thoughts got Hope on her feet and into the beginning of a plan.

Later, as Luz stood at the sink washing up after her breakfast of beans and tortillas, Hope said "Will you teach me how to make Mexican cookies?"

"Which kind?" The girl's brown eyes lit up. "*Cuernos* or *conchas*?"

"I understood seashells, " said Hope, "but what are *cuernos*?"

"Little horns." Luz pantomimed crooked forefingers above her eyebrows. "Or we could make *purquitos*."

"Which are?"

"Little pigs. Soft molasses cookies shaped like piggies."

"Let's start with those," smiled Hope, recalling her morning memories. "While we're baking you can tell me your happy memories and I'll tell you some of mine."

By nightfall they had recalled special days at the beach and picnics in the park. They also baked four trays of *pan dulce* for Hope to take to the Beacons meeting. It tickled her to anticipate presenting the bright pink and yellow *conchas* in seashell shapes, the ginger-bready Mexican pastries shaped like *purquitos*, the pink-sprinkled *galleta* cookies and *pan de muertos*, sweet breads with anise seeds on top. What a tasty way to celebrate Day of the Dead!

ALL SOULS

The Beacon's meeting fell on November first, All Soul's Day. The gathering began sweetly enough, but ended up bitterly.

In a brief liturgy of remembrance, Hope presented each Beacon with one of Luz's colorful Mexican pastries. She demonstrated what to do by saying "Hank," and touching one fingertip to the honeyed teardrop on top of her *pan du muerto*.

"Patty." Beka spoke next, cupping a palm above her delicacy.

"*Gran-Pere*," said Millienne, lifting her pastry as if placing it on a high branch.

"Angela," said Hope. "I am speaking for Paige, whose presence I miss very much tonight." She bowed her head over Angela's teardrop.

"Violet," whispered Dot, touching the sweet pastry to her heart.

"And Nolan." Rev Ruth's voice trembled as she balanced a pastry on two open palms and held it out like the sacred host.

"Amen," said Beka. "Now to the business before us, which is quite challenging." She narrowed her eyes and cast a look in Rev Ruth's direction, then picked up a page from the stack before her.

"The first item of business is from Choir Director Stanley Washington who reports, and I quote, 'Reverend Ruth Salter refuses to let the choir sing anthems composed by people from countries under Communist rule.' Our interim pastor says, and I quote, 'I must protect Christianity's most treasured beliefs and images from the Red Scourge.'"

The Beacons stared at Rev Ruth in leaden silence.

"Is this true?" Beka's face was scrunched in a scowl.

The priest nodded vigorously and opened her mouth to speak, but Beka held up two stop-sign hands. "Not yet. There's more. Our organist, Dr. Wilma Thorpe, reports: 'The current interim pastor expresses deeply-rooted opposition to hymns and preludes composed since 1900. She will not allow me to play them. This attitude places severe limits on our options for worship.'"

Rev Ruth startled the Beacons by thumping her cane on the floor to demonstrate the accuracy of the organist's report, making an audible exclamation point.

Beka went on. "The next report comes to us from WAM, the Worship, Art and Music Committee. It says "The pastor's obsessive resistance to people who speak Chinese has eased

up. She will now allow members for whom English is a second
language to be trained as liturgists so they may read scripture
during worship."

Millienne sat silent as a stone, head bowed and eyes closed
through the hubbub of charges and defenses that followed.
Birkenstocks parked beneath her chair, big bare feet planted
firmly.

Hope watched her lift both heels and press her knobby toes
into the linoleum. Doing her best to ground us, she thought.

Beka caught Millienne's movements, too. Praying as we
squabble, she thought, so I won't call on her to speak.

"Tribalism." Millienne spoke during a lull. "Tribalism,"
she repeated, "is widespread among animals in my home-
land." Her serious tone got everyone's attention. "Tribalism is
a pack instinct. It leads to a double standard of morality, the
in-group versus the out-group. Tribalism is happening in our
church."

"And I don't like it," blurted Dot.

"Saint Lydia's was founded on equality and justice," Beka
reminded them.

"Based on God's love for all souls," Hope asserted.

"Can you hear the problem?" Beka turned to face Rev
Ruth squarely.

The pastor looked away, searching the darkness of a distant corner. She was feeling cornered.

Beka repeated the question. "Sooo-ooo-oo, do you hear
the gap between your attitudes and the values upon which
Saint Lydia's Church was founded?"

Rev Ruth's face showed wariness of a trap she could not
see. "I'm not going to talk about it," she said weakly.

"What do you believe about equality?" pressed Dot.

Rev Ruth glowered. "I told you I am not going to talk
about this."

"Come one, give us some trust." Hope's tone was cajoling.
"You've been our interim pastor for nearly two months. Work
with us."

"What I believe is none of your business," she huffed. "I will not be stalked like an animal." With that Rev Ruth stood, gathered her coat and stalked out.

"That woman needs to do some serious mental housekeeping," declared Dot.

ADAH'S CREOLE

After the recent hot spell, Dot, like any true San Franciscan, felt a sigh of relief when the new day dawned foggy. Long warm stretches were just not natural in her city. This recent dry spell had continued for six days straight, firing up memories of the 1906 earthquake and fire. Hot days still made San Franciscans jumpy and short-tempered.

Millienne said she knew a cool place to eat in the Inner Sunset, so they went there on the N-Judah line. Nestled among liquor stores, taverns and small shops, she pointed to a ramshackle pink bungalow overgrown with purple bougainvillea. The green-and-yellow hand-painted sign said Adah's Creole.

She led the way up rickety steps into a hallway scented with rich, spicy aromas.

"I never noticed this place before," said Dot.

"A lot of people miss it," Millienne grinned, "though it's been here forever. Adah moved here from New Orleans about the same time I came to San Francisco. She's an old friend of my aunt, loves to cook for homesick Haitians. Has a loyal bunch of customers."

Two rooms opened off the central hall. Pink-walled with cracked plaster, they were crammed with rickety chairs and tables covered in worn, flower-sprigged oilcloth. The flatware didn't match; neither did the dishes. Nearly all the tables were taken. Dot and Millienne moved toward one by the window. A single daisy reposed in a jelly jar.

"Adah doesn't mess around with frills, but does make a fine jambalaya. Her grandson," she gestured at the young waiter and held up two fingers. "We'll take two bowls of jambalaya."

Dot picked up the thread of a conversation begun on the trolley. "So, what have you learned by listening to trees?" The two women met in AA many years ago and had become so fully at ease with one another that they could skip the small talk.

"I learned to stop wanting to be a tree." Her voice was almost too soft to hear.

"To stop wanting to be a tree? Is that what you said?"

"Yes. When old folks asked me what do you want to be when you grow up, I always said a tree." She spread her fingers on the oilcloth, wide like tree roots. "On the ridge where I grew up, the soil was worn out, even then; we had to scramble hard to grow enough to feed the family. To my eyes, the trees looked healthier than the people. I can still hear *Gran Pere's* laugh when I told him my wish; it rang out like a song." She turned toward the eastern window.

Dot stayed quiet as her friend's gaze travelled far beyond the herbs thriving in Adah's tidy window box.

"Trees taught me how to stand my ground," Millienne said after a while, "and now—whenever I forget—they remind me to do that." She slid the Birkenstock off one bare foot and wiggled it in Dot's direction. "See, even the knuckles of my toes look like tree roots. But I no longer want to be a tree. I'm glad to be a woman."

"I'm glad you're a woman too. One who learns from trees," nodded Dot, "especially when you bring tree-wisdom back to the Beacons."

The pungent fragrance of jambalaya caught their attention. Adah's grandson set two brimming bowls before them.

"Thanks be to God," said Millienne, beaming up at the boy.

"Thanks be to God," echoed Dot, picking up her spoon.

CASTOFFS

"Rummage!" Scorn scorched Rev Ruth's tone despite her recent resolution to behave herself. "We are doing an important social justice ministry here at Saint Lydia's. Why would any self-respecting church lady want to be a junk dealer?"

"This church was built on rummage!" Dot shot back, eyes narrowed. "Saint Lydia's is known across the city as the house that junk built!"

She was steamed, ready to spar, but Beka put a calming hand on Dot's shoulder and interrupted. "Around here, our Hope Hudson is known as the Queen of Rummage."

Hope's face pinkened with pleasure, quickly replaced by a scowl. "What have you got against rummage, anyway?"

Rev Ruth was on the spot. "Well, " she huffed, "where I come from, nobody in the Ladies Guild would dirty her hands with castoffs from people she does not know."

"What about from people she does know?" Millienne asked softly. "All year, members and friends of Saint Lydia's put aside furniture, clothes and knickknacks to donate to our annual sale."

"Well," Rev Ruth admitted in a grudging tone, "in Cleveland, the ladies of my church did hold a white elephant exchange at Christmastime. We wrapped things like English teacups and antique doilies as gifts to our secret pals."

"That may be how the ruling class does things," said Dot heatedly, "but we're not so hoity-toity here in San Francisco."

Once again Beka dropped a warning hand on Dot's shoulder. "Don't forget, Rev Ruth, that nearly a third of our annual church budget comes from the fall Rummage Sale. I'd say that's a good enough reason for church ladies like us," Beka gestured around the room, "to act like junk dealers once a year."

"But only once a year," sighed Hope, wiping a weary hand across her brow. "I couldn't handle the pressure more often than that."

"Nobody manages the annual Rummage Sale as well as you do," Beka assured her, "but we don't want to wear you out, so everyone will pitch in and make it work."

An audible blast from the pastor's nostrils signaled her feelings on the matter.

Beka shot her a look. "Everyone but you, Rev Ruth. You are exempt from the dirty work."

"Because YOU" —microscopic pause by Dot— "are still on probation." Her raspy voice and wicked grin poked Rev Ruth in the ribs.

The pastor's sigh came out like a penance.

NERVES

Rev Ruth had developed a puzzling aversion to Luz, with her lyrical laugh. The girl was far too dramatic for the pastor's taste. Luz also moved like a dancer, warm and vigorous, which annoyed Rev Ruth, perhaps because she felt so shaky these days. She could do certain routine things, but her head was often filled with terrible thoughts, vengeful, even sadistic thoughts, directed at prostitutes in general and Luz in particular.

Rev Ruth once thought they could be friends, but the Mexican girl was nothing like the daughter she'd imagined. Luz Rivera, pretty as an actress, grated on her nerves. So did the Beacons and many members of Saint Lydia's Church. Truth be told, life itself grated on her nerves, especially when she was drifting on the fog with only a sermon deadline tethering her to the pier.

Last Sunday after worship, as Rev Ruth was taking off her vestments, Luz had knocked on the door of her study. The moment she saw the girl standing there, a vile kaleidoscope of emotions spun her out of balance. She stumbled sideways, banged into the doorjamb and would have fallen if Luz had not moved quickly, caught her and thanked *Jesu Christo*.

Rev Ruth was having none of it. As soon as she regained her balance, she pushed Luz into the hall and locked the door. "Sorry to be rude," she muttered, though she wasn't, not really. She wished this troublesome girl would go back where she came from. Or die.

In better moments she prayed to be kind, but it was hopeless. Rev Ruth did not know why she resented the young immigrant; she might have confessed her vile thoughts to a priest but did not have an Anglican confessor in San Francisco and could not bear to tell anyone else. She plunked into her chair, heard the casters squeal, buried her face in her hands and prayed for forgiveness. She prayed as long as she could, but her eyelids grew heavy and she dropped off to sleep, head on the desk.

By mid-November, darkness came early. It matched the shadowed dreariness that had plagued Rev Ruth for too long. Damp weather said put on thick socks and go to bed, so she did. Soon the storms arrived, tossed by towering clouds. Occasionally a shift in the light brought a sunbeam, bright and operatic.

In the shock of one such beam, she remembered another girl who looked like Luz. That one had chestnut-brown hair worn in a braid, eyes so dark the pupils didn't show, black lashes and brows; full sensuous lips. Ruth could not recall her name but would never forget the swivel of her hips. Nolan had an affair with the girl, a grad student at University of Chicago, though he denied it when Ruth confronted him.

The Salters' marriage, which she thought was sweet and green, quickly turned cold and muddy. The student held a work-study position in Nolan's office. Ruth had seen her twice; a Jewish girl, expansive and yeasty, as if she knew things Ruth did not know. Luz was the same way. Beautiful. Fertile. Uncontained.

Nolan's affair would have ended the marriage, except Ruth was pregnant and he quickly became overly attentive. No more cold glances when she entered his study. No further reason to doubt his fidelity. They both refused to discuss it and, in time, she forgave him. Their marriage worked like a mostly reliable car. They might lie down grim, but their bodies returned soon enough to old habits. In bed they spooned; sometimes they made love. And so the Salters chugged through their days and eventually things between them sweetened up.

STRENGTH OF HOPE

It was four-thirty in the afternoon when Millienne shuffled across her bedroom in unlaced sneakers. She refused to wear slippers; they were for sick people. She hated robes and pajamas, too, especially bed jackets. Fear of cancer left her hating anything that smacked of illness, so she wore gray sweatpants and a maroon SF STATE sweatshirt. The elastic ribs of her white athletic socks left pencil-thin indentations on her shins.

One sneaker bumped a stack of murder mysteries on the floor. Several slid off the top, but she ignored the books and bent to turn the radio off. Tinkling music drove her nuts these days. She found harp music particularly insulting.

She peeled off her sweats and stood in front of the bathroom mirror, naked except for faded socks and sneakers. "Come out where I can see you," she demanded, gritting out the words. "Come out, you damned cancer cells." She balled up her fists and held eye contact with her own dark pupils for as long as she could stand it. "Quit hiding in lumps," she growled. "Look me in the eye."

Oh, the stubborn strength of hope. Millienne let out a long breath and looked around her bathroom. It was small but lovely. She'd painted the walls a pale mango and placed a few beautiful shells in the sink to hide the rusted drain. She'd also arranged a cluster of statues on top of the toilet tank, Haitian saints grouped together for strength.

She moved into the bedroom and looked around. It was a woman's place, plainly and unapologetically. In the corners, she kept baskets filled with elegant seashells and beautiful rocks. Vivid Haitian primitive art adorned the walls. She burned candles at night, four or five grouped together on bold ceramic platters like lit bouquets. Her entire apartment pleased her. Each room seemed to breathe, welcoming the shy soul.

She kicked off her sneakers, peeled off her socks and lay her naked body down on top of her green and white striped comforter. Four pine-green pillows matched the dust ruffle. She arranged two fat pillows under her head and two more beneath her knees. She thought of Caleb, wanted his warm body beside her but Caleb would not be back. With a ragged sigh she admitted the hard truth: we didn't so much fall in love as fall in bed.

Millienne got up and rummaged in the dresser until she found the flowered handkerchief her mother had embroidered long ago. She held it to her face. Softer than Kleenex, it smelled like nutmeg. Once again she stretched out on the bed. This time she spread Mama's handkerchief across her bare breasts. She extended her arms, palms up, and offered her fears to the overcast sky.

Letting go.

Letting God.

SCISSORS

"I'm coming over, girl." Dot's commanding tone on the phone startled Paige. "And I'm bringing something that's good for what ails you."

"How do you know what ails me?"

"'Cause I've had the blues, too. And I've missed you. Time we talked."

"My ailment feels bigger than the blahs."

"Well, I 've got medicine for the blues and the blahs. Be there in ten minutes."

"Licorice ice cream! From Swensen's!" Paige came to the door wearing thick socks. "How'd you know this is my favorite?".

Dot wiggled her eyebrows like Groucho Marx. "My secret." She slipped off her Earth Shoes. "Two bowls, please. This high-priced ice cream is getting melty."

After they'd licked spoons and stacked bowls in the sink, Paige said, "You didn't come just to eat ice cream, did you?"

"Very astute, my friend. Something's going on with you and I am here to hear about it." Even with her friends, Dot could sound like a social worker.

"I'd hate to think you're here to rescue me. I'm not one of your damaged kids."

"No, but warning bells are going off in my head. Why'd you stop coming to church? Beacons meetings. Lydia Circle." Dot counted out the facts on her fingers. "And I want you back!"

Paige looked glazed, arms limp at her sides. No response.

"What is going on with you?" Dot's tone was measured, face composed.

Paige's face flushed. A dark trace of licorice ice cream lingered in one corner of her mouth. "Let's go for a walk. Walking helps me find the words."

She poked sock-clad feet into open-backed blue plastic sandals. Dot put on worn brown Earth Shoes and off they went. Evening shadows lay dark on the sidewalks. Milky ribbons of mist clung to bushes. The air was colorless and cold. There was no wind.

Paige had a reputation as a thoughtful contributor at Saint Lydia's, and a well-read woman. There was something about her, however, that puzzled her friends. Dot sensed a mysterious element in Paige, but could not quite put her finger on it. The truth of the matter might be revealed if she could be patient enough.

After two blocks, Paige stopped and stood perfectly still. "During my nap this afternoon," she said, "I dreamed about scissors." She held the position of one listening to a call from far away. Thoughts of scissors brought a terrible load of grief, a cement truck on her chest. Time had not softened the weight of loss, morbid images of her tender girl-parts buried in damp earth, her dearest flesh cut into tiny bits, moldering in decay.

"Scissors," she repeated, shaking her head. "Scissors."

Dot wait until her friend's voice got steady, then asked "What did you dream? What happened with scissors?"

They passed beneath a streetlight that momentarily brightened Paige's pale face. Her nostrils flared. "I dreamed I stole a pair of scissors from dad's bathroom cabinet. Hair-cutting scissors; teeth so sharp and cold they could cut molecules of air."

"What did you do with your dad's scissors?" Dot sounded tentative.

"Operate on my baby boy. His testicles." Her eyes were watery. "It was urgent, they said I had to cut off his genital sac, so I lined up scissors, scalpels, clamps; nice and straight like pencils on the first day of school. The baby boy asked me not to cut. I told him I had to." Her voice went wavery. "He had so much fear in his eyes."

Her voice broke and she stumbled over a crack in the sidewalk. Dot took her arm and pulled Paige close. They stood hip to hip in the chilly air.

Paige continued in a shaky voice: "In the dream I looked at scrotal diagrams in an instruction book. Snip here, fold there. Looked easy enough, but I couldn't trust my hands." She held them out. They both watched her hands shake.

"Did the dream stop there?"

"No, it got worse." She tugged on her jacket, pulled it more firmly closed. "I turned into the naked one, terrified, screaming. Shame stung in the genital parts of me, wasp bites in hidden places where the doctor's cold scalpel cut away my girl parts."

"Ohhh," murmured Dot, clasping an arm around Paige's waist.

"My fists balled up tight, tiny legs kicking, but nobody held me. Nobody."

Paige closed her delicate white eyelids. They stood beneath the arching branches of a tree. Dot gathered Paige into her arms.

After the tearful trembling was over, Dot asked "How did you pray?"

"Since I was little, my body made me pray. Inside my polo shirt and blue jeans, I prayed to be girly. Pink. Squealy. Mother prayed I wouldn't be queer, but I grew up to be her worst nightmare. Can you imagine a teenage storm cloud sprouting pubic hair?"

Dot smiled over her friend's shoulder. She kept still. They rocked back and forth.

"I prayed for breasts, couldn't wait to wear a bra, wanted to look normal to God or whoever was looking. Please God, I prayed for years, make me into my true self and these days— sometimes, anyway—I can thank God for my femininity."

THE BLUES

When did the blues sweep over you, and how did you get through it?

Dot told the women her opening question a week in advance so Lydia Circle members could think about it. On this foggy evening they stepped into welcoming hugs, then settled into orange vinyl chairs.

Hope, puffing from the climb to Dot's fifth floor apartment, smelled of yeast.

Paige's hug was redolent with peppermint.

Millienne's sweat gave off the scent of pine.

A whiff of Beka's breath conveyed Thai chilies.

Rev Ruth had not been invited.

"Tonight's theme is *Getting Through*," Dot reminded them, "and Bessie Smith got me through some very tough times." She flashed an LP cover with a photo of Bessie Smith, hair up, nails done, strutting her stuff. "This woman sings the blues straight to my gut. She says you gotta plug into the passion of sorrow if you wanna light up the room with the blues."

"You could electrocute a person that way," shivered Hope.

"You were once wild, too," Paige reminded her, and others began teasing Hope.

Dot shimmied and stamped a foot to regain their attention. "Back to Bessie Smith. She danced me through my fury at Rev Ruth. Challenged me to break the rules and make up my own verses. So I got a song for you, but first...." With a dramatic flourish, Dot threw open Dick's big work shirt to reveal her dress, a skin-tight number, shimmery with red sequins. The Beacons broke into spontaneous applause, but Dot stopped them.

"Hold on, there's more." Dot struck a pose like Bessie on the album cover, took a big breath and belted out her song:

Lookee here, Rev Ruth, I wanna tell you
Please get outta my sight
I'm playin' tough now, from this very night
You've had your day, don't stand around and frown,
You've been a good ol' rev'rend honey
But now you've done broke down.

The Beacons applauded long and loud; Dot took an exaggerated bow.

"Be patient with Rev Ruth, she'll learn," said Beka. "Meanwhile, my friend, you may have a future on stage."

"So do I," said Paige, "with angels to help me get through the tough stuff." Her twinkle softened her assertive statement. Posing beside Dot, she placed one hand on her heart and flung the other toward the sky. "Quoting Emily Dickinson, my favorite poet, 'If I can stop one heart from breaking, I shall not live in vain.'"

Millienne raised a hand. "The blues help me get through. Blind Willie Johnson on his slide guitar. *"Trouble will soon be over, sorrow will have an end."* Her dusky alto faded out. "And Muddy Waters," she said, "One More Mile. It was the blues—Hope and Paige too—that got me through my cancer scare." A glance passed between them. The Beacons nodded and readied themselves to share at a lower pitch.

After a long, electric silence, Hope folded her arms. Her foot tapped out a coded message against the floor. Even in the dim light it was clear she was troubled. Smudges darkened her eyes, the frayed edges of a woman who hadn't been sleeping well. "I'm still trying to find some way of getting through…" Hope touched her throat as if the hand of grief was squeezing and would not let go.

The fraught silence had to end and eventually Beka broke it. She had a big need to take charge, even though it was against Lydia Circle rules to do that. "For example?"

"When I was shamed and sent away, the Psalms got me through." Hope's voice came out small and wounded. "All Lutheran girls had to memorize some Psalms. *'My God, my God, why hast Thou forsaken me.'*"

Slowly the story tumbled out, an innocent girl, a sweet boy, a summer meadow shaded by cottonwoods. First love. Pregnancy. Family scandal. A dreary home for unwed mothers. A difficult birth. A newborn taken away too soon, given to adoptive parents. "They wouldn't let me see the baby; wouldn't even tell me if it was a boy or a girl."

The room was thick with emotions. Eyes misted with vapory memories. Not a single sound trailed through Dot's apartment, but inwardly each Beacon heard her own blues tune of sorrow or shame.

THANKSGIVING

As the season deepened toward Thanksgiving, folks at Saint Lydia's glowed with gratitude over the results of the Rummage Sale. The church had pulled in more money than any sale in thirty years. Hope's son Cody and his boyfriend Harvey did so much heavy lifting and charmed so many customers, they wound up selling more castoffs than anyone else. The Queen of Rummage couldn't help basking in their reflected glory, even if everyone could see they were gay as geese.

"You can't put a price tag on love," announced Harvey, "but you can charge a fair price for the accessories." His quip became a quotable quote, repeated by church members during the Rummage Sale and long after. The eloquent couple entertained neighborhood shoppers and befriended two well-dressed men with matching French bulldogs. The gay pair lived on Pacific; they had simply stopped to browse but Cody and Harv made such a good impression on behalf of Saint Lydia's that the local men began bringing their dogs to worship, making friends among the congregation and serving on the Altar Guild

By Thanksgiving, the Beacons had grown accustomed to the ways of the interim pastor; they seemed to have forgotten the earlier upsets. Church members continued to invite Rev Ruth home for dinner or out to brunch in local cafes. There was no more mention of probation.

For her part, Rev Ruth heeded Mother's advice of 'fluttering on, little bird.' She bucked up, following in the boots of her sea-captain grandfather, reaching out to people who were in worse shape than she was. Once, just before the Beacons arrived for a meeting, she even made the coffee. In private, the interim pastor offered pastoral care; in public, she managed to curb her tongue. And if folks wondered why Rev Ruth had not taken young Luz Rivera under her wing, nobody asked.

Beka Ash, on the other hand, spent endless hours with the immigrant girl. Apart from Hope Hudson, who sheltered Luz and tutored her in sewing, everyone could see it was Beka who did the most to ease the girl's suffering. Luz was Saint Lydia's most complicated lost sheep and the Head Beacon was given the most credit for bringing her into the safety of the fold. Folks even began referring to Beka as the good shepherd of Saint Lydia's.

CHAPTER 10

THE MISSION

Animation

SUNLIGHT

A Mexican baker needed her help, that's what Beka came to tell her. Señor Tomaso Santos needed Luz to keep the *panaderia* going. His wife was sick, his sons were gone and he needed her. Needed her. This news brought sparkle to her eyes. San Francisco fog made her sad, but the prospect of baking made her happy. Luz was ready to be happy. And she was ready to work, even ready to stop making trouble, ready to make Hope Hudson proud.

Beka took her to Mission Street to meet Señor and Señora Santos. Walking into their apartment above the bakery, the first thing Luz saw was a picture of Jesus with his sacred heart ablaze. Every house in Hermosillo had the same picture, even the same dime-store frame. This Jesus with his fiery heart and steady gaze made her feel right at home, right away. So did a pair of miniature Mexican and American flags thrust into a beer mug on top of the boxy television, next to the rabbit-ear antennae.

Hanging beside Jesus in the narrow hallway was a photo of Tomaso and Lola Santos decked out in wedding finery, posing on the steps of City Hall. She'd seen that grand gold-trimmed edifice during her time on the streets; it dominated

San Francisco's Civic Center. She was impressed they'd been married there.

Oval frames held baby pictures of Rico and Mario, prompting Luz to smile back at their moist expressions. Snapshots showed birthday celebrations on the merry-go-round in Golden Gate Park, sons in softball uniforms and later, on Pier 39 with arms around girlfriends. The Transamerica Pyramid loomed in the distance.

Senora Santos touched the cheek of her eldest in a formal photo, golden tassel swinging from his Mission High School mortarboard. "Rico said when he got his diploma we had to start calling him Rocky," she said, "because it sounds more American."

Luz and Beka joined in the mother's sigh. They caught a brief glimpse of the sons with serious faces and buzz cuts, standing tall in Army uniforms, eyes fixed on Vietnam, before Senor Tomaso hurried them away.

"Come now and see the *panaderia*." Tomaso pressed a hand against Luz's back. "This good lady"—gesturing at Beka—tells me you are looking for work just when my Lola," patting his wife's gnarled hand, "is hurting more with the rheumatism."

It was a good day for Luz, the day she met Tomaso and Lola. She liked them and they liked her. Their confidence in her gave Luz hope. Their need for help—her help— was a kind of sunlight for her, assurance that she could earn cash without giving kisses.

I LIKE YOU

"Want some banana bread?" Hope asked.

Luz waved it away. "No, I hate banana bread. It's full of cricket legs."

"Show me," said Hope.

Luz lifted the plate to eye level. Silently, they studied the bread.

"You're right. Mashed bananas do look like cricket legs in the bread." Hope met the girl's eyes. She liked the easy way they got along.

Luz's face softened with the wide relief of hearing an American *Abuela* say 'You're right.' *Muy bueno* to have someone believe her. "I like you," she said, with such honesty and innocence Hope wanted to hug her.

"For a moment there," said Hope, "you looked to me like an angel."

Luz stood still for a heartbeat and stared down at her hands. When she looked up again, she shook her head. "No. You are wrong. I am not an angel."

Luz seemed to have lost interest in the past, Hope's past and her own. To Hope, it seemed her mind reached ahead with an urgency that made her seem self-centered, but the grandmother understood, or thought she did. Her youth meant she had to look ahead, had to focus intensely on the future in order to make a life for herself in this new city.

"Do you think I can do it? Keep my job?" She sounded doubtful.

"What do you think?" Hope's blue eyes kept a tight hold on Luz's brown ones.

"I don't know. I've messed up so much already."

"What's going on between you and Senor Santos?"

"He bosses me around too much."

"You know, that's part of being an employee." Hope needed to tread softly, yet firmly. "Being bossed around goes with the job. Any job."

"Well, he treats me like a servant," sputtered Luz.

"The more you learn, the better you'll do and the better he'll treat you."

Luz pooched out her glossy lips, on the way to a teenage tantrum.

"I'm sure you can succeed at the *panaderia*. And I'll help you."

Before Luz could get going on a snit that would end the conversation, Hope tilted her head and said "I could sew a new outfit for you. Would you like that?"

The girl's head came up. "Would you really? What kind of outfit?"

"Several kinds." She was thinking fast. "Skirts and blouses for work. Good dress for church. Maybe a fancy dress for dancing."

Luz's lovely brows lifted like angel wings. "What colors?"

"You get to decide. Shall we go now and look at fabric?"

They spent two hours wandering the aisles of Cole Valley's Fabric Shoppe. Luz, as it turned out, shared Hope's joy in the tactile pleasures of running fingers across cotton and corduroy, stroking lengths of nylon and silk. They enjoyed paging through pattern books, settling on just the right styles and sizes. Luz found racks of buttons enchanting. She chose sensible navy-blue buttons for her denim skirt, shy pearl buttons for her church dress and flamboyant rhinestone buttons for her dancing dress.

"What if we also buy some soft yarn for baby blankets?" suggested Hope "and, what if, after I finish your new outfits, you would learn to knit?"

"Why?"

"Knitting for babies makes me happy. I think it will make you happy, too."

"Whose babies?"

"Women we don't know. Mothers at SF General whose newborns die too soon, during birth or right after."

"Ohhh, how sad."

"The hospital chaplain spoke at Lunch Bunch last week and said hospital blankets won't do when newborn babies die. Sad mothers need soft, delicate blankets to wrap around the baby so they can hold it close. Mourn for it."

"What if I can't knit?" Luz looked doubtful.

"It's easy. You can knit if you choose to learn."

"Why do you want me to knit blankets for dead babies?"

"I know it sounds terribly sad, but the chaplain told us a hand-knit blanket is a big comfort to a grieving mother."

"What if I cry while I'm knitting?"

"Your tears will soak into the blanket. Tears are a sign of your tender heart."

"I like you." Luz said it again as they carried bundles into the house. "And maybe I'm beginning to like your idea about learning to knit. Helping mothers I don't know."

This time Hope hugged her without saying a word about angels.

SAINT ANTHONY

All was not perfect in her rescuer's *panaderia*. The work was heavier than she'd imagined, and hotter. Tomaso kept after her to work up to his pace, and held her to strict five-minute breaks. He questioned her about where she learned to bake. She described her uncle's panaderia in Hermosillo, air dense with flour mist, scented with sugar and lard. Luz had to help out when Papa missed work during his drunken binges.

Uncle Raul used to tell her she made the best buttery horns, better than his own. "You have the gift, senorita," he would joke. Customers agreed. Word got around that Luz Rivera made flakier empanadas than Papa could manage even on a sober day.

"As for me," Luz told Tomaso, "the holiest scent in the world is not incense. It's the smell of baking bread."

The day dawned sunny for a change, and the birds chirped outside her window, but Luz woke up missing home and family, God help them. She prayed, fingering the rosary Reverend Ruth had given her. Before the prayers were done Luz realized her nipples were taut and her belly stirred with desire. She missed Juan's kisses on her neck, his fingers stroking her face.

From a very young age, boys caught her attention. For reasons Luz did not care to explore, she had a propensity for giving herself to males who were not good for her. School did not interest her nearly as much as boys. She rarely studied because Luz thought herself smarter than her sisters, and prettier too. When she was small Papa called her 'my flower.' She liked being Papa's favorite.

As a teen, she spent hours preening before mirrors, vanity getting the best of her. She pouched out her lips to look sexier and exaggerated her stride, showing off her round derriere. At Mass, when she looked up at the altar, she pretended she was in the circle of angels nearest to God, trailing long ribbons of pink silk. When Mass was over, she liked to see men following her with their eyes.

Papa thought she went too far, raised a lightning bolt eyebrow when he caught her making eyes at a handsome fellow, grabbed Luz tightly by the wrist and hauled her back to the house, where he beat her with a belt. For three days she could not sit from the pain, but that didn't stop her from pining for love. She lived for dances in the *zocalo*, twirling with different partners, laughing and shaking her body.

One half-moon night, the sultry Juan invited her to go walking and she told him about her too-strict father. Juan gave her rum from a flask, and hot kisses. She let him fondle her, then move her to the edge of the *zocalo* where he leaned her against the wall and lifted her skirt. And because Luz was tired of Papa's severity, she opened her legs, fixed her eyes on the starry night and let Juan have his way.

At four in the morning Papa was waiting with a belt. After breakfast, despite all the women of the household begging for mercy, he kicked her out. She never saw Papa again, but every time she bathed she saw the scar on her hip from his buckle.

Lola Santos seemed shy and rarely spoke, but one afternoon she went upstairs and brought back the figurine of a saint. She drew Luz past the two industrial ovens dominating the bakery and into a corner with two cracked vinyl chairs. They both sat. She put the saint in the girl's hand. "Take him. Saint Anthony is strong for you."

"Don't you need him?"

"He's done plenty for me. He brought you." She leaned close to Luz' ear and whispered "Keep him upside down and he will find a man to love you."

Lola watched as Luz inspected the statue. Saint Anthony was made of plaster, with shiny eyes and human-hair eyelashes. He held a baby Jesus in his arms and gazed down so tenderly, Luz just had to kiss the top of his black-painted head.

Tomaso beckoned her back to the counter, pointing at yeasty dough rising over the edges of huge stainless steel mixing bowls. She glanced down at Saint Anthony. Tomaso gestured with his knuckles. She tucked the saint into her handbag, upside down, crossed beneath buzzing fluorescent lights and began punching down the bread dough.

"Will you really find me a good man to love?" she asked Saint Anthony that night, holding him upside down above her face. Luz could not imagine how he could do that, surrounded as she was by women at church and home, and guarded at work by Tomaso. Single guys her age never attended worship at Saint Lydia's and seldom came into the *panaderia*. Nevertheless, she put the statue upside down on a cloth beneath her bed. She laid her head on the pillow, closed her eyes and tried to see her future with a loving man, but the screen was blank. She remembered sleeping with Juan, the twitch of his muscles and the rasp of his breath.

She opened her eyes and discovered a bright half-moon peering at her from the edge of the world. Suddenly she knew she could shed the skin of that bad life with Juan, shed it like a rattlesnake. Rev Ruth, Hope and Beka saw her as a girl with potential. Tomaso and Lola saw her as a real baker, more than her father's bad daughter.

Maybe she wouldn't have to wait for Saint Anthony. Maybe she would look for a good man on her own.

MEMORIES

Ruth lifted the teacup to her lips, vapor rising, the aroma of English Breakfast firing her nostrils. The dark, earthy taste reminded her of summers at Grand Lake in Michigan when the boys were young. Sipping, she remembered Timothy making fun of her tea habit, said it tampered with the Lord's design, but she didn't pay him much mind. Such a scamp. Ruth did like her tea on a crisp morning, the smell and the bitterness. Liked the lift she got from it.

Nolan took his coffee black. Such a traditionalist. At breakfast he'd sit slumped over his bowl, champing at his Grape-Nuts. Most mornings, the ring of his spoon and the grind of his teeth were the only sounds she heard out of her husband.

The scent of tea brought memories of Simon at twelve in the green cottage on Black Bass Bay, showering her with "good mornings" and lavishing her with compliments on the color of her cheeks. So different from his father.

And then there was James, bits of sleep in the corners of his eyes, rumpled and shaggy. Always last to breakfast, especially on vacation . She was lucky to hear six syllables from her oldest as he bent silently over his bowl and spoon. Just like his father.

Distant memories came easily on this San Francisco morning. Ruth leaned back and gazed at the pale wash of light and shadow on the beige wall. She awoke feeling better, on the mend she thought, from a recent bout of confusion or amnesia, or whatever it had been. It was a pleasure to close her eyes and picture Grand Lake with its tall pines and rustic cabins. Nolan rented a place on the shore for two weeks each summer, giving the boys freedom to run and climb, canoe and swim. She had to cook over a two-burner Coleman camp stove, but also had the joy of floating in cool water and sunning herself on big, flat rocks.

Current memories, though, had become a problem. Ruth hunched her shoulders and decided she was developing a perpetual slouch. She rubbed her wet eyes, stared at a line of rooftops sitting serenely along Larkin and sensed, in a vague and incremental way, that all was not as it should be.

Case in point: yesterday when she thought she was losing her mind. It had turned chilly in the afternoon. The bare branches of the trees made sharp filigree patterns against the silver-gray sky. By dusk, the sky had turned pale violet. Rev Ruth had tried to practice her Beatitudes sermon for Sunday, but only a dry rattle came from her throat. She stood before the mirror and tried again, but could only speak in short bursts. Her mouth trembled and her eyelid twitched. She found this terribly disconcerting and was even more distressed to realize that she could only remember half a line at a time.

She rubbed her eyes again, and felt the strain of her churchly duties. She imagined others could see it, too, the bruise-like circles beneath her eyes and the waxy yellow color of her skin. Her wrinkled face, habitually tense, had recently developed a tic. Spasmodic twitches in her right eyelid gave her a strangely paralyzed expression.

Rev Ruth ached to understand what was happening to her, countered by an even stronger ache to escape from her troubles, which she did by focusing her thoughts on Easter. Though it was weeks away, she tried to tantalize herself by imagining how she could compose such a striking Easter sermon that they would remember it long after she was gone. Not so long ago, she could spend hours poring over the Concordance and paging through the Bible for inspiration, but not even scripture could inspire her these days. Today she took a desperate shortcut, leafing through old notes from General Theological Seminary and reworking a sermon from her course in Homiletics.

In the old days, Rev Ruth prided herself on her memory. Infallible, she liked to say, but last Sunday something unexplainable attacked her in the pulpit. Her mind had gone blank in the middle of a sentence about Augustine's *City of God*. It must have been a touch of amnesia. Not only did she totally forget the remainder of her sermon, but even the familiar faces of people in the pews seemed strangely unknown. For some moments she stood dumbly with her hands on the pulpit until she finally found the presence of mind to say Amen. Fortunately, she'd been close to the end by the time her lapse occurred. Even more fortunately, the organist caught on to what was happening and launched into a rousing rendition of "Nearer My God To Thee."

The threatening rain held off that day until Rev Ruth was almost to her apartment. She walked slowly, stiffly, careful to keep her spine straight, as if processing in liturgical vestments. Her arms moved as if they would not bend at the elbow; she kept eyes on her narrow black oxfords. Dour storm clouds hovered overhead but down near the horizon she thought she saw a silver line of light. She'd been within twenty yards of her door when the first drops fell. The distance was little more than the length of the central aisle at Saint Lydia's; by picking up speed she could easily have reached shelter, but her dragging footsteps did not quicken, not even when the torrent poured onto her bare head. By the time she made it up the stairs, she was soaked, shivering and dull-eyed.

What had happened in the pulpit? Her face and her mind had gone as blank as the sidewalk. She could not—would not —face the fact of her disorientation, nor the burden of memory loss. She pressed her knuckles to her eyes and repeated the name of Jesus over and over, as though this frail scrap of language held a mysterious power.

What had happened in the pulpit? On this question she was still confused. She sensed the answer hidden somewhere in the shadowy recesses of her mind, but the more she thought about the matter, the sharper her uneasiness became. Her throat, dry and raw, squeezed tight as the truth threatened to come over her. Her tongue tasted as if she had pennies caught in her throat.

Oh my God, I can't be losing my mind.

LIMBO

Ruth Salter was used to picking herself up after losses. She had survived many, and had begun to pick herself up from this one until the EKG came back inconclusive. She would have felt better, even liberated, if only the doctor would tell her what was ahead. The problem was, he couldn't. She hated not knowing.

My dear, you are in limbo. Nolan spoke from beyond the grave, in that wry tone of his, the tone he'd used whenever she refused to face the obvious. *Don't you feel better, my dear, having an authorized place in limbo?*

He could be smug, and she could be sarcastic, but this time she smiled instead of rolling her eyes. She missed his dry wit. *All right, Nolan. Much as I want medical reassurance, limbo has become my official habitat.*

It had never occurred to her, she realized, looking out the window and wishing she still smoked, to let her sons know about the amnesia attack. James, Timothy and Simon had simply not come to mind. She wondered why not.

She had been deeply involved when the boys were young, but had grown distant as the years went by. Ruffians. They'd been such ruffians. She resented their wild behavior, the scenes they caused at school and church. Ruth was the type who wanted to be in control, but her boys' mischief left her feeling helpless. And she was still furious at Nolan. So passive. Never disciplined the boys. It had all been on her shoulders.

James, Simon and Timothy had become such opinionated adults, she felt quite overwhelmed by their forcefulness. Difficult enough individually but totally insufferable as a pack. She hated being ganged up on. Yes, she loved her sons, but had to confess she preferred remembering them instead of encountering them.

LOVE GUIDANCE

Wordy prayer had never been Millienne's way. Silence seemed more holy than pleading words, so she leaned against the tree trunk without uttering a sound. What to do? God's love would guide her if she waited in silent prayer.

Cloud cover was so thick that not one seam of sunlight showed through the morning gray. She stood quietly, opened her arms a bit, tilted up her face and remained as still as the pines. That's when it came, an intensely lucid thought.

Between one heartbeat and the next, she knew how the Beacons could step into Rev Ruth's heartbreak. How they could become part of her suffering, and part of her salvation. How they could bring peace to the end of the story.

When the love-guidance session felt complete, she bent down, slipped on her Birkenstocks, strolled through the Arboretum and went out through the gardener's gate. Now she had to figure out how to explain her crazy idea to the Beacons.

Millienne could think more clearly outdoors than inside man-made structures, even bus shelters, so she stepped away and stood in the cold wind blowing up Lincoln. Feet planted, arms open, she lifted her palms and her eyes toward the mysterious source of light and love beyond the clouds, breathed a silent prayer of thanks and waited for further guidance.

When she finished filling the Beacons in on the plan, Hope and Paige wilted at the knees. Beka and Dot leapt up and slapped palms. Thank God the Beacons were connected again. She wanted to savor this lovely sense of harmony before everyone went into action. She was also scared, or maybe awed, by her strong urge to protect Rev Ruth. Millienne tried to sort out what was going on in her belly. Was it fear? Excitement? But no explanations came, only breath, quick and shallow.

VERBENA

"*Miralos.*" Luz enunciated to Hope as they stood at the counter of Tomaso's Panaderia. "See them," Luz repeated in English.

Hope nodded and repeated "*Miralos elotes,*" gesturing toward a tray laden with handcrafted pastries like ears of corn. It made her happy to learn a little Spanish, and to see Luz baking traditional Mexican confections under the supervision of Senor Santos. Soon, said Lola, she would train Luz to serve customers at the counter. "But first," she whispered to Hope as the girl returned to the kitchen, "a word with you, *senora.*"

Lola's mission, as it turned out, was to convince the American *abuela* that it was time to arrange a special worship service for Luz, a ceremony to deepen her bond with God and her new family at Saint Lydia's. All the people, said Lola, must gather in the church to thank God that Luz was saved from fiery hell and returned to the good life. After the ceremony, she insisted, they must have a *verbena*, a festival of gratitude where everyone would eat and dance. At the end, everyone must kneel down and humbly ask the Creator for special blessings in the girl's future.

Hope wasn't sure she could pull if off. "What do people eat at a *verbena?*"

Lola would bring her traditional *empanadas,* soft dough pockets filled with pumpkin; also *queso,* crumbly cheese stuffed into zucchini and arranged on top of refried beans. She would teach Hope to make *sopa de polla,* a traditional *verbena* soup of clear chicken broth with peas, cubed carrots and chickpeas.

Hope wasn't sure she understood every word, but did get Lola's sense of urgency. For people in the Mexican culture, it was vitally important to have a *verbena*.

Later, attempting to convey all this to the Beacons, Hope did her best to describe how the Virgin of Guadalupe appeared to peasant Juan Diego in 1531 and performed a miracle for him, the first miracle in American territory. "The Lady asked Juan to take roses from her garden to the Bishop, to appeal to him to build a temple for her at the place where they met," said Hope. Everyone listened attentively. "Next day the peasant was about to show the Bishop the roses, but to their surprise they found the roses and the Virgin imprinted on the peasant's cloak. His *tilma*." Hope felt it necessary to say it in Spanish.

The Head Beacon agreed to bring Senora Santos's request to WAM, the Worship, Art and Music Committee.

"Remember," said Hope, "Senora Santos says this *verbena* needs to be done on the Twelfth of December, feast day of the Virgin of Guadalupe."

TWELVE MADONNAS

They'd all been virgins half a lifetime ago, and Luz just a year ago, yet the remembering made it now. And when remembering leads to a ritual of worship, this makes it forever. "That's why religious rituals are so important," Rev Ruth told the Beacons, "to join the past with the future." She asked Beka to help her design the Ceremony of the Twelve Madonnas.

So it came to pass that on the Twelfth of December twelve churchwomen settled into folding chairs arranged in a semi-circle at the front of the sanctuary. Luz Rivera, wearing a robe of Virgin Mary-blue, sat still as a stone in one circle of light at the center of the darkened sanctuary. Dot Davis, in red sequins, sat on one side of her; Millienne Guillernos, in a mirrored shawl honoring the Haitian saint Erzulie, was on the other.

Adjoining chairs were occupied by Mattie Henderson in lilac polyester and Candace Wong in red and yellow Chinese silk. Dottie Mason and four more choristers donned maroon choir robes. Hope Hudson wore the quilted yellow bathrobe Hank had given her; Paige Patterson's angelic robe was made of pink oxford-cloth.

Shy about public speaking, the Madonnas had been relieved to learn that their part in the tableau was to sit still and look holy, or at least demure, for the course of an hour. Beka and Rev Ruth agreed to do all the talking. Since the church organist and five choir members had to sit on stage, a quintet of semi-professional singers had been recruited to hum music without words.

"Quiet periods are a source of spiritual vitality," Beka began, "because quiet invites us into a deeper fellowship of understanding. The founding fathers of Saint Lydia's Church held periods of meditation before regular worship, so we shall follow their ways by interweaving music, words and stillness."

Rev Ruth led off, reading the Song of Hannah from The Gospel of Luke. *"God has brought down the powerful from their thrones and lifted up the lowly."*

After a period of silence followed by harmonious humming from the quintet, Beka quoted Sarah Grimke. "In 1837, the suffragette said 'I ask no favors for my sex, but surrender not our claim to equality. All I ask of my brothers is that they will take their feet from off our necks and permit us to stand upright on the ground which God has designed for us to occupy.'"

Rev Ruth's voice softened as she read Romans 8:26: "We do not know how to pray as we ought, but the very spirit intercedes with sighs too deep for words." Prayers of thanks, blessing and petition were offered for Luz, many in Spanish.

The Twelve Madonnas, well practiced under Beka's direction, rose smoothly in unison to form a quiet tableau. They remained standing in stillness for a full five minutes, and not a cough was heard from the congregation.

Rev Ruth quietly stepped down to sit beside the Santos family and Luz's new friends. After sighing together in wordless unity for a little while, Rev Ruth led the crowd into Fellowship Hall for the tasty part of this *verbena* celebration.

SOLSTICE

San Francisco was getting a touch of winter. Beka noticed the nip in the air and announced it to Paige.

Millienne wrapped a heavier shawl around her shoulders.

Dot and Hope welcomed its bracing bite.

Rev Ruth was unaware that others shivered, accustomed as she was to blizzards marking the season in Ohio. Everyone felt a touch of melancholy because winter spoke of endings.

Unbeknownst to the Beacons and the Rev, strong westerly winds that blew the city of San Francisco into Solstice were also blowing the congregation of Saint Lydia's through a passage of endings, though none could have said what was coming.

Rev Ruth and Millienne had both been restless, though neither could say why, exactly. The pastor perched on one side of the passage and the Beacon on the other, both seeking guidance though for what, exactly, neither could say.

Fifteen past nine. Two women in different parts of the city sighed in unison, lost in thought. One lay supine on her single bed, bony bare feet raised on a flowered pillow. The other stood upright on bare earth, balanced on the balls of her feet, pressing her weight between the second and third toes. Each sought divine guidance to lead them home, yet it was toward a home neither had ever seen.

Rev Ruth had her share of stubbornness and it could be granted that Millienne did, too. And both had their inquisitive sides. Seekers, but how deeply alike and different were they? This may have been one of the matters they took to God. On this gusty night, prayer shed light on something else as well.

Ten thirty. Both felt homesick and would have been glad to be back where they grew up. Each regretted the day she'd said, "I think I will go to California." Both were women of the devout, achieving sort. Millienne was twenty-two when she set foot in San Francisco; Rev Ruth was seventy. Both had legendary, adventurous male ancestors. Millienne's father was said to have drowned when his fishing boat broke up on a

Caribbean reef. Rev Ruth's sea-captain grandfather was said to have been lost in an Atlantic gale, aboard a schooner en route to the East Indies. Could ancestral disappearances at sea have somehow jarred both women into motion and landed them in San Francisco?

What exact excuses, promises, and petitions each left behind cannot be known, but they likely amounted to a considerable collection. Yet both had completed the pilgrimage and here they were, one uneasily sheltered in a Larkin Street studio apartment with third-hand furniture, the other standing beneath a blue spruce in her Upper Market neighborhood. And both found their spiritual lives sufficiently interesting to do nightly prayers in hopes of making each new day more fully God-shaped.

It was a leaden evening all across San Francisco Bay. On Alcatraz, the lighthouse blinked against the black island and the tide turned to join the quick surf of the Pacific. Far across on the Marin Shore, the lights of Sausalito were scattered like embers atop the dark rim of coastline. Chill winds visited Millienne's favorite trees and shook their high branches. Tonight's gusting had started hours ago, during the gray fade of daylight that is December in San Francisco, marking the beginning of winter.

Christmas was coming. Both women yearned toward the holidays. They shared an appetite for festive food. Rev Ruth's thoughts turned to oyster stew and roast goose. Cranberry sauce with currants and cloves. Pumpkin pie with nutmeg. Millienne's tastebuds hungered for goat stew and fried plantains with cinnamon. Mango chunks with wild mint.

Deep inside these feminine memories and motions on a windy winter night, new patterns were taking shape. A tincture of apprehension may have been mixed in with each woman's sense of homesickness, but unbeknownst to both, Rev Ruth's ministry in San Francisco was shortening.

CHAPTER 11

THE PIERS

Supports

HERESY

The more she heard Dot Davis bragging to church folks that she ate Jesus for supper every evening, the more perturbed it made Rev Ruth. That woman is deluded. Here I thought we'd reached an understanding, but now she's up to her old tricks. Dot must be made to understand why the sacrament of Holy Eucharist requires a pastor to bless the bread and cup. I must convince her to honor the sacred table within the community of faith and only there. It is my job to straighten her out, but how?

Ruth practiced in front of the bathroom mirror. "The *Eucharistia* is the *centrum fidei* of The Church, the visible sign of God's invisible grace," she intoned. The ancient words gave her a surge of pride. Quoting Latin was bound to impress Dot. The pastor straightened her spine and went on: "You're supposed to get everlasting life from spiritual bread, but you're meant to eat it in church, beside other Christians."

Her heart picked up speed. Ruth drew what she hoped was a steadying breath. "Bread and wine are symbols of the power of Christ's sacrificial love. They are intended to draw us together. You're not supposed to eat Jesus all by yourself."

Hmmm, not so good. Dot would get ticked off if she felt chastised. Ruth swallowed with what felt like a lot of effort. She cast her mind to the writings of the Apostle Paul. "In First Corinthians Ten," she pronounced as if preaching to Dot alone, "Paul writes how the cup of blessing unites people in love. 'Because there is one bread, we who are many are one body, for we all partake of one bread.'"

Saint Paul was sensible; Dot Davis was not. The woman was too independent, that was the problem. Her attitude rankled Ruth. Even if she was a Beacon, what made her think she could consecrate the bread all by herself? Ruth had been ordained to do that. But how in the world could she bring one wandering sheep back into the fold of traditional beliefs?

Rev Ruth fixed her eye in an insistent stare, practicing to convince Dot Davis to see things her way. "The sacrament of the Holy Eucharist is meant to write its law in our heart. It is meant to make us into the body of Christ, all of one mind." She'd said all this before, but Dot's ears were deaf to the truth. *How can I get her to agree we all need to be of one mind? My mind!* A surge of aggression made her uneasy. She tensed against the unwelcome moment, glanced at her face in the mirror and did not like what she saw.

Incessant twitching among the muscles of her right eyelid distracted her. Turning her back on the mirror, Ruth practiced her speech again. "The Church is here to keep order among the people. The priest is the only one empowered to turn ordinary bread into the body of Christ. A lowly social worker cannot proclaim the holy words that bring about transubstantiation."

The sag of Ruth's shoulder's expressed her frustration. She needed to voice the truth of the Christian Church powerfully enough to convince Dot Davis that God consecrates the Bread of Life only through pastors. Through Rev Ruth. But how could she force Dot to honor her priestly authority?

She tried again. "The sacrament of communion is the opposite of magic! Eucharist is based on a hierarchy of sacred authority and you don't recognize my authority. When you eat Jesus by yourself, you leave me out ...you...you heretic!"

Fury raised her temperature and mottled her skin. She bit her lip until it bled.

It did not occur to her to pray for help.

ASHES

The next day—Ash Wednesday—began with the slow, grave marking of ashes upon foreheads. Miz Washington, with her furrowed walnut brow, was first in line. Next came Judge Benson, lifting his white eyebrows at the pastor's touch. Annie Baxter coughed into her hand afterward. Jessie Eaton pulled off a ragged knit cap and pushed his stringy hair out of the way. Even Homer Adams showed up, hung over, to kneel in his greasy overalls and receive the cross of ashes.

So it was that many members of Saint Lydia's began the journey into Lent 1977. For traditional Christians like Rev Ruth, Lent was a time to prepare for death and rebirth, though she had heard that some turned it into a display of personal religiosity by publicly giving up luxuries like chocolate and poker.

Yes, the body of Saint Lydia's had sore places and unhealed scars. Our little flock may not be perfect, thought Rev Ruth, but it is beautiful. She liked gazing at these faces, early light glancing off cross-marked foreheads. Ash Wednesday gave the pastor a rare chance to touch them, these unconventional members of Christ's body in San Francisco. She was beginning to love the people of Saint Lydia's, even with all their oddities, clashes and sorrows.

SPARKS

Rev Ruth asked the heretic to come in for a talk that afternoon, but things got off to a tense start.

Dot Davis refused to take a seat. She lifted her chin a notch and looked straight ahead with terrible patience. "I prefer to stand," she declared, hands on hips, taking a wide stance just inside the doorway. Dot avoided Rev Ruth's steel blue eyes. The Beacon did not like the pastor's slitted way of looking at you, as if she'd watched you put on your clothes that morning and knew what you were covering up.

That woman is odious, thought Rev Ruth, and sturdy as a damn oak. She took a deep, deep sniff.

So far as Dot knew, there was no physical reason for this habit, only that the Reverend seemed to feel entitled to more air than anyone else in the room.

"We need to talk about eating Jesus," Rev Ruth began.

"Eating Jesus," Dot repeated. Her expression turned hedgy.

"Yes, well…" Rev Ruth opened and closed her mouth twice, reminding Dot of a trout in shallow water.

"Ahem." The pastor cleared her throat, trying to find her voice. "Dot Davis, while I am in no position to tell you what you must believe…"

"Then do not." Eyebrows arched, Dot gave a grudging grin.

"Well," Rev Ruth cleared her throat again. "This particular sacrament, the Sacrament of Holy Eucharist is, as you know, central to the church." The fancy Latin words left her mind just when she needed them. "It is good and right, you see, to honor the exact wording of the Divine Liturgy."

"That I do." Dot's tone seared like dry ice.

Rev Ruth pressed both hands against her waistband in an effort to quiet the tangled knot in her stomach. She needed all her wits to make the point, but her wits had fled. "It is, rather…I don't think your comments about eating Jesus for supper should be spoken aloud here at Saint Lydia's."

A pang shot through Dot and quivered there, but she tried not to give Rev Ruth the satisfaction of seeing it. "Is that a fact?"

Rev Ruth's lips flattened, squeezing out the pink color. Her steely eyes cast judgment. "The law of the church applies."

"And how, exactly, does it apply to me?"

Rev Ruth could remember nothing of her carefully rehearsed speech. A sharp pain made her reach for her chest. "Uhmmm...the law of the church applies," she repeated, face flushed with heat.

"You don't know?" Maybe Dot sensed the tug of war going on inside the pastor but she had run out of patience. She raised up like a forester's ax, stepped closer to the desk and leaned in from the waist until her face was only an inch from Rev Ruth's. "The law of the church does not apply in my own home. Nor in my office."

The tart smell of her breath was strong. Rev Ruth felt faint.

Dot barged on. "And the law of the church does not apply in the sanctity of my own head and heart."

She left the office like a gust of chill wind.

Rev Ruth slumped in her chair. Despite the palpitations in her chest and the roiling mess in her belly, she knew she must still find some way to convince this unruly parishioner of the truth about Holy Eucharist. Her truth.

The stench of failure made her gag.

The pen exploded from her fingers.

Desperate to rise, she made it halfway to her feet before folding from the waist and collapsing onto the desk.

Her head knocked over the Regency silver chalice, but she did not hear it clatter to the floor because the pastor was unconscious before her forehead hit the metal spine of the desk calendar.

Blood from her scalp wound blotted out the date: February 23, 1977.

Ash Wednesday.

SPARED

Unconsciousness spared Ruth from the clutch of terror that usually grabbed hold when she heard the scream of a siren. Since the summer day she'd seen her three-year-old sister ablaze, high-pitched sirens and girls' screams always tangled her nervous system.

The good reverend was spared the memory of Dot's furious departure and her own collapse. Blessedly, she was also spared fears of her ministry crashing down.

She could, now, feel the sting of a needle taped to her arm. She could smell the heated-up antiseptic air. She could hear the beeps of machines that must be keeping her heart pumping. She also heard an odd stillness, a hush that was not what true silence should be.

No, she gurgled in protest. No, she protested, batting at the tube hanging from a plastic bag of plasma.

The bed tipped at an angle and seemed to buck. She reached out to stop it and felt her palm strike a metal bed rail.

"Forgive me," she panted. "Forgive me."

Next thing she knew, a cold stethoscope startled her chest. Someone shouted for a crash cart.

SORE HEART

Paige picked up the phone. It was Beka calling from San Francisco General. "Rev Ruth, she's in the hospital. It's her heart. Nothing you can do."

Actually, neither knew what the hell to do. Both clung to something already gone. Quiet filled the air on the line. Paige's face stared back in shock from the hall mirror, framed by angels Reverentia and Simplicita. The Beacon sensed the old world of Saint Lydia's leaning in and whispering farewell, then it dissolved.

Paige put down the phone, picked up her keys, went out the door, walked around the neighborhood. She stared at winter shadows between buildings. She watched pigeons spreading their tails in stately dance steps. She wished the sky would split open and grieve. She wanted it to rain and rain, wanted God to flood the streets of San Francisco with tears, but buses still drove and passengers still talked. People still shopped. School kids still joked and pushed.

She walked past Saint Lydia's, where she'd found her first sense of belonging. She remembered telling Rev Ruth her gender truth, boldly confessing her odd admiration for angels, and for Thomas Aquinas.

Any imprint she'd made on her pastor was now in danger of being lost. She paused outside the smeared window of Henry's Café and wished they could have tea there again, share one more conversation about *Summae Theologica III*.

Paige remembered a book on bereavement. After denial comes grief. Or anger. Or guilt. She couldn't remember which, but needed some way to order her sense of loss. She wanted to make it sensible, but there was no sense in it.

Walking was an act of discipline. So was breathing. She did both.

What she noticed: When a part of you collapses, you feel hollow but you also feel lighter. Truer, somehow.

What she wondered: What will happen if Rev Ruth dies?

What she asked God: Who will fill her place in my hollow, sore heart?

What she decided: The bread of Jesus, the cup of salvation and the love of Saint Lydia's will get us through.

MISERY

Darkness had fallen by the time Dot learned what had happened after she left Rev Ruth's office. "My God," she said to Dick after Beka's call. "She had a heart attack. My pastor. The janitor found her unconscious after I slammed out. Something made her collapse. It must have been me. Something I said."

"What did you say?" he asked from the kitchen. Dot was sitting at one end of the dining table, the end nearest the window; the rest of the table was piled with bills and catalogs and clean laundry that needed folding. Rain and wind blustered around the corners of the apartment building. Dick was standing at the stove, dropping pats of butter into a cast iron skillet, toasting ham and cheddar sandwiches for their supper.

"What did you say?" he repeated.

"I said I didn't need her to bless my bread," replied Dot. "I said I didn't need anyone to do what I could very well do myself." Her voice shook. "I told her I intended to keep on eating Jesus whenever I damn well pleased, wherever I damn well pleased. She tried to argue with me, but I cut her off and slammed the door on my way out. Oh my God, what have I done?" Dot heaved a huge sigh and folded forward like a puppet with cut strings. Her forehead hit the tabletop with a thud.

For such a big man, Dick moved quickly. Suddenly there he was, thighs pressed against her back. "You must have given the old girl quite a shock." Respect, comfort and amusement mixed in his voice. He leaned close and stroked the back of her neck. "You're probably the only one who's ever talked straight to the old biddy."

He kneaded her shoulders, stroked her neck. Dick might have even caressed his wife right into bed, except for the shriek of the smoke alarm. By the time he grabbed the skillet off the stove and put out the fire, by the time Dot threw open the windows, all talk of Rev Ruth was swept out into the night sky—along with smoke from the charred bread.

All the next day, Dot berated herself. At times she suspected her anguish might be presumptuous. If she claimed she was too weak to bear the blame for causing Rev Ruth's heart attack, didn't that somehow mean she really had the strength for it? She couldn't make sense of her responsibility, nor could she shake the persistent waves of remorse. That Rev Ruth's near-death experience felt to Dot like the end of the world—or at least the end of her ministry at Saint Lydia's—embarrassed her, because she knew people who suffered far worse. Diphtheria. Falling from windows. Dying from gunshots.

At the same time, Dot had a deep and abiding respect for the idea that anyone should be able to make bread holy, whenever and wherever she wanted. An ordinary woman should be able to bless her own bread—or saltines—whenever she needed to take the power of Jesus into her own body.

But such ruminations brought no relief from the pain, for having shoved her pastor off the edge of a vigorous—if often irritating—ministry and into the abyss where death threatened. Anger and guilt and sorrow continued to distill within Dot. Although her despair threatened to become permanent, Dot still believed that giving in to remorse showed a failure of character.

It soon got to where she didn't want to go outside. Someone from Saint Lydia's might see her; might stop to make small talk. The exposure and the humiliation would be too much to bear.

She had imaginary conversations with Rev Ruth in which the old woman tried to console Dot by preaching a forgiving point of view. The Beacon could imagine agreeing, wholeheartedly, but did not actually feel forgiven. In these imaginary conversations, Rev Ruth would act very convinced, so certain that forgiveness was the providence of Christ, and that Dot was worthy of receiving it. She found it easy to accept the idea that anyone deserved forgiveness, but in turn found it impossible to believe she could ever be one of those loved and forgiven sinners.

She had trouble sleeping. She spent her nights in the murk of brittle memories where she had to watch her tongue and speak very carefully because her strongly-worded opinions might cause her pastor to die. That prospect was too awful to bear.

Dot's misery finally gave way to resolve; she would clean the house. The living room was littered with old magazines and newspapers, stained coffee cups, sticky 7-Up bottles. Cigarette butts overflowed the ashtrays and stuck out of the potting soil around the houseplants. Crusty plates filled the sink.

She spent the day washing dishes, swabbing floors and scrubbing grunge from bathroom tiles with a toothbrush.

By the time the apartment was spotless, her sweatshirt was drenched and she was exhausted. Dot had done her best to cleanse the regrets from her mind, scour the remorse from her soul and purge the self-recrimination that clogged her heart, but true relief was still out of reach.

Dot stretched out on the couch and fell into a strange trance. She saw herself freshly coiffed and manicured, wearing an ivory silk blouse tucked into creased black gabardine slacks, sitting in an armchair upholstered in gold brocade, across from Rev Ruth in a matching chair. She heard two tumblers of 7-Up fizzing on the table between them, and saw two saltines on a Melmac saucer, crystals of salt glistening in the sunlight streaming in the south window. They were having communion. On Dot's lap lay an open Bible; her finger marked an inspiring verse. She read a passage of scripture and it quieted their hearts, no longer troubled by the hurtful words that hurled Rev Ruth into the back of an ambulance.

BROKEN

Ruth's dream was more vivid than life. The air was dark and full of water. Her family home, the house where she grew up, was collapsing around her. Cold rain poured through the broken roof. The floor was all mud.

This was her house but it was empty. There was no family in it.

Water, thin and sour, poured through the holes, ran down her face. Messy mud kept her feet stuck in loss. Her whole body ached.

Loved ones who had lived here were gone. She reached out for Nolan but touched only chilled absence.

Ruth lifted one eyelid and stared into a wet-sifting darkness that seemed to rise and fall in the room. The bed had a mudlike hold on her.

I'm done, she thought. Broken. Useless.

"Hello," then more loudly, "HELLO."

Eyelids flickering. Raggedy brows wrinkling.

Beka had to say everything twice to bring her pastor back from a place of strange visions. "Rev Ruth. Rev RUTH!

"It's Beka. BEKA ASH from Saint Lydia's."

Silence. Incoherent mumbling.

"Rev Ruth, are you in there? Can you wake up?"

The wan priest levered her eyelids up. She managed to lift her gaze, until it jumped the fence and fled into the wet sky.

EMPTY

The Beacons designated Beka as their sole visitor until Rev Ruth was strong enough to handle more people. They gathered at the church to hear what was happening. "So, how is she doing?" asked Paige. "Really?"

"The nurse tried to feed her a little chicken broth but she refused. Wouldn't even take a bite of cherry Jello." Beka's eyebrows gathered in. "Today they got her up to walk but she couldn't take a single step."

"Maybe she's just too tired." Hope heaved a weary sigh of empathy.

"That woman was born talking." Dot gave a sharp nod. Too ashamed to admit her role in the situation, she acted her usual blustery self. "Rev Ruth always has an opinion. On everything and everyone."

"She usually does," Beka agreed. She lifted her hands and let them drop. "Odd thing is, she's not talking, even to me." She formed a steeple with her fingers. "It's not like Rev Ruth to go mute. Her silence scares me."

"Things are never exactly silent when that woman is around, even when nothing is being said." Dot sounded peevish. "Her opinions make noise all the time. The force of her personality makes a racket even when she's not talking."

Paige ignored Dot's outburst. She put down her pen and turned toward Beka. "Do you think she understood what you said to her?"

"Hard to tell." Beka's voice lost power. "Her face looked blank, no expression."

"Maybe there's a lot going on behind her face," ventured Millienne.

"Like what?" asked Dot.

"Like life or death." Paige nodded to affirm the gravity of her own words.

"Maybe…" Millienne paused and raised her gaze to tree-top level. "Maybe she's been shocked out of her body. By the pain of her heart attack."

The Beacons fell into a thoughtful hush. This was a new idea.

"I wonder," Millienne went on, "if Rev Ruth hasn't yet decided whether to come back into her body. Whether it's safe."

"She's a damn feminist, remember, not a masochist." Dot spoke rapidly, intent on maintaining the status quo.

Millienne flinched and slanted her body away from the accuser. "Maybe Rev Ruth doesn't yet know whether she can stand to be that vulnerable again."

Paige nodded vigorously. "I know. I think I know." Her friends exchanged glances. They knew Paige kept a close alliance with pain and death.

She gave Beka a searching look. "Did she seem frozen in some way, as if she was trying to decide whether or not to stay with us? To stay alive?"

Beka's focus was far away. "She did seem as if she'd…gone somewhere else. She kept her eyes closed. She looked small to me and somehow…deflated."

"As if all the life had leaked out of her?" asked Paige.

"Yes. Like an empty balloon." Beka wiped a hand across her forehead. "I didn't know what to do."

THE SNIT

"Be honest," Dot challenged Beka. "Doesn't some little part of you feel relieved that Rev Ruth is off the job?"

"You mean on account of her secret heart condition?"

"And her personality, the way she blows hot and cold. If she hadn't collapsed, things would have gotten worse. She might have blown up in public and caused another citywide scandal."

"Oh Dot, we never would let that happen. The Beacons would come in and... settle her down."

"And exactly how would you do that!"

"Oh, I don't know, stage a coup or something."

Dot made a little puffing sound of amusement. "Right, I could sock her in the kisser while you wrestle her into handcuffs." She stared at her fist, imagining scraped knuckles, then shifted her gaze to Beka. "I'm sorry." She swallowed. "I want to apologize for that."

"Forget it. Fact is, I am kind of relieved you spoke up. Far better to blow off steam with me than punch our contentious pastor in the kisser." They shared a little charge of laughter.

Beka and Dot were in the pastor's study cleaning up the mail. Or rather, Beka was slitting envelopes and stacking papers.

Dot was pacing around, picking up random objects and setting them down.

"Do you dislike her that much?" asked Beka, narrowing her eyes.

"I don't dislike her! Jeez!"

Beka tossed junk mail into the wastebasket and stood to look Dot in the eye. From the way she lifted out of the chair, all businesslike, it was clear she had something to say.

"What, you don't believe me?" blurted Dot. "We get along fine! I mean, it's true Rev Ruth can be a goody-goody, like 'See how much holier I am than you,' and she talks way too much, in a super-theological way, but I have no problem with her."

Beka smiled one of her mysterious smiles.

Dot picked up the silver Regency chalice, turned it over, looked at the bottom and set it down on the desk.

"Can you hand that to me?"

"You really want to serve communion in Rev Ruth's precious antique chalice?" Dot raised both eyebrows.

Beka gave her a look.

Dot passed the engraved chalice across the desk, then picked up the scrolled silver paten and balanced it on her open palms.

"You're not the only one who's in a snit over Rev Ruth," said Beka, "and–".

"I am in a snit, as you call it, because—"

Dot broke off and stared back at Beka. "Sorry," she said in a small voice. "Sorry. Again. You were saying?"

"I'm thinking the Beacons need to do something sacramental for Rev Ruth, and do it together, something to mend our hurts. And hers."

"Bread and wine?"

"Not yet, since her nourishment comes through an IV. Not strong enough for solid food." Beka gave Dot a long, measured look.

Dot stared down at her tangerine fingernails, picked at a cuticle.

"You and Rev Ruth treat each other like oil and water, so maybe that's the kind of communion we need to take to the hospital."

THE LIFELINE

"Rev Ruth needs a lifeline. Needs to know we need her," declared Hope.

"Do we?" Dot could be brusque.

Hope had cooked supper for the Beacons so they could talk about what to do next. They were spooning up tomato-basil soup made silky with Mexican *crema* (Luz's idea), paired with Hope's savory grilled tuna-Swiss cheese sandwiches.

"I need her," said Paige, "because she's the only one around here who knows my friend Thomas Aquinas."

"Our kids need her, that's for sure," Millienne added. "The junior high girls need a better role model than you know who."

Reminders of Pastor Peacock's dastardly deeds made them mutter in unison.

"Luz needs her, too." Hope fanned her face. She was breathing too fast. All eyes fastened on her.

"Since when?" snorted Dot. "And where is Luz, by the way?"

Millienne glanced at the mirrored wall of the dining room, remembering that Luz avoided looking into it, but Hope didn't notice.

"Working late tonight," said Hope. "Told me she tried to get Rev Ruth to baptize her, but was sent away. Since then, she's been too scared to ask."

"That girl should've talked to me first," Dot glowered. "I would've made sure she got baptized."

"There's more." Hope wiped a napkin across her face. "Luz whispered in my ear that she loves Rev Ruth." She touched fingertips to her chest. "She's so sad she never got to tell her, and now she's scared it's too late."

Paige tipped her head to one side, facing Hope. "When our pastor hears how much she matters to the girl, more than she ever realized, it's bound to give her strength." Moisture made her eyes shiny.

"Amen sister, amen," caroled Millienne.

"That's the medicine Rev Ruth needs now." Beka's jaw firmed with confidence.

"To know we love her. That's what she needs." She tried to make eye contact with each Beacon around the table, but Dot stared fixedly at the floor.

"To know we love her just the way she is," Beka repeated.

"I'll go with you," said Paige.

"Me, too." Hope spoke quickly. "And I'll bring Luz to the hospital. We need to touch Rev Ruth, all of us."

"She's right," said Millienne. "Touch is the lifeline our pastor needs, to help her get back into her body."

"Sure, go ahead." Dot tossed her hair back. "If you say so." She uncrossed her legs, shot a disdainful look at Millienne, rose to her full height, slung her handbag over one shoulder and said "Thanks for the soup. Gotta go."

THE HAWK

Midmorning sunlight fingered its way across the linoleum squares as Rev Ruth awakened. Her room was stuffy, air thick with disinfectant. Medicinal smells clung to her skin. Her bones felt like rubber melting in August sun.

What day was it? The nurse said March twelfth.

She tried to pull up into a sitting position but there was a bird trapped in her chest. Ruth could feel strong wings batting against the walls of her ribcage. It was a wild hawk; trapped, caught in too small a space.

The bedside phone rang, sending an electric current down her arm. She shook her head. Shook her hand. Reached out and raised the receiver to her ear.

"Yes, James. No, James." She was angry with her eldest son, and firm. "No. I told you NO." But there was nothing she could do to stop his diatribe. Not in her condition. Her hand trembled. She dropped the receiver and covered her ears until it stopped buzzing.

She took one rattling breath, then a deeper one. Felt the wild hawk fold its wings. Breathed through her nose. Hawk settled onto a branch of her ribs where it rested, quiet for the moment. She looked out the window at pigeons perched on a ledge. She raised her eyes to the sky, impossibly blue for March. A wide band of clouds arched above the city. Two treetops bent in the wind, rooted as deep as they'd been since before Ruth was born.

She wanted James to leave her alone. "I do not want you to come and get me," she gritted into the stale air. Hawk banged its wings against her chest. She felt the shudder of heart disease surfacing on her skin. She watched her hands tremble, braced them against her hips.

She squinted her eyes and aimed a mean glare eastward, toward Cleveland. Fear of having James show up in San Francisco came in full-body spasms.

Lord have mercy. Christ have mercy. The prayer quieted her. She repeated it. Her breath slowed down. By now, the day had worn her out. She slipped into a nap.

UNBIND HER

Back in her dreams, a black billboard spanned the width of her mind. Crimson words flashed across it like neon. *THE BUCK STOPS HERE.*

Below the billboard was an open tomb. Inside was a corpse bound in black. Ruth recoiled, ready to run, but was halted by a commanding male voice. *"Unbind her. Unbind your mother."*

She knelt on the ground to unwrap three black silk scarves wound tightly around Mother's body. The first scarf was a maternal black mood, familiar from childhood. Once she worked it loose, a chorus of ravens chirped a single word: *Pettiness.* The truth of the mother startled the daughter; she rose to her feet, ready to flee.

I instruct you again: unbind her. An angel? Or God Himself speaking in a Charlton Heston baritone?

Ruth did as bid. The moment she unbound Mother's body from the second black scarf, the ravens chirped two words: *Parsimony, parsimony.*

She wanted to get away but there was no way out; she had to continue. The third black scarf was tightly knotted. She struggled to work it loose and flung it up where a current carried it aloft, a black smudge against high white clouds. This time the raven chorus chanted *Scorn, scorn, scorn.*

As the volume intensified, Ruth came fully awake, wracked with pain. She shaped both palms into hollows, pressing cupped hands against her ribs, trying to release Hawk trapped inside.

The world changed then. No more black moods. No more arguing. No more temper. The cage around Hawk became a blue scarf on a warm breeze.

Mother, robed now in light blue, became Rosie, her dead twin.

OIL AND WATER

They entered quietly, on tiptoe. Three Beacons and Luz carried tiny bottles of essential oil into Room 303. If Rev Ruth sensed their presence, she gave no sign.

Luz carried *Citrus senensis,* essence of orange, intended to lift Rev Ruth's spirit. According to the owner of the *apothecia* on Mission Street, citrus oil stimulates the brain and eases anxiety. Luz brought it to amplify the pastor's sense of well-being.

Hope had noticed Rev Ruth's mental lapses and chose a tiny bottle of *Callitris intratropica.* They said essence of blue cypress improves circulation and increases the flow of oxygen to the brain. Just what our poor old pastor needs, she thought.

In Millienne's large hand was a miniscule bottle of *Cinnamomum verum,* the oil Yahweh bestowed upon Moses, according to Exodus Thirty. Wary of hospital-borne diseases, Millienne chose cinnamon bark oil for its antibacterial, antiparasitic and antiviral properties. Since this was the oil that protected Moses in the desert, she figured it could protect Rev Ruth in the hospital.

Dot had decided at the last minute that she, too, would go to the *apothecia* with the others. There she chose *Tanacetum annuum* to cleanse Rev Ruth's liver and lymphatic system. Blue tansy, she was told, worked emotionally to combat anger and negative emotions. Dot figured this oil would benefit giver and receiver alike.

Rev Ruth remained still, eyes closed, breath barely audible, as the hushed women circled around her bed.

Uneasy about touching the pale pastor, Beka stayed back, leaned against the wall and stared down at her fawn suede Famolares. Paige stood beside her, eyes closed in prayer, as four oil-bearers stood around the patient's bed.

Hope began by mixing blue cypress oil with a little water and massaging it into the sole of Rev Ruth's right foot. As her fingers moved across the papery skin, she spoke quietly, reminding her pastor what they shared as widows, still learning to get along without husbands.

Millienne added a little water to her cinnamon-bark oil and rubbed it into Rev Ruth's left foot. She silently infused each stroke with the strength of a Haitian pine.

Luz whispered into Rev Ruth's ear as she mixed fragrant orange oil with a bit of water and tenderly massaged the mixture into the woman's right hand. The Beacons couldn't hear what Luz said, but the look on her face was sweet.

Last of all, Dot gently cradled Rev Ruth's left hand in her strong ones. Placing a few drops of blue tansy oil in her palm, she reminisced about their walk through the Fillmore and the hilarity they'd shared with two old colored men.

And all the while, Rev Ruth lay flat as an empty balloon, unresponsive amidst bouquets of fragrance and reminiscence as essential oils and water absorbed into her dry skin and also, the Beacons hoped, into her soul.

When a black nurse in a crisp white uniform stepped through the door, Millienne greeted her with a half smile. "We're sharing communion with our pastor," she said, extending her palm to reveal a tiny bottle of cinnamon-bark oil. "We're exploring how oil and water can mix at Saint Lydia's Church."

GRANDMOTHER'S LAP

The next day, a soft knock. Hope entered the room with an expression of genuine concern. She skipped the small talk, leaned close, rested a warm hand on Rev Ruth's arm.

The patient put a hand on her chest. It was stopped up. Her breath was weak.

Hope had a shifting feeling near her own heart, a pang. "Tell me how things look to you." She spoke gently, invitingly. "What do you say to yourself? What's going on in your head?"

Slowly, Rev Ruth began, things she'd never before admitted. Recently losing her balance, then her bearings. Traumatized, seeing her twin burn to death. Anguished, seeing her newborn daughter die. Helpless, not able to save them. Totally powerless.

Hope nodded, patted her pastor's arm.

Rev Ruth described suffering when her father died of the heart disease he kept secret. Closed her eyes. Fell asleep for a bit.

Hope prayed without words, in waves of emotion. Empathy, they called it on TV.

The patient spoke weakly without opening her eyes, how her mother had faded into vagueness, how nobody could reach her even though Ruth did her daughterly best.

"I know," said Hope. She couldn't fix things, but she could listen. Empathize.

Afterward, Rev Ruth said she felt lighter. Somebody knew her hardships. It made a difference. "You're a good listener." Her voice was lower-pitched, steadier.

Hope gave a small nod. No words could improve on listening.

After a quiet spell, Rev Ruth asked "How's Luz?"

"Luz loves you."

Rev Ruth's throat tightened.

"She wants to be baptized. Wants you to baptize her."

Rev Ruth turned away and fanned her fingers across her breastbone.

"Not today or tomorrow." The Beacon's light touch on her arm was meant to be reassuring. "Don't worry," Hope hastened to add. "Only when you're strong enough."

Later Ruth remembered back when she was ten, when her cocker spaniel Goldie died. Sobbing into Grandmother's lap. Being with Hope felt like Grandmother's lap.

GAUNTLET

A day later when Dot stepped into Room 303, Rev Ruth opened one eye, closed it and tightened her jaw. Knew she should greet her adversary, but did not want to do so.

The Beacon paced the room for three minutes, trying to decide what to do. She settled on confrontation.

"Beka tells me you've gone mute. If she were here, she'd say she accepts you just the way you are. She'd let you lie there feeling sorry for yourself, but I won't put up with that crap."

Rev Ruth's eyes flew open. She wrinkled her forehead, stared hard at her visitor.

"What I want to know is, are you going to say anything today?" Dot made a wide gesture with her wrist, flinging down a gauntlet between them. "To me?"

This time, Rev Ruth decided to meet the challenge. She was weak, but ready. She opened her mouth to argue, then stopped. She was about to say you can no more win a war with me than you can win an earthquake, but it didn't feel right to fight. Her face took on a pensive expression. She absently rubbed her arm.

Dot cocked her head to the side, eyes narrowed warily.

"I think the day of selfishness is over," said Rev Ruth. Her voice shook. She took a calming breath. "I think it's time we learned to get along."

"I usually work well with others," Dot ventured, "just not with you."

"I think it's time we stop blaming each other."

Dot had been eyeing the exit. The topic of blame brought her back into the room. "If you want me to stop blaming," she said, "you'll have to stop trying to make me in your image.

I want to be a first-rate version of myself, not a second-rate version of you."

"Yes," murmured Rev Ruth. "Yes." She pressed her palms together.

Yes was the magic word for Dot, contagious on the subliminal level. Yes made her want to open up and welcome the problematic pastor into her heart.

Open, she said to her heart. Dot always had trouble opening her heart. Today it was a kitchen cupboard glued shut. She had to wedge the doors apart. It was hard work. She had to dust. Toss out some old junk to make room. "Yes," she repeated in a strong voice. "Yes."

"Thank you," croaked Rev Ruth, eyes brimming. She reached for Dot's hand. "Thank you," she repeated, squeezing for emphasis.

"Why are you thanking me?" Dot's tone had turned kind, soothing.

"The doctors are trying to cure me but..." Breathing with difficulty, Rev Ruth coughed and cleared her throat. "Curing is their job but healing....healing me...that's what you're doing."

Dot dabbed at her nose with the back of one hand. With the other, she held onto her pastor. This time the silence was sweet.

Rev Ruth would not have trusted anything less genuine than what Dot had given. And neither had to wonder about the source of freedom from blame. They both knew—without saying—where the healing had come from.

THE KNIFE

It must be Good Friday, she thought. Even the pigeons on the windowsill sounded mournful. How could silly birds know it was Good Friday?

Or maybe it was Ash Wednesday. *Ashes to ashes, dust to dust.* In Rev Ruth's tradition, people made their way to

church early, while the sky was dark. They lined up silently—
the handsome and the homely, rich and poor, arrogant and
humble—for everyone was equal on Ash Wednesday.

All were repentant, or pretended to be. Eyes downcast,
they bared their foreheads for the gritty bits of ash and prepared their souls for harsh words. *Thou art dust and to dust
thou shalt return.*

Today Ruth felt like dirt. Body nothing more than food
for the worms. The soul, though, she'd been taught the soul is
eternal and the sinner could spend eternity in hell if her soul
made a big enough mistake.

Paintings of roaring infernos were done by humans: Ruth
knew that, yet visions of the hissing fires of hell terrified her.
She'd seen Rosie aflame. Her pure innocent sister, devoured by
fire. Please God, don't put me in the inferno. Please God, don't
let my dear twin spend eternity in hell.

Ruth was lost in the immensity of it, leaning halfway out
of bed, rummaging through the drawer in her bedside table
when Dot arrived.

"May I help?" she said.

"Where'd they put my knife?" Rev Ruth sounded furious.

"Your knife?" Dot sounded confused.

"My Swiss Army knife. I brought it to the hospital."

Dot doubted this. An ambulance brought her straight from
Saint Lydia's, but today the pastor's obsession was not about
facts.

"Why in the world do you want your knife?" Dot had
plenty of practice remaining patient with irrational people.

"It protects me," huffed Rev Ruth. "Because it's red. Fights
fire with fire."

"Tell me about fire." Dot had an idea where this might be
going.

"The devil is fire and my red blade can kill the devil."

Dot evaluated the patient. "Kill the devil?"

"The devil killed my twin with fire. My red knife fights fire
with fire."

Before Dot could react, a series of loud beeps came from the hallway. "Code Blue," said a voice over the loudspeaker. "All staff to ER. Code Blue."

Rev Ruth ducked as if under attack and Dot moved quickly to place both hands on her trembling shoulders. "It's okay." She eased the frail body down onto the pillows. "You're okay. Code Blue is not about you. Someone in the Emergency Room needs help, that's all."

"I need my knife." The patient's voice sounded very young.

"No place to whittle an arrow." Dot tried for humor. "You're a sick lady, not a Girl Scout." She smoothed her fingertips across Rev Ruth's forehead, repeating the motion until they both calmed down.

Rev Ruth tried again. "What if I need my knife to clean under my fingernails?"

Studying the patient's face and determining that she was coming back to her right mind, Dot decided to go along. "Wait a sec. I've got a fingernail file in here somewhere." She rummaged through her handbag.

"No." Rev Ruth curled fingers and thumbs into the safety of her palms. The look on her face reminded Dot of a stubborn child.

"No? Why not?"

"Do it myself. With my own knife. The smallest blade."

Dot didn't move. They were quiet together. Dot stared straight ahead, imagining Rev Ruth moving the smallest blade of her Swiss Army knife beneath each ridged and yellowed fingernail. For a moment it was a tender thought.

There had been times when Dot would have pulled away out of judgment, or simply out of the strangeness of the situation, but she didn't. She looked fully into Rev Ruth's face and she smiled.

Something took shape between them, something beyond words. Rev Ruth relaxed back against her pillows and looked at Dot with weary gratitude. Love was there.

"Thank you for coming today. I always get sad on Good Friday."

"You're welcome. I forgot it was Good Friday." Dot wasn't about to set her straight about today's date.

Rev Ruth gave a tentative grin, took a fresh breath and spoke in a serious tone. "Now I want you to do something for me."

"What?"

"Forgive me."

"For what?"

"For everything wrong I ever said to you. Ever did to you."

"You didn't do anything wrong…"

"Yes, I did, and you know it. I don't have time to fix all…" Rev Ruth sighed loudly and kept her eyes locked onto Dot's.

"Okay, fine. I forgive you. Okay?" Dot let the air out of one side of her mouth and grinned lopsidedly.

"Do you?"

"Yes. Now I'll find my file and clean under your nails."

PSALMS and BEATITUDES

Between naps and dreams, she began to think more clearly, which helped Ruth admit she had not been feeling herself for quite some time. She had tried to act normal, but decidedly was not. Sometimes she lost her sense of direction; sometimes she forgot what she meant to do next. Sometimes her hands got the trembles; sometimes she was overcome with fatigue so profound she could not rise from her chair. These troubling events disturbed her greatly. She had tried to keep them secret.

Something dangerous had been happening for months, something she could not name and found impossible to describe. She decided it was like being caught in the claws of a lion, held prisoner by a fierce animal no one else could see. Feeling immobilized by a power greater than her own terrified Rev Ruth, but she had not been able to speak of this terror; she had steadfastly refused to tell anyone.

At the same time, she felt like she was letting people down. She hated it when church folks went on without her and hated to admit she could no longer keep up.

Yea, though I walk through the valley of the shadow of death, I will fear no evil. Rev Ruth repeated the Twenty-Third Psalm, trying to convince herself it was silly to be afraid. *Thou preparest a table before me, in the presence of my enemies.*

Was Dot Davis an enemy? She used to be, but no longer.

The real work of faith lies in putting Christian beliefs into practice.

Who said that?

Grandmother Nelson, in her silky white blouse and long black skirt, held out a hard candy wrapped in cellophane.

The table is prepared FOR you, not BY you.

Grandmother again. *And everyone is welcome.*

But Dot may continue to defy me, she...

She is a woman of sorrows, my dear Ruthie. Your Dot leaves a puddle of tears wherever she goes, and you just step around it without a second glance.

But if she knew what I've been through...if people at Saint Lydia's knew all the hardships I've survived, they would proclaim me a heroine!

Little by little, Grandmother's convincing voice presented the tragedies and comedies of her long life, which wore away at Ruth's contradictory views of herself. One hour she was a tragic figure; the next a misunderstood heroine. In one dream, fury seethed beneath the surface of her skin like an infestation of termites; she tried to stave them off but they ate away at her flesh. In another dream, Ruth plodded—all alone—over sharp stones and through thorny ravines, traversing the valley of the shadow of death until she was totally worn out. She awakened to realize that it was she, herself, who had banished Ruth Salter to the wilderness of her own specialness.

Little by little, old life stories peeled away and sloughed off like dead skin.

Little by little, Ruth replaced tired inner dramas with radical truths from the Beatitudes. *Blessed are the poor in spirit,* she breathed. *Blessed are they that mourn...* In and out, taking longer inhalations than usual, she tried to pray in rhythm with her heart monitor.

Beep: *Blessed are.*

Beep: *the meek.*

Beep: *Blessed are.*

Beep: *the merciful.*

Little by little, the rabbi from Nazareth and the grandmother from Providence led Ruth to actually begin loving her enemies and forgiving those who persecuted her. What they forgot to tell her was that she was powerless to achieve love and forgiveness all on her own. She could recite the Twenty-Third Psalm all night and chant the Beatitudes all day, she could sweep out the furies and do everything in her power to cultivate a loving heart toward Dot Davis, but she needed to meet the God of Love halfway.

You can't forgive without grace, whispered Grandmother, *and grace is not something you can demand.*

Ruth tried to hand over her inner turmoil to God. She did her best to open her heart to grace. She often fell asleep chanting *Prepare a table.* Then one night she woke up to find her heart as quiet as a stone on the riverbed. She no longer felt alone.

Oh! she exclaimed to Grandmother, *when grace comes, there's no doubt. I know I have been blessed. Embraced. Released from blame.*

For a few sweet moments, the God of Love peeked out from behind the curtain and suddenly, every terrible thing that had ever happened to her, and every terrible thing she had ever done, made perfect sense.

It felt like death, she thought; part ecstasy and part mystery.

CHAPTER 12

THE BEACH

Currents

JIGSAW CENTRAL

Beka was browsing at Auntie Mame's Bookshop when she spotted the jigsaw puzzle, an oak grove with a thousand pieces, some brightly colored, many dark and shadowy. Just the thing to get Rev Ruth out of her slump, she thought. Beka liked a good challenge, and this complex design filled the bill.

Rev Ruth was puzzled when Beka presented the gift. "Don't you know I'm too sick to play?"

"It's for your visitors, something people can do together. But they won't know the picture ahead of time," Beka announced merrily, "because I hid the box top."

"You're such a pill." Rev Ruth gave a hand-flap gesture of dismissal.

"Doubt is beautiful, and so are you," chirped Beka, gleefully pouring a thousand pieces onto a table she'd borrowed from the hospital laundry. She pointedly ignored Rev Ruth's gloominess and began piecing together the edges of the design, playfully humming *Amazing Grace*.

"You have an advantage," grumbled Rev Ruth, curious in spite of herself. "You're the only one who has seen the box top."

"But I won't be here very often, because I am busy running Saint Lydia's." She gave Rev Ruth a teasing look as she fit together bits of a cherry-red Adirondack chair.

No response.

"That's life at Saint Lydia's," teased the Head Beacon. "With our pastor away, we Beacons have to put pieces of ministry together without knowing the whole picture." She cocked her head, very pleased with her analogy; it was all Beka could do to refrain from clapping her crabby pastor on the back.

And she was right. Most visitors could not resist stopping to search for a piece or two; a few nurses and lab technicians spent their entire breaks with the puzzle. When the first hint of a pattern became visible—a circle of rainbow-colored chairs— word got around the hospital and before she knew it, Rev Ruth's room turned into Jigsaw Central. Janitors, secretaries and even one surgeon came by Room 303 to try a hand at teasing out the hidden design.

Eventually, the patient took an interest too, just as Beka had predicted. Rev Ruth remembered Mother's instructions about hospitality and turned on the charm as she hosted dozens of visitors and watched hundreds of pieces find their place in the design. Eventually, the full picture emerged; a sun-dappled oak grove, a welcoming table and a dozen bright Adirondack chairs resting upon a carpet of acorns.

"Life provides all the pieces," said the Night Minister, fiddling with the knot of his red necktie. "And every piece is part of the unseen whole."

"Sage commentary," agreed Rev Ruth.

"I have spent many hours with many patients," declared a chubby chaplain whose white collar was beginning to fray. "Whenever a bit of new and previously unsuspected meaning arises from an old fragment of pain or loss, it confirms that I'm in the right line of work."

"Thank God," said the patient.

ACORNS

"It is so boring to just say hi, how are you," declared Paige. "We should greet each other like the Hindus do." She pressed

palms together in front of her flat chest, fingertips pointed skyward. The rest of the Beacons, gathered for a meeting in Fellowship Hall, tilted their heads and pursed their lips.

"But we're Americans," scoffed Dot. She could be impatient.

"We could learn a lot about being better Christians from
Hindus." Paige could be insistent. Ignoring Dot, she bowed
slightly toward Hope and intoned 'Namaste.'

"What does 'Namaste' mean?" Dot's classes at City College had been thoroughly practical. She had no tuition money
to spend on World Religions. She sent a coveting glance, a
tightening under the eyes, toward her academically privileged
friend.

"It means I see the soul in you and I greet the soul in you."
Paige held Dot's gaze and patted her own heart. "I see the
Christ in you."

Dot blinked rapidly and glanced around the room, trying
to see where Paige was going with this.

Hope poked her tongue into her cheek and gave her head
a slight shake.

Paige forged on. "I think we should remind people that
we see God in them. I think we could help Rev Ruth get well
by showing her that we see her divine nature. Like the Hindus
do." She ducked her chin and lowered her eyes, a signal she
was done trying to convince them.

"She would hate that!" snapped Dot. "Rev Ruth is too
traditional. Too Anglican!"

"I agree," said Hope. "It bothered me when you," nodding toward Paige "bowed to me. And also, I don't like being
talked to in foreign words I can't understand."

Three Beacons goofed around mispronouncing 'Namaste,'
curtsying to each other and bowing with big exaggerated flour-
ishes but Millienne sat with chin in hand, looking thoughtful.
After a bit, she slapped her fingers against her cheek and rose
to her feet, towering over the others.

"Like a mighty oak," murmured Hope.

"Perfect analogy," Millienne nodded, "because I am thinking about acorns. Even the tiniest acorn knows it has the potential to be a great oak, even if it never gets planted. Even if it never gets to grow into the tree it could be."

"What do acorns have to do with Hindus? Or with us?" scowled Dot.

"Or with our problem pastor?" Beka was ready to get the meeting back on track.

"The way I see it," said Millienne, "if we treat Rev Ruth only as a sick person, if we focus only on her symptoms, she'll think she's headed for the grave."

"So," interrupted Dot, "what does that have to do with the price of tea in China?"

Paige stood. Millienne gestured with her wrist, yielding the floor. She sat.

"There is a huge difference," asserted Paige, "between a bit of wood carved in the shape of an acorn and a real, living acorn. It's clear to me that Rev Ruth's weakness has raised doubts in her..."

As the surprise—and the truth—of Paige's analogy hit her, Beka jumped up and put a hand on her friend's arm. "So, do you mean Rev Ruth is afraid she's a fake pastor? Not the real thing?"

"She could be," blurted Dot, jerking her head back. "You could be right, Paige. We have been tough on her, putting her on probation and all..."

"Shaking her confidence in herself," added Hope.

The Beacons nodded in unison. They sensed, rightly, that Dot was not ready to admit her part in escalating the communion conflict that led to their pastor's heart attack, but felt it was a step in the right direction.

"And Paige is suggesting that the way we treated her might have shaken Rev Ruth's image of herself as a good pastor." Beka widened her eyes for emphasis.

More nods among the Beacons

"Back to 'Namaste." Paige spoke into the silence. "If we greet her with a praying hands, a holy word and a little bow, it would convey that no matter how weak she looks at the moment, we see a great pastor in her."

"I wouldn't go that far," said Dot, cutting her eyes toward the cross on the west wall of Fellowship Hall, "but I will collect acorns in the park and take her a handful."

CAPTAIN GRANDFATHER

Something was wrong. The ocean was curling up on itself, rising into a frightful tsunami of water. Ruth grabbed onto a strong man who shouted, "God Almighty!"

The wave hit like a hammer blow. It separated them and she surged forward, banging into rocks until finally she landed flat on a rocky beach, lacerated and bleeding, amazed she wasn't dead.

In the morning, what remained in Ruth's memory was the sheer power of the Pacific. The freak wave. The strong man. The bleeding body. The hard landing struck her to the core. And now her stomach hurt, as if the almighty power of God—or Jonah—had rearranged her insides.

Oh! The strong man was Grandfather Nelson. She peered at the image of his grizzled face as if she'd seen a ghost, which she had. The Captain, she realized, had given her a dream-preview of her own death by taking her through his own. The whole episode left her feeling that time had stopped.

Much as Rev Ruth liked to think she had come to San Francisco under her own pluck and power, she could no longer deny her true vulnerability. A puny human who couldn't walk more than six steps without support, she belonged to God's green earth and God's blue sea; one was sure to claim her.

Today the Captain's dream had claimed her as forcefully as the Pacific breakers claimed the boulders at Fort Point. It had taken getting sick, and slowly getting better, to wear down her independence to the point where she could acknowledge the intense, ancestral presence of her long-dead Captain Grandfather. His fierce protection was only half the story. Despite many months in San Francisco, the Reverend Doctor Ruth Ridley Salter had barely begun to take in the power of the place.

Fresh waves of revelation washed over her as the day went on. The remainder of her story was still being written by the force of belonging—belonging in San Francisco and belonging to Saint Lydia's Church. God's gravitational power had come to claim her.

Another revelation: God sent Grandfather Nelson to bring her home to herself, and to the fullness of her ministry among the people of Saint Lydia's.

THE WHITECAPS

"She'll soon be ready for release," said Doctor Tamadi. "Missus Salter will definitely need placement in a convalescent hospital unless," he looked pointedly at Beka and Dot, "either of you is able to take care of her full time."

Both Beacons shook their heads.

Rev Ruth was pointedly ignoring the conversation.

Driving home, Beka said "She gave up everything to come to Saint Lydia's. How can we even think of putting her away in a nursing home?"

"I don't think I can do it."

"Me, neither."

They drove along. Neither could think of anything else to say. Finally Dot spoke: "Anyway, its just until she's stronger."

"But what if she's never stronger?"

Dot, always practical, sighed. "We have to figure this out as we go along. And the first step is to go out and look at some convalescent hospitals."

The director of The Whitecaps on Ocean Avenue was warm, sympathetic and hearty. He gave them a sales pitch and left them in the waiting room. Framed photos of 1940s movie stars covered the walls. Big-band music played from a speaker high in the corner. They gazed up at the ceiling like people waiting for an eclipse. Or a tidal wave.

"It's like he's trying to sell us a used car," Dot whispered.

"No matter how nice it looks, it's all about urine," said Beka. The odor was strong and sharp. Dot covered her nose with one hand. The big band music played on.

The director returned to show them around. The first resident they saw was tall and well dressed. She paced the hall, black pumps squeaking on the shiny floor. She seemed to be with it until they got close enough to hear the song she repeated over and over: "*Daisy, Daisy, give me your answer do. I'm half crazy all for the love of you.*"

Beka's heart sank lower with each step. The Whitecaps was as good as convalescent care got, but the whole building was inhabited by vacancy. You could hear the hum of vacant minds. People parked in wheelchairs sat staring. One feeble man called "Gladys, Gladys, Gladys," his plaintive voice trailing them down the hall.

"Here we go." The director held open the door to a room marked Activities where four people sat slumped over. "Hello" the director called cheerfully, and two of the four looked up.

"Excuse me," Dot asked. "What would you call this activity?"

Beka knew the answer. It was called sitting. And sitting, even debilitated sitting, was different from lying flat, staring death in the face. Sitting with others in weak sunlight filtering through gauze curtains was different from lying down and staring at nothing, which is what most people here seemed to be doing—except for the drooping man calling for Gladys and the shrill woman singing her love song to Daisy.

A few days later Beka and Dot put their pastor in The Whitecaps, against her desperate will and their own. "It's just for a few days," Dot assured her, "till you're strong again. I promise."

Rev Ruth was not assured. She held her nose against the smell of urine-soaked nightclothes and bad food. She smoldered, glared and shrugged off their hands when they tried to console her.

Beka held back tears. "My place has too many stairs. You've been there; you know how steep it is. And I can't give you what you need, Rev Ruth. You need to get strong," she said, repeatedly. "You need to get strong so you can go home."

Suddenly, Dot felt as if she might faint; she had to sit down in the room's only chair. "And I can't take care of you properly. You'd have to climb five flights of stairs to my apartment. You need more care than I can give you. You just need to stay here until you get stronger."

The pastor looked over at a roommate who appeared to be dead. Dot and Beka looked at her, too. A puzzled expression appeared on Rev Ruth's face, as if she heard someone calling her name from far away.

The Beacons exchanged anguished looks on their way out. Would the old woman ever get her freedom back?

Rev Ruth turned her head slowly as they left, like a little girl whose balloon was floating out of reach and heading for the open sky.

REGRETS

Subject to death without notice. They were good lines, she thought; they had shock effect. *Subject to death without notice.* Those words should be tattooed on the foreheads of infants.

Rev Ruth imagined saying this to her respiratory therapist, a sallow young man with no sense of humor. The idea provided her only smile that day.

Why didn't I stay in chemistry, she thought, not for the first time. Why in the world didn't I keep my old job? Chemical formulas don't change. Physical elements don't abandon people.

Whatever made me think I'd be good at ministry? Personal relationships are fraught with far too many unknowns.

ANCESTRAL GUIDANCE

Sea met sky in a misted vista at the edge of San Francisco. Rolling breakers from the distant horizon splashed foam on windswept beaches. Wind whistled westbound along Ocean Avenue and wrapped around a modest building called The Whitecaps but for Rev Ruth, the tumult of wind and waves was centered in her own chest.

Back in Cleveland, she had imagined San Francisco as a place of happiness and security, not stormy inner turmoil. She had scrimped and saved for the passage, but the hard journey to a church of her own had left her shipwrecked on the rocks. She watched as her promised land—ministry at Saint Lydia's—dissolved in cold mist.

"Be ye the Captain," he'd commanded in a dream. "Your church people need a strong Captain." His *basso profundo* voice erased her sleepiness. How charming, Ruth thought, Captain Grandfather insisting she must become her best self. Grandmother used to call her lost husband a legendary commander.

Dawn glimmered on the horizon. The patient sensed a shimmer of anticipation, rousing her into a state of palpable excitement. He'd used a three-part meter, which made the details easier to recall.

"Get to know your vessel, the angle of the sails, the creak and strain of the ropes." The Captain had addressed her quite poetically.

"Get to know the lean of the tiller, the pull of the tides, the salty sting of the seawater on your skin.

"Get to know the hum of your crew, the shout of folks in trouble, the song of your congregation."

There was something familiar about this pattern. Why, Grandfather must have been a Trinitarian. She liked knowing they shared such a central belief.

"You can't captain a ship with sheer, bloody-minded willfulness. Lead with a firm hand, but do not trample. Use your expressive imagination."

Ruth stared hard at the western horizon, barely visible through the trees, seeking celestial clues on how to follow his advice. What was expressive imagination?

How could she use it to learn what he meant?

Engage the Captain in dialogue? Worth a try.

"What do we do after leaving port, Sir?"

She heard a quick laugh, followed by a silence that felt deadly serious.

"What strengths are you hiding? What unspeakable fears?"

Oh dear, she was not expecting such searing questions.

"You must find the elemental goodness within yourself if you are to assume your own captaincy," he declared. His rumbling bass voice sent shivers up her spine.

"Take an inventory of what you have on board. List not only your strengths and fears, but also the gifts you are afraid of receiving."

She had no idea how to do what the Captain wanted her to do.

DARK NIGHT

"No one chooses to go into the dark night of the soul," Rev Ruth complained to her visitor. "The dark night drops on your head like a collapsing roof. Darkness so black, it tests your puny soul."

To Hope, the patient was beginning to sound like her old preacherly self, which seemed like a good sign despite the topic.

The pastor moaned. "The dark night imposes circumstances beyond human control. This illness has taken me almost to the point of losing faith."

Hope made what she hoped was a comforting sound. Rev Ruth's lament reminded her of an overly-dramatic Job on the ash heap and Hope certainly did not want to sound like one of his so-called friends.

"Losing faith in God, you mean?" She was tentative, half afraid that was exactly what Rev Ruth meant.

"If God is light, then God's been gone since I landed in this dreadful place."

"When you're stuck in the dark, what do you wonder about?"

"Who the heck is in charge? It sure isn't me." Rev Ruth sounded glum.

"Could it be…" Hope paused until words arrived, and prayed they were the right ones. "Could the one in charge… maybe…be God in disguise?" She wasn't sure what she was talking about, and prayed Rev Ruth would not make her explain what she meant.

"Have I been hearing voices? Is that what you're asking?"

The old, familiar sharpness was back; it gave Hope an odd shiver of reassurance.

"Have you?" She peered closely at her pastor.

"Yes, as a matter of fact." Rev Ruth's pale face had turned as pink as a petunia. "One voice—which sounds annoyingly like my mother—warns me when I'm about to do something stupid. Another voice, in a much lower range, instructs me how to become the captain of my own ship."

Hope wiped her brow. "I wonder if maybe…God's voice could come disguised as your mother's, or …"

"Never has before," snapped Rev Ruth.

"Can you tell the difference between a mental disorder," ventured Hope—quoting a doctor she'd seen on television—"and a divine disturbance?"

Rev Ruth stared at Hope as if she'd gone nuts. "Divine disturbance?"

"I'm out of my depth here…"

"Oh. My. God. "

Rev Ruth moaned and clapped a hand to her forehead. "Maybe this heart attack wasn't a punishment after all;

maybe…" She tilted her chin to the sky and took one long, deep breath, then another.

Hope filled the noisy silence. "It seems fairly natural to see a serious illness as a test, but…"

Rev Ruth interrupted her. "One of the hardest things to decide is whether to resist or surrender. But I haven't had strength to resist. And I couldn't stand to surrender." She ran out of breath.

Hope handed her a glass of water and waited for her to drink it. "Maybe," she ventured, "that's why they call it a dark night, because you can't see what's going on…"

"I don't even know who God is anymore," whined Rev Ruth. "I used to have a big old treasure chest stuffed with ideas about God, big notions about sin and salvation, repentance and grace. Now I just don't know…"

She fiddled with a tiny cross on a gold chain and fixed her gaze on the bit of sky visible from her bed. "I've become more and more devoted to some holy, distant… something….that I can say less and less about."

"Maybe your faith just got worn out," smiled Hope. "Maybe you're clearing out the junk in your God-closet and getting ready for a big rummage sale. Of the soul." Hope's thousand-watt grin lit the room. She felt inordinately pleased with herself for coming up with such a grand idea.

"A rummage sale of the soul! I had no idea you were so smart," chortled Rev Ruth. "Are you saying things aren't so dark after all?"

"Yes!" Hope was on a roll. "I think maybe you're just having a cloudy evening of the soul."

FOOT COMMUNION

Ruth was again lost in confusion and despair when they trooped in, all five Beacons plus Luz, lugging armloads of towels. *Uh-oh*, she thought, spotting the plastic basin. She rose up on her elbows and started to protest.

Hope cut her off with a merry grin. "Jesus started it. We're just followers."

The pastor curled her bony toes and sputtered "But...but..."

"Remember who else said but, but?" Millienne raised one charcoal brow.

"Peter." A look of chagrin came across Rev Ruth's face.

Paige held up a leather-bound Bible. "John thirteen, eight. Jesus said 'Unless I wash you, you have no share with me.'"

Rev Ruth got into the spirit by grabbing her flyaway hair in both fists and crying dramatically "Lord, not my feet only but also my hands and head."

Luz couldn't suppress a nervous giggle.

After a round of cleansing laughter, Beka put on her Head Beacon voice. "May we proceed with the sacrament of foot washing, your Grace?"

Rev Ruth met Beka's eyes and nodded. In silence, unusual for the formerly vociferous pastor, she met the eyes of each woman circled around the bed and solemnly nodded yes. Six times.

Hope untucked the sheet, revealing feet white as roots. Luz, close beside her, placed warm hands beneath blue veined calves and lifted so Hope could place the thickest towel— Royal Cannon, navy blue— beneath Rev Ruth's legs. "The navy towel with white piping is in memory of your grandfather, the one lost at sea," said Hope.

Vulnerability washed over Rev Ruth's sharp features. "I'm touched that you remember the Captain," she murmured.

Paige held the basin—Rubbermaid, powder blue—as Beka and Dot filled it with warm water from the sink.

Millienne thumbed through the Bible and marked a place with a Kleenex pulled from a box on the nightstand.

Hope offered towels and each chose a different color, leaving the daffodil-yellow one for her. They folded towels into thick pads, placed them on the floor and knelt before feet and hands humble as tree stumps. Rev Ruth lay stiffly, corns and calluses exposed.

Dot, unusually quiet, was first to dip her hands into the water. As she cradled one lanky ankle she said, "Actually, Jesus didn't start it. Mary Magdalene did, when she anointed Jesus' feet with her tears and dried them with her hair."

The Beacons looked at Dot in surprise, startled by her pronouncement.

Dot kept her gaze on the skinny foot. "You should know it was Mary Magdalene who gave Jesus the idea of washing his disciples' feet."

If Rev Ruth heard this theological pronouncement, she gave no sign.

Luz, who'd been humming under her breath, went quiet. No one spoke after that, even Millienne who'd intended to read Psalm One Hundred Thirty Nine; '*You who formed my inward parts and knit me together in my mother's womb.*'

They knelt like sisters of the woman at the well and prayerfully bathed their pastor's hands and feet, each of her bony knobs and calluses. They rinsed away old disputes and toweled away old arguments.

Enfolding Rev Ruth in the holy hush of foot-washing on a spring afternoon in 1977, the Beacons' sacramental act soothed the soreness bound up in each others' journeys and gave everything back cleansed.

Rev Ruth turned toward a puzzled nurse in the doorway and spoke for the first time. "They brought good medicine, better than money can buy. This is how we do communion at Saint Lydia's."

THE OPENING

*What fortitude the Soul contains, That it can so endure
The accent of a coming Foot, The opening of a Door!*

Rev Ruth's door opened, and the footfall turned into a Beacon quoting Emily Dickinson. This person was Paige, extending her arms wide as she repeated the poem. For someone who lived mostly behind closed doors, Paige understood the nature of solitude and the illusion of private comfort. This had served her well for much of her life—private solitude can be very insulating—until the illusion came to an end, which happened more quickly than she had ever imagined.

Her pastor had fallen sick, and in that interruption, something mysterious had also happened. Long ago, mortality hit Paige when her sister Angela disappeared, but Rev Ruth's recent fragility touched Paige differently, more viscerally. Whole-body empathy led her to extend her sympathies to the elderly priest, which meant leaving some parts of herself behind, particularly the Anna Karenina part that could dramatically collapse into pretense. Paige sought angelic guidance and received the right angelic touch at the right time, in the right spiritual place to open a door she had kept firmly shut until now.

"I open the door of my home to you," said Paige without prelude. "The doctor says you're ready for release, if someone can give you continuing care. I can. Please come live with me."

Rev Ruth went nearly speechless with gratitude. "What… how…why….?"

Paige mixed metaphors in an effort to explain what brought about her sudden invitation. "A heartfelt desire," she told Rev Ruth, "is like a seed—or an acorn—that needs dark and cold to help it germinate. Whatever emerges, then, from the combination of acorn and soil, arises from desire itself— desire for the new life that awaits us in God." Paige did pretty well at describing her desire, rooted and grounded in a love much larger than personal.

In offering to open her home—her sacred *poustinia*—and being willing to take Rev Ruth into it, Paige joined forces with the great surging sea, the gravitational pull of the tide flowing in the direction of belonging. This was a direction both women longed to travel; Paige and her angelic host prayed with the deep tidal current and this combination brought Rev Ruth to a new home with the quietest Beacon.

"But where…where did this idea…this invitation come from?" asked Rev Ruth. Nearly overcome with gratitude, she was barely able to follow Paige's metaphorical ideas, let alone form a coherent sentence.

"Out of the silence," said Paige. "It came from insights that arise in silent prayer, and from the right action that flows from silence."

So it was that the pastor and the Beacon found themselves on the threshold of sharing a home. It came about very quickly, and despite everything they had done to arrive at this spiritual threshold, they were still not prepared to live together.

FIRE

The next morning Paige's phone rang at dawn. It was Rev Ruth, hysterical about a terrible fire at Paige's house.

"No, no," Paige said. "There's no fire. You just had a bad dream."

Rev Ruth did not believe her.

"There is no fire here, believe me." She kept her voice low and slow, hoping to reassure the nervous pastor. "I'm fine, the house is fine and your room is almost ready."

Rev Ruth hung up on her.

Paige's hands shook as she made tea and toast. *What was I thinking?*

Hope came to help clean house, and Paige told her what had happened.

An hour later, Rev Ruth phoned again, her words tumbling out in a panic. "There's a terrible fire at your house," she said breathlessly. "Get out while you can."

Once again, Paige assured her there was no fire. "Hope is here with me," she said, "and we're both okay."

Hope watched her friend's face. When Paige hung up, their eyes met.

"What are you going to do?"

"I thought about telling her I'd changed my mind," said Paige, "but I can't disappoint her. She's too frail. Let me catch my breath, then we'll finish up and go fetch her." She reached for the dust mop.

In Hope's car, Rev Ruth rolled down the window and breathed the clear air, which, she told them, smelled fresh and old at the same time. She'd been breathing stale old urine-scented air for too long. The outside air smelled grandfatherly to her, she insisted, as bracing as breathing on the deck of a sailing ship.

The sky was wide and blue, like the sea. Light breezes lifted the branches of oaks and bay laurels along the way; the leaves fluttered, nervous and playful. Rev Ruth said she thought the limbs of passing trees looked like Japanese dancers.

Her worried talk about fires had been put out.

On the way home, a sweet treat appeared. Paige pulled a small brown bag of M&Ms from her jacket pocket and held out a cupped palm full of colors. Rev Ruth took the red ones and Hope chose yellow. They popped the candies in their mouths and let them dissolve slowly, like communion wafers.

The End

POSTLUDE

A Conversation with the Author

Beka Ash, Head Beacon, pulled up a stool alongside Judith Favor at Swensen's Ice Cream Shoppe, a few blocks from Saint Lydia's. Beka had a rocky-road fudge sundae and Rev Judith had lemon sorbet. They both had a lot of laughs.

Beka   First things first. I've been interviewing new attenders at Saint Lydia's and writing up their profiles for our church newsletter, but this interview with you merits a special issue. Is it okay with you if I print our conversation in the next issue of JAM?

Judith   Sure. But why have you renamed the church newsletter JAM?

B   JAM means **Jesus And Me**. That's what the kids call our early Pancake Worship.

J   Well then, let's JAM! I'm glad you're cooking pancakes for hungry kids, interviewing newcomers and introducing them to Saint Lydia's old-timers. I always figured you to be a good writer.

B   I only write the first draft. Paige edits everything before JAM goes to press.

J   Good to collaborate. Paige can give things a poetic touch.

B   Speaking of poetic, I loved your book, especially
        the way I looked in THE BEACONS OF LARKIN
        STREET. Well, not the part about lying and stealing.
        By the way, I stopped shoplifting after I read that part.
J   Glad to hear it. Lying, too?

Noise from the milkshake machine drowned out Beka's reply.
When things quieted down she said, Let's change the subject.
What's it like for you, living in LA after all your years in San
Francisco?

J   The freeways are jammed, but Claremont has more
        trees per block than your city by the bay. It took me a
        few years to quit comparing the culture of Los Ange-
        les to San Francisco, but I still complain about the
        heat and air quality.
B   People at Saint Lydia's thought you got things pretty
        accurate about our history, except you changed the
        name of our church. Did you mean to do that?
J   As a fiction writer, I get to invent people and re-imag-
        ine places, so I turned Saint Lydia's into a mix of the
        real historic church and the church of my heart. And
        since you Beacons are becoming known for feeding
        hungry folks in San Francisco, I named your church
        after a biblical woman who practiced hospitality by
        feeding Saint Paul and the apostles.
B   Speaking of names, the rest of the Beacons agree with
        me. We're pretty sure the characters in your novel are
        based on real people and we're still trying to figure
        out who's who. Obviously, I am me, but who is Rev
        Ruth?
J   She's herself.
B   Yeah, but who? People around here think she could
        be based on … Oh, I better not name names.
J   Good idea, since Rev Ruth isn't just one person. She's
        an amalgam of women known in Episcopal circles as

The Philadelphia Eleven. Rev Ruth's character honors all those women—and a few men—who worked together to break the stained-glass ceiling. Rev Ruth and the first generation of female pastors had to enter parish ministry without female mentors or models.

B   What about Hope?

J   She is based upon a San Francisco friend of mine who was a lot like Hope in real life. During a hard patch in my life, she took me into her home. I slept in Luz's room and ate at the same kitchen table. So I enjoyed describing how Hope (not her real name) looked and talked, dressed and dreamed, cooked and sewed. Hope Hudson's character honors many ordinary women who express their faith through caring for others. I loved putting my friend in the book.

B   What about Luz Rivera?

J   She, too, is a combination of immigrants and women forced into the sex trade. I think readers will be surprised when they find out what happens with Luz in the sequel. This is why I find fiction so powerful. As the author, I get to open my heart to the place where ideas are born, pay attention to what my characters say and do, then put their stories on the page as faithfully as I can.

B   Speaking of the sequel, I was fascinated by Rev Ruth's granddaughter but you didn't tell me nearly enough about her. Any chance I might get to know Caro better?

J   Oh Beka, you are in for a delicious surprise. In the next book, Caro Salter comes west to be with her grandmother and things get very lively.

B   I can hardly wait. Caro sounds a lot like my Patty.

J   A word of caution: Caro thinks of herself as totally unique. You might not want to tell her she's like someone else.

B   Okay, I'll remember that. Now, I've given copies of your book to some of my lesbian friends and if you don't mind, I'd like to ask you their most common question. Why would Paige, a solitary if I ever met one, invite Rev Ruth to move into her house?

J   Well, I guess your friends have a small point. Paige is a female whose parents tried to turn her into a male and whose God did turn her into a contemplative. Why would Paige give up her privacy, especially with someone as sparky as Rev Ruth?

B   Yeah, we couldn't figure out that part.

J   Paige's decision startled me, too, but whenever imagination ushers me into the soul of the Beacons and the Rev, I record whatever comes alive. At that point in the story, the action got so full of twists and turns that Paige's revelation totally surprised me.

B   So you're telling me you're not in charge of what your characters do and say?

J   Far from it. The motives that drive the actions of Saint Lydia's folks are often hidden not only from themselves, but sometimes also from me.

B   What I like about Hope and Millienne is they don't seem right for each other, yet they have an undeniable connection. I hope your sequel explores more about their relationship.

J   It will. You probably also noticed how Millienne and Paige are deeply connected to the natural world. Humans who foster a vibrant relationship with creation are brought more fully alive in matters of faith and practice.

B   So connecting with nature is important for church people in urban areas?

J   Absolutely. And books are good places to explore such themes.